Under My Skin

Alison Jameson lives in Dublin. Her first novel, *This Man and Me*, was published in 2006.

Under My Skin

ALISON JAMESON

PENGUIN
IRELAND

PENGUIN IRELAND

Published by the Penguin Group
Penguin Ireland, 25 St Stephen's Green, Dublin 2, Ireland
(a division of Penguin Books Ltd)
Penguin Books Ltd, 80 Strand, London WC2R ORL, England
Penguin Group (USA) Inc., 375 Hudson Street, New York, New York 10014, USA
Penguin Group (Australia), 250 Camberwell Road, Camberwell, Victoria 3124, Australia
(a division of Pearson Australia Group Pty Ltd)
Penguin Group (Canada), 90 Eglinton Avenue East, Suite 700, Toronto, Ontario, Canada M4P 2Y3
(a division of Pearson Penguin Canada Inc.)
Penguin Books India Pvt Ltd, 11 Community Centre, Panchsheel Park, New Delhi – 110 017, India
Penguin Group (NZ), 67 Apollo Drive, Rosedale, North Shore 0632, New Zealand
(a division of Pearson New Zealand Ltd)
Penguin Books (South Africa) (Pty) Ltd, 24 Sturdee Avenue, Rosebank, Johannesburg 2196, South Africa

Penguin Books Ltd, Registered Offices: 80 Strand, London WC2R ORL, England

www.penguin.com

First published 2007
1

Copyright © Alison Jameson, 2007

The moral right of the author has been asserted

Set in 12/14.75 pt PostScript Monotype Dante
Typeset by Rowland Phototypesetting Ltd, Bury St Edmunds, Suffolk
Printed in Great Britain by Clays Ltd, St Ives plc

A CIP catalogue record for this book is available from the British Library

ISBN: 978-1-844-88096-6

For Kathy and Rachel

ONE

1   *The Yum-Yum Girl (January 2001)*

Sweetheart n. Something or someone who is cherished and often considered one of a kind.

Whenever Larry is late I make spaghetti. He says he'll be here at three now, and instead of answering I catch the sun with my watch and make a bright dancing spot on the sitting-room wall. The flat is old and dark. It has dark green walls and the furniture is oak. The fabrics are corduroy and velvet, dark green again and stained yellow and brown. It's like living in a forest, a strange underworld on the second floor. People died here. They must have. Old people or maybe even youngish people like me and my flatmate Doreen. The poster of *Les Misérables* belongs to her. So does 'Famous Pubs of Ireland'. So does all the cutlery and the giant steel saucepan. The half-dead cheese plant and the boyfriend who is late belong to me.

'OK?' he says and then 'OK?' again. The first time he says it he sounds impatient. The second time he is smiling into the phone. In the flat downstairs, Mr and Mrs Costello are moving around. Larry owns the diner on the corner. There are red leatherette seats and rows of white tables and all the walls are painted turquoise-blue. He wanted it to look like a 1950s cinema and so the name 'Vertigo' hangs in small dizzy letters over the door.

In my head I am starting to make Pasta Putana. Boiling the water, adding the pasta, opening the fridge, and asking the anchovies to step out.

Last night Doreen came home drunk and put our coat-stand into the neighbour's skip. I met our neighbour once, a nice man in a Foxford dressing gown and slippers, *pleading* with us to turn the music down. This morning Doreen went out in her pyjamas and brought the coats back in. As I watch from the kitchen window now a young man in a white raincoat comes and lifts the coat-stand out. He walks down the promenade with it resting on one shoulder and then the sun blinks out and it picks out some fresh glistening spray. There is something about this and the idea of warm Mediterranean tomatoes that make my Saturday feel more complete.

We took the flat in Bray because of the location and because we are all officially poor. All around us, there are people getting rich in this city – the *'Boom'* is everywhere – except here. Doreen moved in two months ago. She's my best friend and she can also pay one third of the rent. No one seemed to notice the smell in the downstairs hallway or the green fur on the wallpaper or the hole under the lino in the kitchen floor.

'What's that smell?' I asked the landlord and we stood and looked at each other in the tiny kitchen at the top of the stairs.

'Rising damp,' he said calmly in a voice that told me he had met a hundred girls like me before.

So the giant saucepan gets lifted up from under the kitchen sink and the pasta gets bunched together and then I light the gas heater and lie out on the sitting-room floor. The water needs to bubble up before I can put the pasta in. I am still thinking about the question they asked me yesterday.

'If you were having a dinner party, what four people would you invite?'

I wanted to ask them what that had to do with working in advertising. I had already made up a good story about 'previous experience' and the truth is I have never worked in an advertising agency before. On Wednesdays I visit my grand-mother and I spend the rest of the week managing the vintage record shop – they didn't need to know that we live like three church mice in a damp green and brown flat. I had answered all the questions about brands and my favourite TV ads and now I just wanted to say, 'Please. Just please. Give me the job and get me out of that dump.' They were all wearing after-shave and black suits and one of them had a pair of Bart Simpson socks. But I got stuck on that last question. Now of course I can think of all the great people to ask. Martin Luther King. John F. Kennedy. Even Queen Elizabeth. I mean people you think of just to show you have a brain and have read some books. Instead I jammed and said – wait for it – 'Gay Byrne.' I mean to say, who in their right mind would have him over for dinner? Maybe if I was in my sixties. Sometimes I think I am and actually I am just twenty-two. If I was being truthful the only people I would want are Larry and Doreen – and Jack, if he was home from New York. And my grand-mother – on a good day – and even Matilda – or the guy who took the coat-stand out of the skip – but that's not the kind of answer that gets a person a job and a better kind of home.

Then they asked me if I was mobile but I was still thinking about Gay Byrne.

'We need someone who can get out and meet the clients,' the Managing Director said. And here's the worst part. I actually jumped up and went to the window of their board-room and pointed out my car. It's an original Messerschmitt. A bubble car in red – and it was still shaking a little after the drive in from Bray.

'It's a TG 500 Tiger,' I told them. Actually when I see it now it reminds me of jelly and cream. Larry refuses to go anywhere in it. He says he has never seen a ladybird so big.

Anyway, the boys at the ad agency seemed to find all that rather amusing.

I know I'll be lucky to get this job. I think everyone in the room realized that. I had to ask Larry to check my CV. I have a problem with spelling and the meaning of words. When I hear a word I like I have to write it down. Otherwise they just seem to fall out of my head and sometimes I use them in the wrong places which can be embarrassing. For example, when they asked me how I got to the agency yesterday I wanted to say, I *descended* by car.

The bathroom door slides open. Doreen walks down the three steps from the hall to the kitchen. She's wearing a white towelling robe with white tennis socks and her black suede high-heel pumps. Sometimes she wears a swimming cap in the shower. Sometimes she sleeps in those shoes.

'Nice look,' I tell her, and she says nothing and just starts to make tea. I like Doreen a lot, especially like this, when she is smiling and silenced by her hangover and she has Minnie Mouse feet.

She looks at the saucepan on the stove and then picks up her cup and holds it in both hands.

'I'm asleep,' she says eventually. 'Standing up, like a horse.'

Yesterday we wrote the landlord a long letter and we complained about all sorts of things. Once we got started neither one of us knew how to stop. And the truth is I was just nervous about the job interview and Doreen's allergy had flared up. But we covered everything – starting with the gas and ending with the smell of our neighbours downstairs. We even told him that there was a giant spider living in the bathroom – the bathroom with the weird sliding door and the tiny teaspoon sink.

The pasta is making the windows steam up. When Doreen

speaks her voice is three octaves lower than it should be. I try to talk to her about the interview question.

'Who would you ask if you were having a dinner party?'

'Are you still going on about that?'

'Who would you ask?'

'What are you having? Pasta Putana?'

'What's the difference? – who would you invite?'

'If we were having spaghetti I'd ask Robert de Niro.'

I can kind of see her point.

'And if we're having Indian . . .' and she pours more tea and starts to laugh.

Doreen works at the Indian restaurant on the corner. Last night when we came in she had them all sleeping on our sitting-room floor.

'It's the Indians,' I said to Larry, and he just looked up at the ceiling and went straight down to our room. One of them was sleeping under a duvet that looked a lot like ours. I'm getting used to seeing them pull up in the beige Ford Fiesta and shout out her name in the street.

Larry says, 'You need to build a wall, Doreen,' but I know she has no clue what that means.

Sometimes it looks as if there are more than ten of them packed into that little car. She takes them to the islands and the lakes and once she even drove to Wexford with them for a whole weekend.

When Doreen comes in again she is dressed and her cheeks are rosy and she tells me she's going to the flicks for the afternoon.

'Are you meeting the Indians?' I ask her.

'No,' she says. 'I've had enough for one weekend.'

My least favourite word in the world is *croquet*. Because of *croquet* I was kept back in second year at school. Because of '*a game involving wooden mallets and hoops*' I was told I had a reading age of a ten-year-old, and I was fourteen then – and I have never needed to say *croquet* again. Not even once.

On the other hand, some of my favourite words are *soufflé*, *lackadaisical* and *afternoon*.

Doreen has only been gone ten minutes when the phone rings. I am lifting the spaghetti with a fork and checking that it's not going to stick – and the black olives and anchovies are mixed and waiting together in a bowl.

'Hello,' I say, and I'm using a distracted voice like someone who is slightly bored.

'Hello,' the voice says, 'this is Bandhu.'

I sigh when I hear this because it means one of the Indians is on the phone.

'Doreen's just gone out,' I tell him.

'OK,' he says. 'But actually . . . it was you that I wanted to speak to.'

'Me?' and really what I'm saying is, '*Oh*' and '*God*.'

'Could I come round?' he asks. 'I need to talk to someone. I'm in trouble. I need to talk to someone about Doreen.'

'Well, this isn't a good time,' I answer. And I'm surprised at how firm I can be.

'Are you busy?' he asks. 'It won't take long. Please, I really need to talk to you about Doreen.'

'I'm sorry,' I tell him, 'but I'm cooking spaghetti this afternoon.'

'It won't take long,' he says again and then he puts down the phone. In five minutes the doorbell rings. He must have been parked nearby. He must have sat in the driver's seat and called me on his mobile phone. He must have seen the man lift the coat-stand and he must have watched Doreen leave. He is small and his hair is parted too low down on one side. He reminds me of a tax inspector or someone collecting census forms – and every time I hear myself saying, 'Gay Byrne' I still want to get sick.

He sits down on the edge of an armchair and his hands are placed neatly on his knees. He is wearing the kind of grey pants twelve-year-old boys wear when they're visiting their grandmothers. He is wearing a blue shirt and a grey V-neck cardigan, and everything about him, especially his voice, is apologetic and small.

'Thank you for seeing me,' he begins. I have had to turn the spaghetti back so that it's cooking slower now. In five minutes it will have to come off and if he's still here I'm going to ask him to leave.

'The problem is . . .' and whenever he speaks I am thinking that there is a little boy in our sitting room. He is sitting there on our armchair and soon his legs which are too close to the gas fire will begin to toast.

'The problem is . . .' he says again, and he is slicing the words out in this thin boy voice, 'I'm in love with Doreen.'

And I'm nodding back at him and even smiling and inside I am thinking, 'Oh, beautiful. How lovely. Thank you, Doreen.'

'We've been an item for several months now. I'm in love with her but she won't tell anyone about us. She won't tell anyone that I am her boyfriend.'

I have known Doreen all my life. There are lots of things she doesn't tell me and there are things she tells me that I would rather not know.

'OK,' I say again.

'I don't know what to do. I am so in love with her. But she will not introduce me as her boyfriend. She pretends it doesn't exist. But we have had the happiest times together, at the Powerscourt waterfall . . .' and here he shakes his head and his eyes drift off.

Doreen is at least a foot taller than him and he guesses my thoughts.

'I'm not making this up,' he says and he holds his palms out towards me. 'I'm in love with Doreen.'

And I just sit there looking back at him.

'You know her,' he says. 'Tell me, help me, what should I do?'

'You need to talk to Doreen,' I tell him.

'She won't talk about it.'

'My pasta is ruined,' I tell him, and now I'm towering over him, 'and you need to talk to Doreen.'

When the front door closes the phone is ringing again.

'This is Jonathan Kirk,' the voice says and it is so well behaved and liquid-smooth. 'Can you talk?' he asks politely. 'You're not in the middle of something . . . ? I'm sorry to call you on a Saturday afternoon.'

'No, it's fine – at the moment,' I tell him. I am about to pour some more tomatoes into a bowl. I imagine he is calling me from his big walnut desk at the agency and that he is swinging around and around on a black leather chair.

'We have white smoke,' he says. 'We'd like to see you again.'

Upstairs I can smell the pasta starting to burn.

There are several different songs in my head and I want to sing them all together when I put on a new batch of spaghetti and then Larry calls again.

'It's crazy in here today,' he says, 'I won't make it until five.' In the background Vertigo sounds like it is sliding down a hill.

'Don't worry, Larry,' I tell him, 'and by the way, I think I got the job.'

'You did?' he says, and then quick as a flash I say, 'I love you *muchly*, Larry,' and he says, without even blinking, 'Well, you know I'm *crazo* about you.'

The flat is darker now. The winter sun stretches out and covers me in the dull shadow of five o'clock. I sit on the forest floor with the toadstools and the damp green bark and think about Larry. How he stepped into his old jeans this morning when he sat on the bed. How he left the watch I bought him on the bedside locker. How his old leather jacket hung on the door, the Penguin Classic pushed down into the flap pocket. His notebook, dog-eared. His lucky pen. The small extras thrown in and then – just Larry, the *loveliness* of him. He turned on the radio and Aretha Franklin was singing and then he went upstairs and cooked some eggs for me, something he usually hates to do when he's at home. When he went to work I found one of his little notes which he hides around the flat for me. 'I miss you already,' it said, and if he was here I would have said, 'Larry, I miss you too.'

The only problem is we have no money. *Zip*. We are not even able to buy things like clothes and shoes and on top of that we owe €3,865.00, which Larry lost in a game of Black Jack. He is not even a gambler. He has only ever played once and that was because Doreen and the Indians got him drunk.

But last week someone called to the diner and asked Larry to 'pay up'. The conversation opened with a very nice black eye and ended with a pleasant head-butt. This year we were supposed to go to New York and now we can't afford to do that. We had it all planned out and I even rang Jack about a sublet, and one week later he rang me back.

'Hey,' he said, 'I think I found a place for you. It belongs to a girl called Matilda. She's dating The Chief's best friend.'

'The Chief?' I said and inside I was seeing a picture of Sitting Bull.

'Remember? My brother-in-law,' Jack replied, and I could tell from his voice that he was smiling. 'He's head of the Midtown North Precinct. Everyone calls him "The Chief". I don't know Matilda or his buddy but I hear she's got a really nice place on the Upper West Side.'

Then he gave me her email address and we've been emailing each other ever since. She even sent me a picture of her apartment and now there is a tall brownstone with its own chestnut tree on the door of our fridge. Someday I know we'll fly to New York and Matilda will move out to be with her boyfriend, and me and Larry will start our new life and move in.

The front door slams and I know it's not Larry – or Doreen – or one of the Smell family – I know from the heavy footsteps coming up our stairs that the landlord has let himself in. He's puffing like a madman and his face looks hot and flushed. When he walks down the little landing he wobbles from side to side and he is wearing squeaking shoes and carrying some extra weight.

'How dare you?' he begins and he's completely out of breath. 'How dare you?' and he just puffs the same words out again and then I see he's waving our letter in his hand.

'Dear Mr O'Grady . . .' he begins and he's so wound up and gasping I'm afraid he might just collapse.

'Dear Mr O'Grady, we are writing to complain about the state of our accommodation. For three weeks now,' and here he takes a step towards me, 'three weeks – it is NOT – three weeks' – and he goes back to reading again, 'for three weeks we have been asking you to fix our cooker. Are you aware that this is a danger to our health and the health of the other tenants in 102? In addition to that the bath is blocked again and we are having problems with the family downstairs – there is a bad smell coming from their rooms.'

And this part came from Doreen. 'If things are not rectified immediately we will withhold our rent.'

And then he's off with the 'How dare you?' and the 'How dare you?' again. There is a half-built mews in the back garden. The Smells downstairs have told us that he's run out of money. We probably shouldn't have mentioned withholding our rent – especially when we already owe him more than three weeks.

'Do not write to me,' he concludes in one big town crier's peal. 'Do NOT write to ME,' and then he goes off, Mr Anger and Repetition, back down the stairs again. If Doreen was here we would lie down on the floor and laugh ourselves sick over it. And then we would sit up and look at each other and I would say the same thing I say, every day, 'We need to get out of here, Doreen.'

More than anything I want this job. Not just to have some more money but to have my very own desk and phone and pen. And I think Larry will be later than five today. I guess he'll make it to our place at around nine.

When Doreen comes out of the bathroom she tells me the

spider is still there. Then we both squeeze in together and look down at him and he is really huge.

'He's not from around here,' she says.

'Where do you think he's from?'

'South America,' she replies and then before I can even speak she leans down really close to it and shouts, '*Hola! Como se va?*' But still the spider does not move.

Then we hear a loud bang outside and when we lean out the bedroom window we can see that the landlord is back and has climbed up on the mews roof. He's drunk and shouting and he seems to be attacking the house with an axe.

Downstairs the Smells are all out on the lawn.

'Mr O'Grady . . . Mr O'Grady . . . please come down. You will hurt yourself. Mr O'Grady . . . please come down.'

And all we can hear is our landlord screaming curses and crying like a baby.

'Doreen,' I whisper.

'I know,' she replies and she is beginning to laugh. 'We have got to get out of here.'

In the sitting room we watch the TV with the volume turned down. She is eating a bag of white bonbons and I am eating a chocolate frog. The front door bangs shut and then Larry puts his head around the door. He kisses the top of my head and slides down into my armchair.

'Anything happen today?' he asks. Doreen points the remote control at the TV but the channel does not change.

'Not much,' I tell him. He puts his arm around me and kisses my hair. 'Made Pasta Putana. Watched some TV.'

On Wednesday I take my grandmother to the swimming pool. Her name is Djuna Ethel Hendleberg Swann. She is eighty-three years old and usually we spell her first name with a simple 'J'. In 1935, Juna swam the English Channel. She wanted to beat the record set by Gertrude Ederle, the first woman ever. But it took Juna sixteen hours and forty-nine minutes. Now she says it takes her that long just to get up the stairs. She wears a purple hat that is shaped like a mushroom and when we walk in the park, she runs her stick along the rails. Once when we were in a hotel she got stuck, with a large crate of broccoli, in the service lift. I have to watch her all the time but it's not any trouble. She is happiest when I put her make-up on and she loves blue eyeshadow and fire-engine-red nails.

At the swimming pool she undresses very slowly. She has a black and white striped bathing costume and she looks a bit like a zebra stepping across the room. She wears earplugs and goggles and a tightly fitted blue Speedo cap. Her glasses have to be inside her handbag before she puts her goggles on. Her clothes have to be folded really neatly before her earplugs go in. Her teeth have to be wrapped in a tissue before her swimming cap goes on – and all these things are like a road map or a trail of breadcrumbs to take her back home. Then she begins to move carefully from the locker room to the pool. Sometimes she gets confused when there are too many doors and she always wants to go back out the same door she came in. So I steer her the other way and when she smiles suddenly, she puts one hand shyly up to her face. She looks different without her glasses and teeth, a bit like another person underneath herself. Her white hair is gone under the swimming cap and it turns her into a mad pixie thing. 'This is one way to clear the kids out of the pool,' I tell her and that never fails to make her laugh. I warn her about the steps and stay really close to her and then she stands very still for a moment and with one slow, steady glide, she launches herself in. She can still pound out a few good strokes. 'The American Crawl', she calls it. The same one she used in 1935.

She turns over then and tries the back crawl.

'Now you're just showing off,' I tell her.

'I never lost it,' she says.

Outside the spray flies into the air as the breakers crash up and down and then into one another again. Every week she points out the pink church where her best friend got married and then we take the slope down on to the sand and begin to walk slowly, her arm linked through mine. There is a black cannon on the promenade. A surfer's shop. A hut that sells fishing tackle. A giant plastic ice cream cone. Vertigo is on the first corner into the main street and opposite is my place of work – the vintage record shop.

'Which would you like?' I ask her. 'A cone or some tea?'

'Neither,' she says flatly and then, 'We stayed in the Atlantic Hotel once.' Her eyes rest on a row of new shops. 'Somewhere over there.'

We walk to the first pub and ask for tea. Inside there are men and women sitting on bar stools and children running around the room. We find a quiet corner where there are old-fashioned road signs and a white chamber pot hangs over our heads. We sit away from everyone, where it is peaceful and we are up on a high cushioned form. We sit side by side and we are quiet, our cheeks still fresh with the sea wind. The tea arrives. A giant silver pot. Two big mugs. Pink and blue.

'It is the best tea I have ever had.'

Every Wednesday I say this and every Wednesday she smiles at the size of the mugs.

'People are very generous here,' she says. The rain begins to spatter on the windows beside us.

'Let's stay here for ever, Juna,' I want to say, but she is looking at the pictures on the walls and reading the names of the old street signs. I want to tell her that I will look after her. That I will take good care of her – no matter what. But how can anyone suddenly say this? She would say she does not need me to care for her. That she likes her life the way it is. Living on the farm with a big cat jumping out of every chair. And how will she go in the end? I have begun to worry about this – and still in old age she moves and breathes all around me. On the beach, she walks head down into the wind, and the only part of our lives that feels safe, and has any kind of certainty, is the sea wind, and the giant mugs and the silver pot of tea.

Bandhu calls again and this time, Doreen is at home. He brings her a giant Elizabeth Arden make-up set and a bottle of Campari for Larry and me.

'We can't accept this,' I tell her.

'It's an Indian custom,' Doreen replies. 'It would be very rude to refuse.' Then I call Larry and ask him if he has ever heard about an Indian custom that involves Campari and Elizabeth Arden and he says, 'It doesn't sound very Hindu to me.'

My fear of water began in the shower. It took a whole day to install, my pappy, my brother Daniel and me. There were phone calls from neighbours who asked, 'Is it in yet?' without saying their names or even 'Hello' first. The plumber was stopped and asked questions at our shop door. Dogs raced up and down the street and then barked back over their shoulders like they didn't care, but they did. We were the first house in the town to have one and we boarded it like a spaceship.

'Stand at the back,' Pappy said. And then, 'Are you ready?' and without waiting for an answer he turned the water on. No one told me what it would be like. That I would be blasted by sudden jets of water. That they would hit me on the face and take the wind out of me. I was six and full of confidence then. I could sing every advertising jingle from the TV and when I called into Farrell's clothes shop I did my Irish dancing up and down their floor.

In the shower there was steam and pounding water and noise and no way to escape. I couldn't breathe and I turned my face into the corner and the water pounded my back. I turned around to face it but there was no air anywhere. I gave in quickly. I didn't know how to have a shower so I caved in and sank down on to the floor.

'For God's sake,' Pappy said and he reached in to turn the water off and I climbed out, humiliated, wearing a large floral shower cap and soap on a rope. Daniel looked out from under a white towel and held his hands out towards me. It was a gesture he used to show exasperation, confusion, annoyance, except now he used it and gave that funny infectious laugh of his as well. There was no half-way mark with Daniel's laugh. It was either the funniest thing ever or not at all. Most of the time his own laughter forced him back into a chair.

Matilda knows all about my fear of water. She also knows where to get the best hotdog in New York. When Larry is working late I go to the Internet Café and we chat. She's got a big job with the *New York Post* and I've already told her that I work in an advertising agency. When she asked what I do there I typed in 'Managing Director' and sent it back to her and she replied with one word: 'Wow!'

The funny thing about emailing Matilda is that it's easier to tell her things I still can't tell anyone else. I think it's because I have never actually seen her so I can't imagine her eyes or if there is a smile or a frown on her face. One night I sat down and told her all about Pappy and Daniel and when I pressed 'Send' I thought I would never hear from her again. Then her reply came back with a 'ping' and the screen flashed on and it seemed to light up my life. She only wrote one line back but I printed it out and I still keep it in my bag.

'*It wasn't your fault.*'

That was all she said but it means an awful lot to me.

Sometimes if you blame yourself for something – and you keep it inside like a secret – and then someone says, 'It wasn't your fault' – it seems to save your life.

The best hotdog in New York incidentally is at Gray's Papaya on 71st and Broadway and it's also the cheapest.

Larry is standing near the jukebox. One eye is black and half closed and there is a golden light on his face. He makes me a club sandwich, just the way I like it, toasted rye bread, fresh tomatoes, potato chips and sour cream on the side. I sit at the counter and eat very slowly and in between cracking eggs he smiles and winks over at me. It takes me an hour to eat everything and he always laughs about this. Sometimes I think I don't have enough teeth or else the ones I have are not sharp enough.

'Baby . . .' he says and he is pretending to be sad now. 'You're eating all our rent.' Then he sits down smiling and starts to smoke. When he offers me one I say, 'No thanks – that's last month's gas.' He goes to the freezer and finds two beers and then he hands one to me.

Larry's eyes are very dark and he has wild eyebrows and long bristling lashes and he is more than six feet tall – but when I think about Larry I don't see any of that because there are other things about him that are secret and more important to me.

He has a scar, a thin white line just over his top lip and curling down and around his mouth. Sometimes it stands out like a whiplash on his bright tanned face. A dog bit him as a child and it gave Larry a slightly crooked Cupid's bow. And when he laughs, only I can see that one of his teeth folds slightly over another, and when he is smiling like that, he is really lovely to me. His hair is dark with a slight curl, the kind of forest you can almost hear grow. He reads something once and he remembers it for ever and he sees things about me – that I can't even see. He hates people who are mean with their money and he loves Frank Sinatra and he *loves* New York.

When the last couple leaves he turns the sign and Vertigo is steady and finally empty at ten minutes after three. He smiles at my silence and changes the record on the jukebox. Then he leans on one elbow and looks into my face. When he sits down again his leg leans and rests against mine and I feel his life and his warmth moving towards me, the nearness of it, his golden inner glow.

On nights like this he tells me about his family and the

kind of boy he was growing up – and how his mother is a strong-willed and sometimes angry woman; and how his father had a stroke and lost his voice – and all of his hair. Now he uses a little notebook and pen to write everything down. He tells me how they sent him to university and what a disappointment he is to his family because he left a degree in economics to be a short-order cook.

But tonight things are suddenly different – because Larry looks right into my eyes and out of nowhere there are four really awful words.

'We need to talk.'

Yesterday Matilda asked me who my favourite New Yorkers are and I replied, 'Woody Allen. Art Garfunkel and Meryl Streep.' Then she sent me hers – 'Eleanor Roosevelt, Walt Whitman and Benjamin Cardoso.' The last person is a Supreme Court Judge. Larry told me and now I feel too embarrassed to email her for a week.

Outside it is beginning to rain and inside my whole world is falling apart.

'The thing is . . .' Larry says and then – lucky for me – the telephone begins to ring. He looks at it and so do I and we both know it is probably 'Mr Friendly', the debt collector, again. We listen and count the rings and then Larry gets up and bolts the double doors.

He sits down again and says, 'Listen . . .' and this time I interrupt. He looks like a cartoon character in his white chef's coat, with his black eye and his favourite beanie hat.

'I got you something,' and I pass the black eye patch over

the table. He smiles at this. A real Larry smile. And in that second everything seems to change. He takes off his little hat and puts the pirate patch on. Then he leans over and puts one hand on my head and through my hair I can feel the weight and the warmth of his hand. He swallows and sighs and I am thinking, 'OK, here it comes.'

'It's like this . . .' he says, and outside three girls begin tapping on the glass door.

'We're closed,' Larry shouts but they are not going away.

So I get up and open the door a crack.

'Could you go away?' I ask them. 'I'm being dumped.'

'Oh!' they all reply together and then they say, 'Sorry!' and they hurry off down the wet street.

When I come back to the table Larry has lit a candle and turned off the lights.

'There will never be anyone like you,' he says, and then in a very soft voice he says, 'Ever', under his breath. I feel as though I should say, 'Thanks', or something but inside I am packing up all my feelings and thoughts.

And then he says my name and what a little name it is – and what a meaning and it has never felt further from the truth – but he says it again, whispering it now, and his eyes are filling up.

'Will you marry me, Hope?'

Yesterday I looked up *dyslexia* and wrote it into my notebook.

n. A learning disorder marked by severe difficulty in recognizing and understanding written language, leading to spelling and writing problems. It is not caused by low intelligence or brain damage.

When Doreen read the part about brain damage, she looked at me and asked, 'Are you absolutely sure?'

This morning Larry makes Eggs Benedict with cinnamon toast and blueberry pancakes. For lunch he cooks fresh scallops and roast figs with garlic cream and Parma ham. For dinner he feeds me pink fillet steak with black pepper and cream. We drink wine, three bottles, and make each other laugh. He closes early and tells everyone he meets, 'From now on I'm cooking for my wife.'

Mr Costello stands with his back to the fireplace. There are four candles on the piano and his wife stretches her fingers a little so she is ready to play. They have moved the yellow couch back and closed the curtains and the dark wooden blinds. For three days the rain has fallen and now on a wet Tuesday night everyone stands in a loose circle around the bride and groom. The air smells of warm apple pie and on a table near the window there are eight bottles of Heineken and a jug of mulled wine. Doreen is of course my bridesmaid. She is wearing a white tennis skirt and her nice black suede pumps. Larry has a black top hat he found at Oxfam and the pirate's eye patch. I am wearing my leopard print coat and my favourite red Converse runners. And Mrs Costello is standing by and smiling, ready to turn the music up.

Juna arrives and gives me away. This takes two steps on their carpet – one foot landing on a big red rose and the second on some giant green leaves. We did not want a church wedding because me and Larry don't believe in God or any of that stuff. One day I went into Vertigo and we've been together ever since. In our world everything happens by accident – and so we asked Mr Costello if he would read out the vows and if we could get married in their flat downstairs.

'Do you, Larry, take Hope to be your lawfully wedded wife?' asks Mr Costello.

'I do,' Larry says and he has taken off his hat.

'Do you, Hope, take Larry to be your lawfully wedded husband?'

'I do,' I reply and then our rings are exchanged. These came from a pawnbroker in Dublin. Mine fits on my index finger and Larry has to wear his on his thumb.

'You may kiss the bride,' Mr Costello says and then he looks at us over his glasses.

'Kids, a promise is a promise,' he says.

Email to Hope Swann
From Matilda Vaughan
Hope,
I am so happy for you. I can't imagine anything more romantic than marrying your first love. Tell me everything . . . are there any photos? What is the ring like? I would love to see you in your dress and veil.
(By the way . . . don't tell anyone . . . but I think a certain man in my life . . . is going to pop the question too. He hasn't said anything yet – but I feel so sure . . . when you meet the right guy, Hope . . . you just know.
Much love,
M x.

Jonathan Kirk stands on the cream marble stairs and when he smiles he looks almost as young as me. There is a red carpet in the reception with blue lights on either side. He beckons, he waves and he guides me in. The second interview goes like this. It is just myself and Jonathan and we are sitting on two red couches near his desk. The quote on his wall says, 'If each of us hires people smaller than we are, we shall become a company of dwarfs.'

When he speaks he puts one foot over his knee and talks for an hour. He tells me that great brands need great ads, that great ads come from great clients, that we are all here because we want to make great ads, that there is no overtime system but we all stay until the work is done and how does that sound?

'Great' is the only possible response.

'If you work for me,' he says, 'I expect you to come up with solutions, don't bring me your problems, and if there is a problem with a client – I would rather you told me before the client does.'

This seems like a contradiction to me but my response is to swallow quietly and breathe.

'Why do you want to work in advertising?' he asks and then, 'Let me tell you why I work in advertising. Last night I was watching TV and three of the ads in the break were ours. Now I don't know about you . . . but I get *aroused* by that.

'Is there anything you would like to say?' And now he is leaning forward and being friendly and kind.

'Yes,' I tell him. 'If I was having a dinner party I would ask Eleanor Roosevelt, Walt Whitman and Benjamin Cardoso.'

'I see,' he says and his face is very serious even though his eyes are beginning to smile.

It rains and we throw a party in Vertigo.

We drink the profits and we eat all the food. Larry drinks

to celebrate our wedding and I drink to wish both of us luck. We drink and we dance and he turns me, turns me. We leave the blinds up and when we open the doors people crowd in. We drink because we found each other early and Juna shakes her head and says, 'Too young, too young.'

Arouse v. – 1. To evoke a feeling, response, or desire. 2. To cause feelings of sexual desire in somebody. 3. To make someone angry. 4. To wake up, to wake somebody up from sleep or unconsciousness.

2   1029 *Prince Street – Manhattan*

In time Glassman would grow tired of it, his own face in the mirror, and knowing that he was the last person other people saw before they died. On 2 January 2001 a snowstorm was forecast in New York and the city seemed strong to him then, and safe. On that day he did not think about snow. Instead he stood in his undershorts at the bathroom mirror and looked and looked until he saw himself fail. He was aware of the heat in his apartment and he was aware of Paul Simon coming from the CD player on the landing but he noticed the sleet on the skylight as if the sound came through a third ear he did not know he had.

The disease had begun with a chain of small red spots, delicate embroidery on his spine and around his waist and in some bizarre flamboyant gesture up and over his shoulder again. The first treatment meant that he had a negative charge. Static shocks were an issue. The escalator at Macy's, cab doors, some street signs. On a bad day he could stand still on the sidewalk and put the street lights out. Two doses of radium and every woman he met smiled at him. Later Matilda would say that he glowed. And women were drawn to him anyway. And mostly younger women too. Women who were some-how damaged, and loners like him.

Before Matilda there was a woman from Alaska and before her a Mongolian woman called Boo. One night she took a knife in her hand and refused to put it down. And the Eskimo drove with her baby through snow in a pickup truck to find him at the cottage in Cape Cod. All the hopeless cases followed him like a lighthouse and somehow thought they had found hope in him. Then she went home and jumped from the top window of her house with the baby in her arms, and both of them – 'Why?' Glassman wondered – 'Why?' – survived.

Now there were three kinds of antibiotics, a nasal spray that hit the back sinus wall and went straight to his brain. And binders. Painkillers. Vitamins. Every kind. All like bolts and screws to make a together man. His sexuality was unpredictable and it seemed as though the drugs and the disease had run away with his old life and his happy thoughts. Lately he believed it had taken his passions and feelings and he only seemed to *like* women now. He saw them and he was somehow pleased by them, but there were no real feelings of enthusiasm or desire attached.

Matilda stood on the other side of the bathroom door. She inched it open and looked at his reflection in the glass.

'Arthur,' she asked in a whisper, 'are you home?'

Together they looked into the mirror and only his eyes, slate-grey and considered beautiful, could save him from becoming a shadow now.

In the kitchen he took his meds and she made green tea. She poured some over the spider plant on the window ledge and he watched as she scalded the only green thing he had left.

Plants died around him anyway. Bees buzzed and then spun on their backs until they were gone. But he could not infect people. His physician talked a lot about the pituitary gland and how the disease had gotten itself into the cockpit and taken the controls. 'You may not be fully in charge of your emotions,' he said, and when Arthur thought about this he saw devils in red cars driving his feelings around. Now, as he watched her for a moment over his small silver glasses, he could have blamed these devils but really he believed it was more about him and her.

So she was pretty, Matilda, in a voluptuous 1950s way, but he had no real feelings left for her. He would tell her soon, and without her, some of the headaches in his life would go. Lately women seemed to take from him and just leave a weaker fight inside himself.

She talked about her work and he listened and asked questions like 'Really?' and 'Why?' and 'Why there?'

He was always interested in other people's lives and he liked conversation. He knew how to use words to connect people and how to make them all feel as if they were the centre of his world. With women, that gift – and his eyes – seemed to be enough to bring them down.

The pale winter sunlight came in across the river and New Jersey and they sat across from each other and talked about her parents who were in town.

'Mom bought a scarf in Bloomingdales,' she said, and although Glassman tried he could not think of any possible response to this. His eyes over his glasses were growing warm with amusement and inside he thought, *'She's going to ask me to meet them now.'*

She sounded even younger when she spoke about her mom and dad. Matilda was thirty-four and he was fifty-one. When The Chief teased him about dating younger women he said calmly, 'I would like to date a woman who is my age . . . or *a little* younger . . . but do you know any fifty-one-year-old women who are single and not completely insane?'

He had met Matilda at the local swimming pool. She swam towards him in the shallow end and was beautiful, with pale wet skin. And she could swim, long athletic strokes learned and practised from a very young age. She had large breasts which he admired and he liked the modesty of her old-fashioned bathing suit, and she in turn saw the marks and the scars from the injections and spinal taps, and because she seemed OK with that they slept together at his SoHo apartment that afternoon.

He knew then that it would not last of course, as he always knew, but he was distracted by her raven-black hair, her thick slanted eyebrows, her wit and her smile, and so he let what he called another of the 'undead' slip in. He had read somewhere that orphans could always recognize another orphan in a crowded room. He sensed that she was already broken and read the telling 'Please love me' sign in her eyes. The next night she called at his apartment on Prince Street at 4 a.m. and he smiled at her in his sleep and let her in. And later he stayed up and watched her while she slept in an armchair, like a beautiful blackbird, her shoulder supporting her bill.

The next morning she said she was sorry to have woken him up and when she smiled that lovely smile and asked if he would meet her again, he heard himself say, 'OK.'

And now it was somehow five months later and her Connecticut parents who were concerned and wealthy wanted to meet Glassman. They wanted to see, and he enjoyed the irony of this, if he was good and kind and safe enough. Everyone loved Glassman. Lately he had been loved by a group of visiting German doctors and they had wanted photographs and had stood at JFK smiling broadly with their arms around him. He felt bewildered by their love and found it difficult to react. He told Matilda about it now and he frowned and knew there was a joke hidden somewhere in this.

'German love,' he said slowly, 'is very difficult to reciprocate.'

And she sipped her tea and laughed.

'Mom and Dad want to have dinner at Elaine's,' and here she smiled and looked right into his eyes, 'and then . . . they *really* want to meet you.'

'What Mom and Dad . . . *really* want,' Arthur replied in a deadpan voice, 'is to have dinner at Elaine's . . . and then meet someone who is a lot *younger* than me.'

And again Glassman asked why, why when he was swimming lengths in the swimming pool did he decide to stop and why did Matilda also stop and turn around? And why did he take her home and make love to her and then continue to let her in again and again? Glassman had never met a good woman in a bar. He did try of course but he could not connect with the women he met there. And besides, a certain type of woman seemed to find their way to him anyway and this was something he found difficult to explain. To him they were like wild birds who could fly higher than the Himalayas and no matter what sort of storm clouds they encountered, they would not, could not, turn around. They would not stop until they found him standing – ready to be pecked apart – doing what he liked to do best, walking in the wind and collecting old sea glass on the beach. They found him the same way Matilda found him in the swimming pool – and perhaps he preferred it that way. But sometimes when he was lonely, as he often was, he too, like so many men, would have to go to a bar and drink and hope.

'And what happens if you don't find anyone?' The Chief asked.

'What happens?' Glassman replied mildly. 'I do what any self-respecting fifty-one-year-old man does, get a pint of frozen yoghurt and go home.'

↜

But on that one morning in January when he found himself at the mirror in his bathroom and he was not even sure how he got there, for the first time his spirit waned, and Glassman was afraid he was going to die.

He saw for the first time what he needed to see – a real person, losing strength and growing older, feeling older and not very well in himself.

'I do not look good,' he said and it was the saddest voice he had ever heard. He knew then that he was in trouble but he didn't want to be too harsh with himself. He looked down at his hands and said, 'I promise myself that I will use these hands in a different way – and use these eyes to see new things, other than people who sometimes die.' He promised himself that if he ever got out of it – and 'it' must have meant the special body corset for his back, the injections, the drugs – he would leave the ER at St Vincent's and have a different kind of life. He had an idea around glass. Whenever he found a new piece on Long Island or Cahoon's Hollow Beach he would pocket it and he knew that if he became well, this one piece, attached to many others, could allow him to make something great.

Matilda called him at his studio and she was at Elaine's. He could hear her parents in the background and they were drunk and gung-ho and wanted to meet him now.

He did not want to hurt her, so he agreed, but picked a place where the barman knew him, and where he knew every drink on the cocktail menu and every picture on the wall. The barman was waiting for him and he asked, 'What gives, Arthur?' as he gave a sideways nod to the people at the bar.

'You watch,' Glassman said, 'this is better than the *Jerry Springer Show*.' When he walked towards Matilda's parents he saw – and they saw – that he was almost as old as them. It was embarrassing but soon everyone was smiling. Glassman pulled it off, for himself and for her, and that night when she put her hand in his, he told her that really he wanted to be alone. And what he meant, although he could not say it yet, was that she was beginning to trouble him and that he just wanted her to go off somewhere and leave him by himself. The night before she had woken him by taking a photograph of him asleep.

The trouble with Matilda had begun with Marilyn.

The Marilyn. *Marilyn Monroe.*

One night he said it to her and now she could not let it go. He mentioned it in the afterglow and watched as she lit up in front of him. He made a casual remark out through the dark of his bedroom and she turned into a star right before his eyes. She did remind him of her – the high brows, the red mouth kiss, the sleepy sensuous eyes – but now he was getting tired of her. No, she was making him feel tired – which was a different thing. She was, he felt, somewhat 'displaced'. Maybe even a little 'unhinged'? One night she came wearing a blonde wig and a raincoat and not very much else. Every man's fantasy, wouldn't you think? But Glassman felt uncomfortable and a little afraid. He began to wish, in the most basic terms, that Matilda would simply go away.

'Go buy a farm in Virginia,' he wanted to say. 'Have a cobra, ostriches, a boa constrictor, just find new ways to extend your madness.'

Now when she left her parents at their hotel she came back and banged on his door. And he let her in. 'You're my umbilical cord,' she said and she slept on a chair again. She looked

33

beautiful to him then but this was something that he did not need to know. In the morning after she went to work he drank two cups of coffee and went to the bathroom, and here he cursed the medication for burning up his inners and looking into his own face in the mirror he congratulated himself on managing three rabbit pellets and a fart.

The next day, a businessman ordered chocolate ice cream at Darcy's in the Village. He was celebrating the christening of his first granddaughter and he ate a fillet steak and fries before ordering a poached pear with chocolate ice cream. He did not know that there was a crushed almond in it and within minutes he was in anaphylactic shock and it was Glassman, who was on reduced hours now, who injected the adrenaline, even though he knew it was already too late. And as they elbowed each other around the gurney at St Vincent's it was Glassman that was elbowed closer than anyone else. He was moved up from the end so that he saw the body jump and some kind of aura move upwards and then the man opened his eyes and he was able to tell him that his granddaughter was called Anna Louise. But then the pink and orange aura lifted again and he was gone, and before he died, he saw the face of Glassman.

And 'What a face' – that was what Matilda once said – 'like a younger Samuel Beckett.' But it all seemed too familiar to him now – the metallic grey of his hair, the weathered Cape Cod skin – and the deep lines from temple to jaw and each one with a story of a different woman and a different kind of song.

When Matilda wrote her column she called out to him for spellings and definitions. Whatever question she had he could always explain and then add new words. As he buttoned his overcoat in the hallway he answered her and she made light tapping sounds on her laptop in response. Glassman had the gift of vocabulary. He loved words and gathered them around him – he kept some, used some, loaned some, explained some. He had a word for everything. He had words that could fix a person and a place. His apartment was full of books, read and underlined. And in his bedroom, he had begun typing words on his old Remington typewriter again. Old-fashioned expressions and feelings to remind him of something he once had. 'Ardour', 'lustful', 'woo' and then in his small neat letters a word that he would stare at and could no longer draw meaning from – 'love'.

As she worked he went to see his own version of New York again and quietly visited each favourite place. But when he stood at the Stock Exchange he felt nothing. He was unmoved at the foot of the Empire State. He became bored at Writers' Row in Central Park. He fell asleep during his favourite Broadway play. He even took a cab to Lugar's in Brooklyn and ordered, something forbidden in his diet, fried onions and a red rare T-bone steak.

But in the early evening of the cold winter day he saw it, and he asked the cab driver to stop and he got out in the middle of the biting wind and the honks of commuter traffic on Brooklyn Bridge. He saw the Statue of Liberty and the World Trade Center and as if he had never seen them before, he caught his breath and marvelled at how she pointed upwards and how there were two other man-made giants to care for her – and Glassman felt something at last. At home he lay on his bed and took his medication and when Matilda went out for a run, he typed in small black letters, one word – hope.

He did not believe in God any more. But he believed in the power of the universe and the stars and the cosmos. So that night, because he wanted something very badly, he typed it on a piece of paper and went up on to the terrace and sent his wishes out into the night sky.

'I want my apartment to be empty again.'

'I want to make something that no one else has ever made.'

And finally, without a flicker of emotion, just his blinking eyes and his beating heart, Glassman wrote his thoughts; in pure logic because it was all he had.

'I want to feel something more than hope.'

And he stood looking out towards Ellis Island and watched as his wishes flew away.

When Matilda came home she called out to him from her bath, would he like sushi, or Chinese, or broccoli tempura? She had a knack of keeping her voice light and easy when things were going wrong. She used everyday things like the cable bill and the dry-cleaning and sushi to keep their problems at bay. Glassman hated broccoli and Matilda knew that. Now he wondered why these things were important. Sushi or Chinese or carrots or broccoli. Will anyone ever say that about him when he dies? 'Here lies dear Glassman. He hated broccoli and he preferred sushi any night to Chinese, unless it was from Mr Chow's.' The small details that made one person different from another.

She had already set the table in the kitchen and there were three yellow candles and a box of matches waiting on the windowsill. Somewhere outside the Manhattan skyline flickered, and Liberty stood frozen in New York Harbor and he wondered for a moment if she could feel the cold. 'God bless America,' he thought, 'on a night like this she could catch her death.' The bathroom door was open and he knew that in a little while Matilda would step out, steam lifting from her arms and legs, just hoping that he would see her there. Instead he noticed that she had left the polka dot napkins out with the chopsticks.

'Chinese,' he called. And he could hear the relief in her voice, just because he had answered her at all. Through the open door he watched as she dried herself. He was familiar with this aspect of women and how they needed to display themselves. The power they had and yet how his illness had rendered him and her, powerless. She leaned over and her towel fell so he could see, and in his mind they were labelled and marked down, the curve of her back, still wet, her ass, her thighs and her calves. Heavy oval breasts. Underarm hair. Low round buttocks. White transparent skin – and her best feature, her winning asset, the one that had won him at the start, her old-fashioned lips, beautiful, full, yes, and always red.

In every movement now she called out to him. She cried out in silence for him to touch her. And all the time, the air was cloudy with the small decisions of their short life together – the angle of the couch which they had agreed on, her books and his, the clock and the glass of water on the bedside table – the air was clouded with her hopes and fears and dreams and in her every movement now, especially the long stretch of her neck, which she knew he had loved, she called and called to him and Glassman in logic could decide to hear or not.

He walked the landing, past the ceramic plates from Denmark which she had bought and arranged, and past her blue coat and her blue scarf and her keys and the Persian rug over the dark wood. With each footstep he prayed for him and for her. He did not want to break her or break her heart.

37

She turned and she was smiling before she turned and he pulled her into his arms and kissed her neck in behind her ear. And when she turned towards him he could feel how her smile had changed her flow of skin and how she was breathing and her scent and aura said joy and all because he had noticed her after all.

She did not know that Glassman was only trying because his physician had told him he should. He had told him that the medication would affect him. That things would change, and now three months later Glassman did not know which part of his own mind to believe. So he walked the landing to Matilda and she offered herself up and he was always astonished by this. How big the crime and the hurt from the man and yet how quickly women could fold – and how softly – to forgive and forget and just give themselves. He bit her neck with his lips and she pretended to hurt. He kissed her breasts and left a mark. He took her hand and led her into his bedroom and opened her up and tried to find the way to her and prayed he would not forget. Glassman was a good lover. He knew where to put his fingerpads and his kisses and even his thoughts.

He told himself to get real now and to try to treasure her, and yet his spirit seemed to be somewhere else – and how she tried, God bless her, kissing him, taking him in her mouth, holding him, needing him, loving him and all the time –

'God bless her again,' he thought, 'it must be like fucking a mannequin.'

Outside New York lived and around the city in studios with foldout beds, and under low hanging shades, and with a whore, freezing against a railing, other New Yorkers found their own version of New York Love. Afterwards she curled her body around him and made a neat line of kisses along his spine.

From behind he looked like an old man and he knew this and he also knew how much she loved him then. And they slept, her feeling safe and almost loved and Glassman thinking about the bruise that he had made on her breast. In the morning it might show in yellow and green and faint brown and how they would both be glad, somehow, that he had left a mark. And when Matilda slept he got up and wrote more words – 'hollow', 'warmth' and 'soul'.

Later they ate Chinese that was not from Mr Chow's but he had decided to make this Matilda's night and she wore their love now like a ratty bathrobe. For now he had made her happy and she was flushed with it, and then – as she offered him some broccoli on a chopstick – he finally decided, in that New York minute, that he needed to simply walk away. He would take her to his friend's wedding in early February and after that, he would end it. But that night she glowed and her cheeks were flushed and he could see how beautiful she was and he searched for a feeling, for Glassman knew he had a heart somewhere but it was empty now and not even sad for the hurt he was going to cause.

On Friday Matilda's column was about Starbucks. He read it at the open fire on his taupe couch and that evening she came over again and in his mind he knew she had not been asked.

She sat on the rug and leaned against his legs and he wondered at how she could not feel his indifference flooding out from his every pore. She had written about Ray Oldenburg's theory about the third place and how everyone in New York needed the office, their home and the third place to go. She had decided that it was Starbucks and in between making mind-boggling decisions about lattes and chai and grande and vendi, people had found a third place to be. Glassman only went to Starbucks when he needed the restroom and even then they were never clean enough.

Then Matilda said that her third place was his apartment and he said he knew that and she asked where his third place was and he said he was still trying to find it.

And that night he went to bed before her and he read the words he had written, in a long thin row, reading downwards like a Chinese poem.

hope
anticipate
wish
look forward to
ridiculous
unachievable
inconceivable
unbearable
feel
touch
hurt
need
search
find
romantic
can't live without
Love.

3   The World of Us (February 2001)

Honeymoon n. – 1. A period of time spent alone together, especially by a newly married couple. 2. A short period of harmony or goodwill at the beginning of a relationship.

The flat is freezing again. It is Poland, Moscow and Siberia in here. The gas cooker is on in the kitchen and Doreen is wearing her coat to keep warm. Jack Frost is making flowers on the window and outside there are Russians doing a Cossack dance up and down the hall.

'Will you be home soon?' I asked the telephone in the hallway and when Larry answered I knew he was looking across the counter at Vertigo and into a very crowded room.

'I've just closed up,' he said and he sounded really tired. 'I'll bring some dinner home.'

Doreen is carving out a heart in the frost with a teaspoon. 'What do you think of this coat?' she asks. She keeps looking at the heart and does not turn around. Someone left the coat in the restaurant last night and it walked home with her, along with all of our hats and gloves and every umbrella we have ever owned. We play 'I Wish' which is our version of 'I Spy' until we hear the front door open and bang shut again.

'I wish Larry was at home.'

'I wish the Indians would give me free food.'

'I wish we could go on a honeymoon to the Waldorf Astoria.'

'I wish the Indians closed on Sundays.'

'I wish Larry was at home.'

When the kitchen door opens my husband's eyes reach mine from the narrow hallway. He has been working all day and most of the night and now when he looks at me, we are together and safe and warm. He is carrying our dinner in a brown paper bag and the new blue plaster on his finger means he has burnt his hand on the oven door again.

He hands the first parcel to Doreen.

'Roast chicken, mashed potatoes and sage stuffing,' he says, and she begins to laugh.

'And for you,' he says, and here he kisses my cheek, 'Dover sole, dauphine potatoes and a selection of Mediterranean vegetables.'

We turn up the gas and begin to eat our hotdogs and fries.

When Larry sits at the table he opens his coat and pulls me inside.

'That was the nicest roast chicken I have ever had,' Doreen says and she winks at Larry and goes off smiling down the hall.

'Any plans for the weekend?' he asks and when he speaks he looks away and scratches his eyebrow.

I reach for the ketchup and say, 'Hanging around with you?'

'Better pack a bag then,' he says, 'I've got a surprise for you. First I want you to meet my parents and then . . . we're going on our honeymoon.'

Bandhu calls and asks if Doreen is at home. She stands beside me shaking her head and waving her arms and then he calls at the door and I'm still saying, 'Can I take a message?' and he is still talking into his phone.

'We're going on our honeymoon,' I tell him, and he smiles and bows low but all the time his eyes are watching Doreen. She stands back and he walks up the stairs ahead of her.

'I don't see why I can't come,' she says and she watches as we put our coats on. 'We could have got a good family rate – two adults and one child for free.'

Bandhu smiles and puts both hands on her shoulders. 'Doreen,' he says and his voice is low and gentle, 'you are not a family.'

Outside Larry scrapes the morning frost from the window and when he starts the car the kitchen window slides up.

'Bring me back something,' Doreen shouts and then she waves and waves until we can no longer hear her calling out, 'Goodbye.' Larry drives the car down the main street and in between changing gears he holds my hand.

Wig n. – 1. A covering of hair or something resembling hair worn on the head for adornment, ceremony, or to cover baldness. 2. A toupee (informal).

'Good-looking,' his father says, except he cannot speak and so he writes his words on a notepad and hands it to Larry. He is a tall man with a wig and a neat orange tie. He is a gentleman farmer in shining brown brogues.

'She has small hands,' his mother says. Her grey hair is twisted into a thin knot at the back of her head. There are bare country feet in Birkenstocks and she is crooning at the fire. The Matriarch in all her glory and this house rotates around her. Larry's house is Georgian and it looks as though it is sinking into the ground.

I eat apple pie and it is too dry and I know it is trying to choke me.

'Made with buttermilk,' his mother says and everyone looks at my hands.

The kitchen is untidy. There is a dead plant on the fridge,

sets of keys, a clock, several ornaments. There are bridles hanging from pegs on the wall. A saddle on the table. A carton of milk. The window seat is piled high with cardboard boxes and there are footprints on the black and white tiled floor. They are walking in one door and then, understandably, out another.

Now that I am here I want to go back to our flat. Back into the dark. Back to make tea and light the gas fire and watch something stupid and comforting with Larry on TV. I know I don't belong in a place like this but somewhere along the line I knew I belonged with Larry. I was already in love, with him.

Another face appears and looks me up and down.

'This is my brother John,' Larry says.

'The Doctor,' his mother says, and we shake hands. He has hands like Larry's. Wide, long-fingered, and they have already touched every part of me.

'Small one,' the Doctor says and then with a backward glance as he also leaves the room, 'You won't need a bale of hay at the end of her bed,' and everyone laughs, the soft reluctant laugh that country people have. It starts low and becomes louder as if they are all somehow put out by it. Larry winks at me and smokes a cigarette with his back to the fire.

I wonder if we will make love tonight, if we will sleep together under the same roof where all of these other people were made. He tells me that his parents still share the same bed, eleven children and fifty years of marriage later, the wig on the dressing table, the Birkenstocks under the bed.

The house is three miles outside Ballina. An old country estate with broken-down gate piers and only one stag's head to welcome us in. There are no gardens. Not even a shrub or a hedge. Just muck and sheds and several cars parked up around the door. Grown-up children still pulled magnetically back to the family home.

I was worried about my clothes and what his parents would think of me. 'Believe me you needn't worry,' he said, laughing. 'I'm more worried what you'll think of them.'

We crossed a mucky yard and he started laughing again when I stopped and scraped my shoes carefully at the door.

'Oh,' he said, 'I wouldn't worry too much,' and then, 'Left,' and he steered me through an arch.

'This is Hope,' he said to his mother and as he spoke he was already taking a cigarette out. When I looked at his fingers I saw them give a little shake. His eyes looked into mine though and they said, 'Don't worry, it's OK.' His mother studied me inside out. Her small dark eyes took in my face, my small frame, my small hands. Inside I think she was saying, 'This girl does not belong in a family like this.'

'It's lovely to meet you . . .' I heard myself say and so far there was nothing lovely about it but I used a word she would never use, and that told her she was right.

What I thought was a cupboard door opens and Larry's sister Patricia comes in. 'Well,' she says in a stout mannish voice. She has been walking with their dog through wet fields in the rain. She comes in shaking the rain from her hair and stamping her Wellingtons. She is wearing the vintage-leather jacket I bought Larry for Christmas. I spent hours picking it out. Asking complete strangers to try it on. Asking bewildered shop assistants which colour would be better and there was only a choice of black or brown. He loves that jacket. Now whenever I smell an old leather jacket I think of him. She takes it off and throws it on to the stack of newspapers and then takes the dog's face in her hands and kisses it. Then she begins to pile eggs into a saucepan and puts it on to an electric ring.

Larry carries our bag upstairs. The carpet is threadbare and dangerous and there are children's toys scattered here and there.

'In here,' he says and as soon as the door closes behind us we are laughing and kissing each other. Congratulating ourselves on surviving the experience of being in his family home.

'She says you'd be no good at carrying buckets of water,' and he is laughing himself sick about this.

When he kisses me his arms are wrapped around me. He moves his fingers through my hair and down my spine and under my skirt again. This bare room with the mahogany bed and the plain white linen spread makes us want each other but he turns then and puts his hand on the doorknob instead.

In this house people increase and multiply. Children appear at corners unexpectedly. A little girl with brown hair spoke to us in Irish when we came in. There are strange smells of talcum powder, urine, child and dog. But he is gone. Leaving our bag on the bed and jogging lightly back down the stairs. Whistling softly. There are two white matching pillows, a white bedspread, a nun's bed, and I am expected to lie here with him tonight.

I change into a pink dress and comb my hair and then there is a gentle hand on my back.

Patricia's voice comes suddenly. 'You missed a button,' and she buttons it gently and says, 'There.'

When I look in the mirror I am amazed my hair is not standing on end.

The kitchen window looks out across a bleak wet yard. I sit and have dinner with his family and no one speaks. So far there is only brown bread and hard-boiled eggs and a pot of very strong tea. When Larry tells his mother about Vertigo she will not meet his eyes and finds the middle distance instead.

'It's going really well,' he tells her.

'A university education,' she replies.

He looks at me and I look back. Both of us feeling hurt.

'And what do you do?' she asks then and when she turns and faces me it is as if there is an Alsatian in the room.

'I work at a record shop – but I've just got a new job in an advertising agency.'

His mother looks back at me as if I am speaking Dutch.

'What university did you go to?'

'I didn't go to university,' and I can feel my cheeks going red.

'What does your father do?' she asks.

'He used to own a shop.'

'And your mother . . . ?'

And all the time her eyes are boring into me and I can feel some sort of tears moving up from my toes.

And then Larry suddenly begins to speak.

'Mum . . .' he says and his voice is low and calm, 'Hope is my wife. I don't care what you think of her. I don't care what you think of me. But I expect you to treat her with respect.'

'We . . .' she says and her mouth is in a straight stiff line, '. . . are your family.'

And Larry looks over at me and takes my hand.

'Hope is my family now.'

Larry's father comes in and pulls up a chair at the head of the table. He takes off the wig and puts it on a plate near the bread. In my mind are the words 'Holy Mary Mother of God' and I haven't wanted to say them for years.

Then from nowhere I want to say it – and it is just because it is the one thing I am not supposed to say.

'Who owns the rug? Who owns the rug? Who owns the rug?'

'Another egg?' Larry asks and now we are trying not to laugh at his father's bald head.

'Pass me the bread, please,' his mother says and Larry lifts up the plate and passes her the wig instead.

A dog wanders through the yard and sniffs. When I turn I find a little blond boy smiling up at me.

'What age are you?' I ask kindly.

'Four,' he replies but his cherub face stares sadly out the window instead. When the dog lifts his leg the boy keeps on staring and then both of us look.

'He's taking a piss,' he says.

Tonight we lie side by side without speaking. There are no curtains on the window and the stars are dotted across the night sky.

'This was my room,' he says softly. 'I would sit up here, with the leaves at my window, and read and read and read.'

'What did you read?'

'Anything I could find, anything that took me to another place.'

We don't speak for a little while.

'And then?'

'And then . . .' he replies.

'You met me,' I answer.

Larry turns over and puts his arms around me.

'Yes,' he says. 'I met you and I lived happily ever after. The End.'

He sits up on his elbows and asks me what I think of his family.

'They're a bit like *The Munsters*,' I tell him and we both start to laugh. Then he throws back the covers. It is cold now and it's almost 3 a.m.

'Let's get out of here,' he says suddenly and he's still laughing and pulling his jeans on.

'Now . . . ?' and inside I'm thanking my lucky stars.

'Hope,' he says and he sits beside me on the bed, 'I promise you will never have to come here again.'

'Thank you, Larry,' and now we are both packing our things and laughing as we begin to tiptoe down the stairs.

'And if you ever lose your hair . . . Larry . . . I want you to know . . .' And here he turns in the stairwell and says, 'I know . . . you'll still love me when I'm bald.'

The hotel is in Galway. It is a two-hour drive and it seems a little longer because there are two of us in the bubble car. Our heads are close together and we are like goldfish driving around in a goldfish bowl. There was no hot water for Larry's shower and he still smells a bit like sausages and chips. We have all our things in one carrier bag. I have just brought underwear and Larry has brought his razor and an REM CD.

We stop and ask for directions in Galway.

'Excuse me, please,' Larry says, 'we're looking for the Clarinbridge Hotel.'

'Oh,' the woman says, 'that used to be the Mental Hospital,' and now there is silence from the car.

'Do you know where it is?' I ask.

'Turn left,' she says. 'It's on Mental Hospital Road.'

'Of course it is,' Larry says and he turns the Ladybird around on the street.

It is a tall grey stone building and there is a nice red and yellow creeper growing on one side. Larry manages the check-in and I wait in the foyer with our carrier bag. In the room, the windows seem to be very high and there are no sharp objects and no minibar.

At six o'clock there is a knock on our door and the manager comes in and stands with his back to the TV. We are lying on the bed watching some ice-dancing from Bulgaria.

He tells us that he is very sorry but he had no idea we were on our honeymoon. He says 'a lady' called Doreen rang and asked for a bottle of champagne to be delivered to our room. 'The honeymoon suite is booked,' he says but he would like us to take the penthouse and have a complimentary dinner and a bottle of wine. 'I'm sorry,' he says again, 'I hope this will help and that you will enjoy the rest of your stay at our hotel.' I sit up and look at him. 'It's a bit like a hospital,' I tell him, and he looks back at me and cannot think of any reply. Two chambermaids come to the door to help us to pack.

There are two white fluffy bathrobes. The heat is turned up and the bathroom is full of hot water and steam. Larry has a shower first and then we have a bath. This is the first time we have done this. In the bathroom we have a conversation about hotdogs and Larry says he ate his first hotdog ever after visiting the Empire State Building in New York. Then we have a chat about which is taller, the World Trade Center or Sears Tower, and he says, 'The World Trade Center – it measures 1,368 feet.' Then we talk about our favourite cities and I already know Larry loves New York so I tell him my favourite city is Baghdad and he starts to laugh. We talk about memory and why we remember some things but there are others we completely forget.

'It's something to do with the hippocampus structure,' Larry says and he is sponging soap on to my back.

'I want to tell you something about me,' I tell him and I am saying the words out into the steam.

'Is it about your dad?' he asks.

'Yes,' I tell him, and he kisses my shoulders and his arms move down into the warm water and around my waist.

'It's about Dad and Daniel – but I'm going to tell you about Elvis first.'

'OK,' he replies, and we stay there for a very long time, talking and talking together and Larry adding more hot water by turning the tap with his foot.

When we fall asleep under the white sheets we seem to melt into each other and when we speak again it is as if we are both in the same dream.

'Larry?' I ask and my voice comes out into the dark of the quiet hotel room.

'Yes, Hope.'

'What's your favourite word?'

He pulls me closer.

He kisses my lips.

My cheeks.

My hair.

The moon casts a long white shadow across us.

'Canoodle,' he replies.

4 A Wedding in St Bart's

On Saturday morning Glassman walked down Park Avenue with Matilda. She put her hand into his coat pocket to warm it and together they saw the first tight green buds of spring. His friend, who was four years older than he was, had decided to marry the Parisian – who was only twenty-three. He had planned a springtime wedding for her. He had invited Glassman and The Chief. He had bought his black morning suit at Barneys. He believed he could turn the clock back for her and he had even dyed his hair.

'He looks like a crow,' Matilda whispered, and Glassman felt her lean closer and how her breath was warm on his ear. He smiled because he was enjoying the charade of a wedding and because The Chief had just lifted one eyebrow to say 'Hello'. The two couples smiled at each other and when Matilda sat down again she took Glassman's hand.

In the nave of St Bart's they listened to Mozart and watched the young bride as she glided up the aisle.

'What does he expect?' Glassman wondered. 'In five years' time, making love to her will give him a heart attack . . . and waking up beside him will give *her* a heart attack.'

The bride had asked them to blow bubbles after the vows were exchanged and he tried not to laugh as he began to whip the mixture up. When the groom put his ring on the Parisian's finger, Glassman looked up and saw the bride's mother throw her head dramatically into her hands. And in celebration of the madness of this love and of love in general he scooped and blew a giant bubble up over their heads.

Both he and Matilda watched as it wilfully brushed over hair and clothing and seemed to grow and grow until it landed, elegantly and in complete silence, on the groom's left shoulder, like a second glass head. And Glassman and Matilda and even The Chief, who sat on his other side, began to laugh helplessly over this.

On the way home they went to Zabars and bought smoked salmon and cream cheese and chocolate croissants and with every item she put into their basket he wanted to tell her it was over, and then he would see her eyes, and soften and think, not yet. And for a moment he stopped and saw that all of New York was there and shopping – one person to represent each member of their world – all moving in perfect time as if choreographed and on the ice-rink in Central Park.

And there was Matilda holding up a jar of pickles for him to see and she wore that look of eager anticipation on her face. She was also on the ice but she had stopped because he had, and he hated her for loving him in that puppy dog way and then another thought crashed right into this one – why would he hurt her and why would he break her heart?

The flour machine had pulled up at H&H Bagels across the street and they both stopped and wondered at it. 'Look, the flour machine,' she said and they watched the floating cloud of magical white dust, but when she said 'flour' he thought 'flower' and imagined a million pink petals falling into the street, and Glassman wondered if this was the beginning of his first real feeling or thought. They stood side by side on Broadway and 80th Street and she talked about H&H bagels and how they were shipped to San Francisco and Chicago and Seattle and she spoiled it so that his petals turned back to white, never-settling dust.

Matilda talked about her Irish friend over breakfast and how her husband ran a diner and how she worked in advertising – and how funny she was – and Glassman listened with one ear as he usually did now when Matilda talked. He liked the idea of a young couple in love without knowing anything about the complications of it. He liked the idea of diapers flapping on a line and no money for food and how at night they had no radio or TV and got into bed to read books and keep each other warm. He liked the idea of a woman who could not spell but wanted to write anyway. Matilda told him that her friend had a scar in the shape of a star and even this fact could not sink into him and he did not understand why she could not see that he was really somewhere else.

He knew that she was taking things. And that for everything she took she left something of hers in its place. His pyjama top – lime-green silk – for a box of Tampax in the medical cabinet. His black sweater – for homemade meatballs made at her place and left in his refrigerator. Three pieces of glass from his studio – for a pair of socks left under the bed. His copy of *The Good Soldier* – for her copy of *The Picture of Dorian Gray*. He let it all slide in and out like a game of checkers in his head – and he let it happen because as usual he did not want to hurt her. He did not want to hurt anyone at all. And he let her stay out of kindness, and allowed her to steal from him, and this he believed was the last remaining shred of his good self.

It happened with Matilda as he expected.

After they had made love.

That was how every real conversation happened with her. For five months they had been sleeping together, and breaking up and then sleeping together again, and that morning she wanted what he would describe later to The Chief as a '*personal statement*' from him. She needed to hear 'I love you' and 'I miss you when you're gone'. He knew about this from other women and he knew how to answer it now. Simply and to the point but in a gentle voice. And he was gentle with all of them, he hoped.

'I can't,' he said.

And she turned her face into the pillows and then pulled her legs up, and rolled over to take every part of herself away. He knew about this too. The action women used, curling inwards towards their wombs, bringing their hearts downwards so they could be nurtured. The blood changing direction and going into a colder, more needing place.

At first he could not understand any of it. How he wanted sex and then felt nothing at all. It was the disease, his doctor reassured him. The devils that attacked his pituitary gland affecting, controlling, heightening and then diluting every mood. It meant that words like 'love' and 'need' were missing from his vocabulary now, and it was funny but women were never put off by his pain. They seemed to think that it was sent to him because he was able for it. That with it, bizarrely, he was somehow a stronger, more magnetic man.

So Matilda turned from him. And he was ready to explain. He knew the answers because he had tried to explain it before. To Boo. And she had listened – and then she had laughed, and he liked her more for that.

'The disease has taken my endorphins' – that was how he explained it to her, and the black woman who actually towered over him listened carefully.

'I have no ardour,' he said quietly, and with great sadness he gave the final part of his excuse.

And she looked at him with her eyes laughing and said, 'Well, it's a hell of a way to get dumped.'

Now with Matilda he waited and they both lay there apart and listened to the cars and dump-trucks of New York. Outside two jays were in courtship and he watched with sad dead eyes and envied their mad flapping wings and their screeching and their lust. And most of all he envied how they stayed together on the ledge after they made love.

The next day Matilda moved her things out as he knew she would and his apartment became empty again, and when he sat on his kitchen floor eating a carton of raisins and yoghurt he felt nothing, only the cold of his mosaic floor, and some lower back pain.

Later he finished some cottage cheese and noted with some mild questioning and wonderment that she had left her diaphragm in the refrigerator.

On Tuesday he called The Chief and asked him to meet him for lunch. On his way to Franks on Sixth Avenue the wind felt cold and it got in through his coat and clothes. He waited at the counter and as he drank a black coffee he tried not to think too much about his life. He wanted to shut off the memory of her last sad monosyllables and turn up the noise of New York. Any minute now and The Chief would appear, his broad shoulders and surly face reminding him that life was still OK. Today he would feel safe with Gallagher because he had no time for self-pity and he had no time for romance.

'Walk away.' That was his favourite piece of advice and when the glass door squeaked open he saw him, his grey hair brushed straight back from his forehead and his face red with cold. He nodded to Arthur and then stopped for a moment and spoke to someone he knew.

'Hey, buddy,' he said to Glassman by way of greeting, the words coming out quietly under his breath, '. . . decided to come up higher than West Houston, huh?'

And Glassman grinned and felt himself slip comfortably into the male pattern that they both already knew. They would order lunch. Rare hamburgers. Fries. Coleslaw. Black coffee. Vanilla ice cream. All the things their women and their doctors told them to avoid. They would talk about The Knicks. They would talk about the cold. They might venture towards Glassman's new heating system or The Chief's new barbecue flown up from Maine. They would not mention blood pressure – or cholesterol – or their women. But in the last few minutes of their conversation, as Glassman walked beside his big bear friend, the problem would finally surface – and only for a minute and then it would die again. That was what he needed. He wanted to ignore it. To downplay it. He needed hamburgers and basketball and vanilla ice cream and none of the drama of his female friends.

'So you and Matilda . . . ?' That was how it would come out. The question barely tagged on at the end.

And that was how it did come out and at the same time Arthur felt the gentle slap on his back from his friend.

He stopped and over the noise of the traffic he looked up at Gallagher and only had to shrug and shake his head. At times like this he loved his friend's company. No more questions. No more emotion. No more analysis of things that should never have been said.

The Chief looked away. He put his gloved fist deep into a coat pocket again. He squinted in the cold. He turned quickly for an instant as a police siren flew past.

'Probably better off,' he said and his words were spoken up into the wind. And Glassman nodded without looking at him. They watched the street for a moment, both wondering what the other man would say.

'Are you watching the fight on Friday night?' The Chief asked then.

'Yup.'

'I'll guess I'll see you there.'

And with that The Chief turned and walked towards the Precinct. He had said exactly enough to leave his friend feeling calm and safe and on that day in February Glassman felt normal again.

The next day there were three messages on his answerphone and they were all from Matilda of course. He knew as soon as he opened his hall door and stood with the key still in the lock and the red number 3 flashing in his face.

He listened to the first one.

It began with her taking a slow deep breath.

'Hey . . . it's me . . . I know we said we wouldn't do this . . . I miss you, Glassman . . . could you come over? . . . I'm just finding this really hard.'

He knew he shouldn't listen to the second message but he did.

'Arthur, why didn't you return my call? Look. I'm sorry. I just . . . I'm having a hard time with this. I miss you and I don't understand why we can't be friends. I love you – Arthur? Are you there? Please pick up . . .'

And the third message was just the sound of her breathing and an angry little click as she put down the phone.

5   Elvis Has Left the Building (June 1991)

Melancholic adj. – 1. Feeling or tending to feel a thoughtful or gentle sadness 2. Experiencing psychiatric depression (archaic).

Pappy stands behind the counter of our shop. Behind him there are white chocolate mice, clove drops, bonbons, Love Hearts. On the other side there are boxes of red apples, cooked ham, stacks of eggs, today's bread. The morning sun comes through the open door in a long white beam, like a searchlight. It is Saturday so we stand in a row behind the counter but no one says a word, not my pappy, not my brother Daniel, not me. There is a red leather barber's chair in the corner of the shop and next to it a small white sink. There are three pairs of rusty scissors standing in a glass and an electric clippers. But since summer we only sell sweets and groceries, we do not cut people's hair. In the background The King is singing and outside our shop seems to overflow and spill itself on to the footpath. We live in Oldcastle, on the Main Street. The shop is painted shiny red and outside there are two chewing-gum vendors, four cylinders of gas chained together and a plastic ice cream. And Elvis croons. He is always with us, a sort of wallpaper, a fourth member of the family now.

Every day Pappy gets up at seven and he puts a low side parting into his hair. He does this with a new brown plastic comb and then he drops the new brown plastic comb into the bin. The bin is beside his bed and because it is made from metal there is an odd rattling sound. It is the first sound we hear every morning. Except on Sundays when Pappy stays in bed. There is a picture of four white horses pulling a carriage on the bin and every weekday morning when he drops the comb the horses pull it and some of his stray hairs away. They take them away to Comb Mountain and then they make a giant haystack with his hair. He runs a bath at 7.15 and when he sits down in the steaming water, he holds his wet knees and talks quietly to himself. Through the thin walls, his voice travels up and down, light and soft, in and out, on and on. Pappy is persuading, he is coaxing, he is laughing, he is teasing, and he is praying my mother will come back home. I know this because he sounds so kind and sweet and gentle about it and now and then he will say her name.

'Leonora,' he says and the sigh hangs in the air with the steam – but she could be in the water with him. She could be sunbathing on the flat kitchen roof. She could be standing on the wardrobe – wearing a yellow ballgown with a diamond tiara. She could be flying. She could be gliding. She could be driving a red bubble car around his bed. She can be anything she wants to be now. My mother is invisible. She is a spirit. Since last summer, she is with the angels – also known as '*Dead*'.

Pappy puts on a fresh cotton vest. He does not say any prayers. Every week he buys a new white shirt and these are the sounds that wake us. The comb in the bin, the squeak of the bath taps, the cellophane wrapping – and lastly his footsteps and a little fart on the stairs. Even though he has the depression Pappy still makes farts. And they sound like Noddy's car – 'parp-parp'.

His room is at the end of the back landing, a long narrow stretch of dusty oak, and there is a rose-covered rug and a brass fruit bowl on the windowsill. We also have a jar in the kitchen that still has Mum's handwriting on it. '*Lemon*

Marmalade' it says. Pappy eats his All Bran at ten minutes to eight. After that he makes his tea and has one slice of wholewheat toast. His braces make a snapping sound on his shoulders and then he puts on a long white apron and he opens up the shop.

On Saturdays we help him. Standing in a row and waiting for the first customer to come in. Only Pappy wears the white apron, Daniel wears his lumberjack hat and this year we are twelve. We were born on 2 March – but Daniel is fifteen minutes older than me. We have a grandmother too who lives in the country. She lives thirty miles from us in a place called Devlin in Westmeath. So far we have never met but we know her name is Djuna, which she spells with a 'J'. She's my pappy's mother and he says she has snow-white hair now and that she was a famous swimmer 'in her day'.

Pappy keeps the notes in a box under the counter. The loose change goes into an old red OXO tin. I ask him if we can have an ice cream for breakfast and he says, 'Go ahead.'

Daniel has an Orange Split and I have a Gollywog. Then we sit on the front step eating them and making fingerprints on the soft tar in the sun.

Mrs Deegan crosses the street. She is old and does not have to look left and right. She always walks with her chin stuck out in front of her, like she's being led on a rope. She lives in the blue house on the corner. When she opens her front door she steps right on to the street. Her only son, Martin, is now called Martina. He had a '*S-e-x C-h-a-n-g-e*' but no one is supposed to know this. Everyone has a secret, Pappy says, something they keep inside – something that they stay really quiet about and still everyone else seems to know. Mrs Deegan steps over us and goes into the shop. She buys tomatoes, four slices of cooked ham and a loaf of white bread.

She speaks very slowly and chews over each word before it comes out.

There is a white suit in Pappy's wardrobe. It hangs on a wooden hanger and it is covered in a clear plastic sheet. It is a large one-piece outfit with long sleeves, and trousers with flares. There is also a wide pointed collar, high up at the back, and a beautiful sparkly belt. The suit has gold sequins all over the shoulders and silver glitter that runs down the legs. At night I think it comes out and stretches itself, and then it begins to dance and jive. I remember Pappy wearing it. He used to have long black sideburns and a big quiff in his hair. Before my mother went off with the angels, he ran the shop and he was an Elvis impersonator as well. And on summer evenings he would take down some paints and a brush and sit outside and paint. I can remember how Mum would stand at his shoulder and how he would say something and she would smile and they would have some private talk.

Our secret is not the white suit – or the paints – everyone in the town knows about that – our secret is that the Elvis we know is always sad.

From the shop window we can see Brady's pub, the church, the doctor's house, the chemist and the Presbyterian Hall. There are two old beech trees in the town square, and they are scaly and grey, like big elephant's feet. Once, when my pappy was feeling well, we stood at the window and talked about those trees and then we tried to guess the number of leaves. And then he said something really nice to me – and he also said my name.

'Hope,' he said and his voice was quiet and smiling, 'only God can make a tree.'

When Pappy is having a bad day he looks at us strangely – it's as if he can see we are children but he is not really sure who we are. Today he is having a bad day and that means he will never call us by our names. I am thinking about the angels again and there are questions I would like to ask. I am wondering where they took my mother first of all and if they are all living together now in a white mobile home. I am wondering if they play Scrabble the way we do and if they laugh when they come up with low-score words, like 'cat' or 'God'. I am wondering if they have end-of-term discos like us. And if they like spaghetti with meatballs. Do they wear white wings and ski-pants? Do they like Joan Armatrading? Because I do. Do they ride around on white bicycles? Do they have big cloud dogs with muzzles? Do they crimp their hair?

The paints are kept in the attic. There are worn-out brushes and a pallet with different daubs of colour. Before Mum died he used to sit inside the window and paint the different colours of the evening sky. Now he paints dark clouds over grey water or usually he just sits and stares. He picks up a brush and stirs the water until it turns grey too and then he puts the brush back down and looks at a picture that is just not there. I wish he would make something. I wish he would put red and yellow and blue on the canvas just so he can see that those colours can be out there too.

Our kitchen table is covered in a plastic cloth. There are pictures of small bottles of wine on it and then some apples and pears. Pappy has no time for washing-up and so we use plastic cutlery and paper plates. There is no conversation and we each have different ways to amuse ourselves. Daniel eats his food alphabetically – first the broad beans, then the potatoes, and the smoky rasher last. I think about all the ads on TV that I like and my favourite is for Cadbury's Flake.

'Only the crumbliest, tastiest chocolate, tastes like chocolate never tasted before', and I think these are the most beautiful words I have ever heard. Pappy leans over and pours milk into Daniel's glass and other than that he just eats and never says a word.

'Pappy . . .' I say, and he just keeps chewing and chewing and looking out over our heads. Another ad I like is for Ariel washing powder. I like that they always start out with stains like jam and chocolate and then the same clothes end up dazzling white. I am sure the angels use Ariel and now and then they also have a Cadbury's Flake.

Pappy finishes his lunch and dabs a paper serviette to his lips. He lifts the picnic ware and he glances at the clock.

The shop needs to be opened again.

Tick-tock-tick-tock.

'The nun asked me if you would sing at the school concert again this year,' and then I look down. There are three broad beans left on my plate.

One – two – three.

Three – two – one.

Tick-tock.

Tick-tock.

Tick-tock.

Pappy watches me.

Oh please, and I say this down low and inside myself, but the word that comes back is 'No'.

The red history book shows a dead body being taken away in a wheelbarrow. There is also a woman in a green shawl and she is crying and waving her hands in the air. We are learning about the famine and thinking about all the people who died. Doreen draws a speech bubble from one of the people. 'Can anyone tell me the way to McDonald's?' it says. Then there is a test and we are asked to list 'the effects of the famine on Irish society'. We consult each other and Doreen writes her only answer in very faint pencil –

a lot of people died

I do not have any other answers so I write –

Apple drops

Fizzle sticks

Marshmallows

Bonbons (lemon, strawberry and white)

Chocolate hearts

Milky teeth

Coconut mushrooms – and

Flogs

Bright patches. There are some. Today I am walking up the street with Daniel, and Pappy is standing smiling at the shop door. On a sunny day like this he might come out and meet us or sometimes he will sweep the dust from the step. On a bright-patch day he might stop and lean on the brush a little and then talk to the mechanic from the garage next door. He does not know that there is a notebook in my bag where I save all my questions for him and for this kind of day. They are mostly about ads on TV, men and women, love, angels and death.

At lunch Daniel will not eat his potatoes.

'I have the famine,' he says.

And today there are words everywhere. They fly out of Pappy's mouth and run up the stairs. They fill the saucepans in the cupboard and fall out of paper cups and plates. On days like this he likes to talk and talk and sometimes I think he will never stop. He talks about my mother and how beautiful she was – and how romantic it was when they first met – and then he goes back to his schooldays and growing up in the countryside. He talks about his mother and the animals on her farm. He tells us about pigs and sheep and goats, and even rats and mice. He stands at the shop window and whenever anyone passes, he waves. And it is a big wave with two hands and sometimes they get a fright. He buys too much of everything at the Cash and Carry and there are boxes of Love Hearts and lemon bonbons under our beds.

'He's on a high today,' Mrs Deegan says, and she sticks her head out and she is led back across the street.

Daniel sits quietly in the barber's chair. The double red doors are bolted and the blinds are down. When I walk inside with Doreen he does not look around. Instead he looks at our faces in the mirror and says, 'Pappy told me to wait here, and not to go upstairs.'

The house is quiet and when I walk down the landing to his bedroom the boards do not even creak. I turn the handle quietly and when I open the door Pappy is wearing the white glittery suit and standing on a white painted chair. The sequins from his suit catch the light and make small white spots on the bedroom walls. He looks just the way he did on the stage, except there is a leather belt around his neck and he is facing my mother's picture on the shelf. His eyes are looking into my mother's eyes and her eyes are sad and looking away.

'What are you doing, Pappy?' I ask, and he turns around very slowly. He looks at me as if he does not know me.

Again.

Again.

'I'm changing the light bulb,' he says

Yesterday I made my first phone call to my grandmother. I called her and when she answered I read everything out from a copybook page.

'This is Hope Swann calling,' the first line said.

'Pappy is not well,' the second line said.

'Please send help,' and then without waiting for any answer I put the phone down and tried to imagine her setting off with her huskies and a sleigh.

6   *Is This What I Get for Loving You?*

Matilda said goodbye to Glassman and watched as he leaned down to open the cab door. She stood still and managed to smile when he kissed her cold cheek and when the cab moved away she turned and pressed a small red-gloved hand to the glass. Without noticing people or streets or shop fronts she found her way to her apartment and giving her keys a little shake, she quietly let herself in. Glassman did not understand that after he had told her the news she had felt her own breath slip away. That as her body seemed to curl and then stiffen on the sheets beside him, she felt something real and full of happiness and life just die inside. She had no way to tell him. No means to explain. There were no words big enough to show him that her life, all of it, every day marked out on the calendar, had been for and around him.

Her cat Godot had not been fed for two days. Any longer and he would start chewing on his own tail. She opened the windows and a light snow shower came in and she sat there on the end of her bed and felt the cold wind on her face.

When she got up she saw that she had creased the sheets and she was somehow glad of this. It was in her mind a sign of life she didn't know she had. She had been let down before and she knew the mechanics of it. How she could begin to move on again after losing a love. It had happened only last year too and now she had a cat, knowing that there was an agreed limit on their love. She would feed Godot and in turn he would stay. He would live with her, asking for nothing, just a roof over his head, a handful of Go-Cat and a clean litter tray. Without Glassman she would have to go back to love in dry handfuls now.

She closed the window and seemed to pause and watch her own every move. She had loved this apartment. The curved tongue-and-groove panelling. How the room curled and how her bed, a wide cream expanse with Egyptian cotton sheets and pillowcases covered in blue cornflowers, had kept her safe until now. The bathtub with the shining taps. The goldfish swimming on her shower curtains. The specially chosen walnut doorknobs and the French windows in the kitchen. The previous owner had left a red antique scales and Glassman had helped her to paint the kitchen door to match. Her crockery came from Denmark. In summer she grew sunflowers on her balcony. Until now, when she closed her door behind her, she moved to Europe and said goodbye to New York. But that was before she went swimming and forgot about loving water and instead seemed to fall into him. Her friends said she was crazy and then they saw it too and could only stand by and watch how her life began to turn and turn around his. How nothing mattered. How everything, her work, her home, her family, were all just things to be passed on a road that led to him. He had a way of making her feel *cherished*. That was it. He would lay one hand on her shoulder as he walked from the kitchen to the bathroom and she felt alive. He could look at her and smile over his small silver glasses and make her feel like a three-year-old.

She was not beautiful in any conventional way. She knew that. But he had wanted to touch her from the start. He made her feel wanted and gave her a real sense of place. And now, without him, her whole life would become an irritation. The phone could not ring now unless it was him. The doorman could not give her any message unless it was from him. Even

69

her parents who lived in Connecticut were in the way. Her friends, giant obstacles to her thoughts. At least if she could not have him, she could be alone with her thoughts of him. Perhaps she always knew it was all going to end. He did not want her to sublet her apartment. He had baulked at making promises. Told her about his illness. That in ten years he would be sixty, but nothing mattered to her. Matilda was in love with him. There were red hearts being puffed towards him and they kept coming even when he looked away.

The first item was a piece of glass from his workshop. She had taken it on the first night he showed her around. She had turned it over and over in her hand and when he was not looking she did not put it back down. Then she took his black sweater and he knew about that. It was one of the regular transactions of love. Like the sock left in the bed. The undershorts on the radiator. Small symbols to reassure the other person that you intend to come back. Like all women, though, she marked these things down, and truth be told, Glassman was just careless and tended to leave his things lying around and Matilda, because she wanted to, mistook his untidiness for love.

Then she began to forage and collect.

And everything went into an old suitcase in the closet in the hall. A band-aid taken from the trash can in his bathroom. She treasured it. And a black silk tie from his wardrobe, never worn but taken out once and run through his hands. His empty meds bottles. The plastic caps prised open so she could smell inside. It seemed sad – but she had begun to associate a pharmacy smell with him.

The first photograph she took was of his hands. Strong, long fingers. Made to draw things and carve wood. They were not a doctor's hands at all. Much less a doctor working in the

ER. He would not know that one night she went there. That she got up and dressed at 3 a.m. and went out into the snow and walked twenty blocks until she found him, in green scrubs working on a traffic accident. She stood silently behind the glass and watched him give orders and move quickly and silently and all the time save lives and then she went home and masturbated to the thoughts of it. The next day she knew his patient had lived. He was always different when someone died. Not blaming himself but just looking puzzled and quiet and his eyes full of questions. It was always, 'Why?' With Glassman everything ended in 'Why?'

Matilda took the trash out. Fed her cat and ignored his sulks.

'You think you have problems,' she said, and they would not even meet each other's eyes. Godot walked to the window and watched the snow as if it was new to him. He had seen it for two winters now and yet he sat with his back to her, his head looking up and down as he tried to watch each and every flake. 'Another break-up,' he would say, if Godot would ever talk. She did her laundry. Changed her sheets even though they were almost new. She opened her post and paid her cable bill. Then she checked her mailbox and her heart sank a little further when she saw there was no email from Hope. She tried to practise returning to her old life. And then she turned off her phone and went where she had wanted to go all along.

Matilda kept the wig in the closet in the bedroom. It was short with loose curls and peroxide blonde. She painted her lips red in her favourite MAC colour, which was Rage. Then she put the wig on and took a pill and went to the walk-in closet in the hallway. The inside of the door was covered in black and white prints. Glassman smiling at a barbecue – he hated barbecues. Glassman with his favourite Ben and Jerry's

– Caramel Chew-Chew. Glassman on the beach – he got a great tan – and on the sidewalk after the concert in the Beacon. Then his hands again. His fingertips. His smiles. His face. His eyes – his eyes, and it all came together to make a montage and a shrine to Glassman.

He had told her and was direct about it – and yet in a simple clear moment in her hallway closet she decided something else. He said 'Yes' to releasing her. He said 'Yes' to ending it. He said 'Yes – yes – yes' as she packed all her little things and 'Yes' when he followed her down the stairs and on to the street. It was *his* arm that went up for the cab and he breathed 'Yes' to the one that swooped into the sidewalk straight away. Glassman said 'Yes – oh yes' to the final goodbye of it, but high in the dark shadows of her closet, when Matilda could not manage the word, Marilyn said 'No.'

7 No Running No Jumping No Diving (December 1992)

Alter ego n. – 1. A second side to an individual's personality, different from the one that most people know. 2. A very close and trusted friend.

Daniel climbs the first snowdrift. His feet are sliding, his dark eyes blinking, white sky and white earth meet. The peacock is dazzled by it and flies up and sits on the roof. When my brother sees this he laughs, a bright shouting laugh that comes up from his feet. He walks on top of the drift, as high as the ash trees, and then jumps down and crunches into the frozen snow on the lane. The water tanks are frozen. There is no water for the house. One lamb is dead. A second one in my arms. The lamb's brother, in a small pink cardigan. He makes himself at home in the warm kitchen and gives short sharp bleats, stepping around.

My grandmother's house is pretty, an old falling-down place, painted a very pale blue. There are trees, every kind, silver birch, Dutch maple, horse chestnut and pine. When Daniel passes the kitchen window he is singing honky-tonk, Benny Goodman, I think, and I put some hot toast into his hand. This year I am thirteen years old. In March we will both be fourteen.

'Juna has a glass eye,' he says. 'That means she can see you inside and out.'

My grandmother has driven up the front avenue with her little car puffing out lots of white smoke. It is a long winding gravel path, hard like concrete now, through wide-open fields. So she gets the best of it, the duck pond frozen in the hollow, the old-fashioned wooden fences and gates, the swing with snow on the seat. And in the distance she would have seen Ghost Lake between two hills, and then the house, beginning to crumble, with the stone arches into the stables, the old red-roofed byres and the grey tractor frozen in the yard.

Juna is a tall woman with broad round shoulders and a shock of snow-white curly hair. When she gets out of the car she beams at us, first Daniel and then me. There is something raw about us. I already know this about myself, but she takes all of this in and absorbs us. The Wellingtons worn in the house. The holes in my elbows. The dirty jeans. We are all dressed in layers like onions to keep warm and my hair is in two long blonde braids, several days old. She smiles again at the hen who has decided to leave the kitchen and the lamb who puts his head around the door. She takes a look around the yard and then begins to carry groceries towards the house. Today she reminds me of the Snow Queen, with her white hair and mittens, except she is driving a Robin Reliant instead of a sleigh.

Outside Daniel sits on the pink cart. It is rotten now. Left to die in the long frozen grass. There are two wooden shafts pointing upwards and I go and sit next to him. It is not a nice place to sit. There is a smell of old wet wood and underneath, a place for yellow fungus, frogs, slugs.

'She's cleaning,' I tell him, and he kicks at the ground. A loose stone skitters across the frozen earth. He looks worried. We are both wild but Daniel is worse than me.

He scrunches his face up in the cold and refuses to come inside. His knuckles are red and blue with a summer suntan still on the backs of his hands.

'She's like a white tornado,' he says and we both start to laugh. And from the window she watches us as she piles old newspapers into bags for burning. We have grown up on toast and cornflakes and we eat everything from paper plates and she sees us now, exactly as we are, in the mess of our lives and how we stand in the middle of it, laughing.

Upstairs Pappy is painting again. The older canvases are turned away from us now. There are paintings of grey stormy skies over the lake, with rolling clouds and pale yellow shafts of sunlight pushing through. Everything is the colour of a wet autumn, always damp and dark. Or as Juna says, 'The colour of a bog.' His new paints came down on the Dublin bus. They were wrapped in brown paper and different to before. They have flashy lipstick names – 'African Dust', 'Rhinestone Blue' and 'Lemon Ice Cream'. He is using acrylics and crayon instead of oils. We collected them for him along with Juna's three-day-old chicks. They arrived with their little feet sliding, in another brown box, one that felt alive and warm. He wears an old white shirt when he paints. There is a red splash of paint where his heart is and some yellow flecks up near the collar. He stands in his socks with the shirt on over a jumper and there is a hole in the heel of his sock. His bedroom is used as his studio now and there is a two-bar electric heater sitting in the grate. Old canvases lean on every wall but there is something different on the easel today. Sometimes he goes to it and makes a lot of tiny brush strokes – but mostly he just stands still and stares. He puts his hands to it and mixes the colours and blurs the harder lines with his fingertips. Then he pulls the corners of his mouth down and nods and shrugs and then he sits down on the chair. After supper I bring him some of Juna's special walnut cake and a pot of coffee on a tray.

In the end the painting is of two leather slippers. Soft calfskin slippers with pointed toes. They are covered in as many colours as he could think of. Blue rhinestone, ruby-red, hot pink, azure blue and emerald-green. There is turquoise and jade – a million tiny jewels perfectly positioned and formed. *Indian Slippers* it is called.

Daniel. Origin, Hebrew, meaning – God is my judge.

It is September. Almost one year later, 1993. We are standing at the lake. 'Ghost Lake'. It is calm. Warm. Quiet. There are smooth grey and white rocks near the shore. Two small wooded islands. A ramp with worn-out wood, pounded for years by children running in bare feet. I can hear the hollow call 'Geronimo!!!' They whooped it out like young braves going to battle, the words flying up and echoing in the trees and hills as they ran and bombed off the end. The trees where we found the charm bracelet. The red and white sign that says, 'No Running No Jumping No Diving'.

It is Daniel's idea to take the boat out.

'Come on,' he says. 'Just a little way and we'll come straight back.' He watches me for a moment and smiles at my face. The sun is going down. Late afternoon. No cars. Not even the grey-haired lady who swims for her arthritis. Behind those hills, the house. Behind those trees there is an orange tent. The swimming coach who leaves tomorrow morning. A dental student from Dublin. A young, muscular man in Speedos who has taught me, amongst other things, to swim.

Daniel walks to the edge of the lake.

He makes a stone jump six times over the water.

'Six,' Jack says and he frowns into the sun. The boys are wearing shorts. Denim cut-offs to their knees. Both darkly tanned. I am wearing a new sky-blue bikini made from towelling material and it soaks up the water like a sponge. For a moment the boat is forgotten and Daniel walks to the end of the ramp. He stands on the first diving board. His hands are on his hips as if he couldn't care less. His legs are tanned. Even his toes. My brother is more beautiful than I am. Jack waits with me near the shallow part. I know nothing about him yet except that he is a tall, silent boy and Daniel's first real friend after me.

At fourteen I am growing. 'Coltish,' Juna said. An awkward country girl with red cheeks and tangled blonde hair. There are bruises on my knees and a star-shaped scar over my navel. I could not say Daniel as a child, so I called him Danny and Daniel called me 'Star'.

He jumps lightly on the diving board. It is at least ten feet over the water. He stretches. Yawns. We watch. He lifts his arms. Out by his sides like he might flap and fly. And then he swings them back quickly and with one single bounce – and in his t-shirt and shorts – he is diving in. The water splashes back and then there is silence again. Daniel cuts through the water, taking several strokes before surfacing, and by the time he comes up Jack has looked right into my eyes and I have blushed and looked away. Daniel's black hair is sleek and shiny when wet. He swims towards the red ladder and begins to pull himself up. He is panting and he stands for a moment watching us and sees that something has changed. He looks at Jack and then at me as if we have betrayed him.

'Hope, come here to me,' a voice says and when I turn I see

Juna standing on the shore. Sometimes my grandmother is like a vapour. A bright streak of light. She just appears out of nowhere and I think she must be able to fly and get in under doors.

I lift myself with my hands and drop easily into the water. I swim slowly because I know they are watching me and I keep putting one foot down because I am terrified I will drown. I swim as far as the red buoy and wait there, my eyes turned to the horizon, away from him and away from her.

Jack offers Daniel a cigarette. My brother grins and then wipes the water from his face and puts one between his lips. They stand then as they usually do, saying nothing but liking the fact that the other one is around. I had never seen two boys who are good friends until then. How quiet and calm their friendship was. When my friendship with Doreen is built on laughter and talk and sound.

Daniel turns towards the boat again and blows cigarette smoke towards it.

'We'll row out to the first island,' he says casually and all the time he refuses to meet my eyes.

'Come on, Star,' he says suddenly, and his face breaks into his bright happy smile. He knows I will not go out there with them, that my fear of the deep water will keep me on the shore. He knows he will win with this and he also knows that there was somewhere else I want to be.

'Teach her to swim,' Juna said, 'and I'll bake you a flan.' The dental student thought we were mad. He arrived at her house when we were trying to get a cow off the front lawn. He came on a five-speed racing bike and Daniel, for no reason, began calling him 'Doc'. In the middle of our tea Pappy came in smelling of sweat and manure and ordered everyone, including Doc, outside to help bring a heifer in. 'Get a bottle of treacle,' he said to Juna, 'she's bound up.' I was mortified. My family are generally embarrassing people and I already thought Doc was the most beautiful man I had ever seen.

When we came back there was a cat on the kitchen table with his head stuck in the milk jug. 'Get down, you bastard,' Pappy said without even blinking, and I felt like crawling under a chair.

'Doc . . . Hope's afraid of water,' Daniel said. We were sitting around the kitchen table eating salad with all the windows opened up over the fields. Everyone was passing the real plates around and being helpful and polite.

'Daniel,' I said, 'please shut your cake-hole.'

Sometimes I have no time to check myself. I am always saying that sort of thing. And Granny Juna was looking at my father and shaking her head. Doc, who has just turned seventeen, looked at me and gave me a smile.

'I'll have her swimming by the end of the week,' he said.

My grandmother always pays in food. Tomatoes from the greenhouse. Heads of lettuce. Gooseberry jam, and she is very good at pies. Fish pie. Steak and kidney pie. Chicken and ham pie. Shepherd's pie. Cottage pie. But it is summer so she offered Doc her aquaphobic granddaughter and a flan.

He stood on the ramp wearing a t-shirt over his Speedos. Sometimes he jumped up and down lightly on the diving board but he never got wet. His blond hair fell to his shoulders and his Speedos were like a postage stamp at the top of his legs. I waded in, terrified and delighted that it was just me and him and the lake. Every night he stood on the ramp and gave orders. He swung his arms around as if getting warmed up for a race. He told me to stand two feet away from the bar and then throw myself towards it.

'The water will carry you,' he said. 'You just have to let it.' And he watched me doing that for a long time and then he told me to move back another foot and do it again. And that is how I learned to swim. Standing up to my waist night after night, the sun going down, shivering, sometimes freezing, hugging myself against the cool evening breeze, and always looking up at him.

'Back another foot,' he said, 'and do it again.'

At the end of the first week I made my first proper stroke. And that night Juna made the flan. It had lots of mandarin orange slices and cream on it and I carried it down to him under an umbrella because it rained. I wore a new swimsuit with trainer straps and a heartbeat pattern across my chest. I let my hair loose and it got wet. 'Relax,' he said and this time he got into the water with me, and as it grew dark and with the water still warm from the sun of the day, he balanced me on his arms. He smelt like salt and suntan lotion and later I watched as he dived from the highest board and clapped when he surfaced again. We ate the entire flan inside the tent and listened to the rain on the canvas and he asked if he could kiss me then.

The boat is old. It is wooden with a flat bottom and dangerous in a lake like this. A lake called 'Ghost Lake' because it has no bottom. Imagine a lake without a bottom. A place that could take you right down into the centre of the earth. There are no life jackets. We are not allowed to take it out. We have been told often enough. But Jack is here and everything is different. Sometimes Pappy rows out to the middle of the lake to fish. He takes us with him and we are not allowed to talk and we like the respect for the boat in the water. We like the sound of the oars when they first touch the surface and the rub of the oarlocks on the wood. The knocking of wood against wood. We are not supposed to take the boat out but Jack is here and we are all able to swim now.

The boys row out towards the first island and I stand watching. I envy them and their adventure and the cigarette is held between Jack's teeth now as he rows. He messes it up too and one oar misses the water completely. I want to be there with them but I can't go out that deep. Daniel takes over and Jack moves unsteadily to the stern. The lake is so calm and silent and in a little while I can't hear their voices or the sound the oars make as they fall. I walk to the end of the ramp and sit and watch the boat. I hug my knees, my wet hair pulled into a ponytail. The air is growing colder. What happens? I don't know. That is the truth. I grow tired of sitting here and turn and walk towards the shallow part. I am thinking of skipping stones. Of going home. Of hot tea. Of salad. Of Pappy painting in his studio. Of Juna's nice kitchen. Of our red shop just on the edge of our town. Of hanging wet swimsuits on the line. Of falling into bed and sleeping in wet hair. Of the orange tent behind the trees.

Doc is waiting near the fire. It crackles and sends sparks into the air. He holds the flap back and without a word I creep inside. He begins kissing me and no one says a word. At one point there is a voice. Somewhere far away. 'Star,' it calls and then 'Star' again. The boys. It is almost an hour later when I come back out and when I walk out on to the ramp I am dizzy and jelly-legged and carrying the empty flan plate.

The boat is upside down and there are hands and splashing near it. I almost laugh. I think I do and then the laugh is swallowed until it disappears back inside. There is one head. Dark hair. Who? Daniel or Jack? And then I know that this is different. That something has happened and I am running to the end of the ramp. I can hear Jack's voice, 'The buoy!' and then 'The buoy!!' again. His voice breaks into a cry the second time. He is in the water and somehow crying now. My hands begin to shake when I untie it. I want to pee. My stomach feels as if it is suddenly opening up. My left arm aches badly. My limbs are heavy and from nowhere I am crying too. Whimpering. Crying because the flat-bottomed boat has turned over and because it will sink now and because it is my brother Daniel I cannot see.

The boat is too far away. It is too far to throw the buoy.

Too far. Too far. I would have to swim. The buoy is hollow, old. It won't hold me. I will throw it. I won't throw it. If I swim I will have to go out into the deep water. Deep green cold. The lake without a bottom. Water filling my lungs. Covering my face, my hair, my head. Going down. Down. Down. Goodbye, everyone. In the water Jack leaves the boat and disappears and now both boys are gone. There is a sudden silence and then the boat is going down too. Total silence that chills me to my bones. I begin to whimper and still I am frozen on the ramp. Why? Jumping up and down. Crying. Whimpering. Then I remember Doc. And I run, run away, run away down the ramp. Bare feet smashing over stones. Into the trees over nettles. Grass. Tree stumps. Crying, screaming now. The tent is gone. His fire still smokes. A pale yellow rectangle on the grass but his bike is there, on its side, and when he appears I can only point. My speech is gone and my body gives up and I sink down into the grass. My left side agony now. My breath gone. Where is Daniel? Where is Daniel? Jack is back up again. I can see him. Hear him. Sobbing. Big girl cries. I can hear his crying from here.

It happens close to autumn. I will always remember the light, not really summer or autumn or winter, it is another season in another kind of day – and how there is no breeze at all here, the perfect stillness of it and the leaves that fall on the lake and how they move away slowly, in red, yellow and gold.

Jack knocks softly on the bedroom door. He stands awkwardly in my room with his bag in one hand.

We stand and face each other and as we watch our eyes begin to fill with tears.

'I have to go now,' he says and then he sits on my bed and begins to cry. They have taken Daniel away and there is just an empty house, filled with water and so cold. The guards came. Father Brady. Doc, who stood behind me with his hands on my shoulders. Pappy took the news in silence and then got up and walked away. He drove straight into the town and put a note on the shop window and pulled the blinds down. I put my arms around Jack now and we are still strangers in a new and strange place. He puts his arms around me. We put our arms around each other, clinging for our lives, both knowing that we have shared something together that we can never forget. We both saw his happy suntanned face on the shore.

'Come on, Star.'

We heard his voice. We saw his face. We were the last to know it.

Daniel has left his name in every room. On the wall in my bedroom. In blue chalk half-way up the stairs. On the side of the dresser in the kitchen, on the back of the piano and inside the hall door. In his own room he has left it on the window, etched delicately into the glass. He used an old nail to do it. It is strangely breakable and flimsy-looking, with wispy white letters to remind me of him. And now when I read my books they mean nothing. The letters jump and rearrange themselves – and the words move around like mice on the page.

TWO

8   Big Sky Country (February 2001)

Zoo n. – 1. A park where live wild animals from different parts of the world are kept in cages. 2. (informal) A place characterized as being full of noisy obstreperous people creating confusion and disorder.

A picture of a light bulb means we have 'Ideas'. A picture of a smiling face means 'We love our work'. A picture of a blue sky means 'There are no limits to our thinking'. Our ideas are like Montana, our brains are Big Sky. Jonathan says that growth here is organic, but there are no trees and no green leaves. Our receptionist is from Rwanda. She is like an ad for a holiday with her beautiful white teeth and coloured beads. There are emails about pitches and brainstorms and revised creative briefs. I have no idea who I am today or what I am supposed to be doing here. On Monday there is an early meeting in the boardroom. Everyone comes in and says a cheerful 'Good morning' to someone else. They talk about the weather at the weekend, the football match on Saturday, and after a little while they begin to talk about the work.

A young man with a suntan smiles and starts us off.

'The client would like us to revisit the brief. He feels the work we presented is wide of the mark.'

And then the Creative Director responds – and this is almost a shout.

'What exactly does the client want?'

The man in the suit and the suntan frowns now, but only very slightly, and he says, 'He wants something *edgy*.'

87

And then the Creative Director gets very red and now he really shouts.

'If one more person mentions edgy I'll scream. That client hasn't a fucking clue what he wants. We've already presented twice and I'm not tying up two more teams until we have a clear brief – and what the fuck is edgy when it's at home?'

Here the man in the suit swallows and smiles again and this time he says, 'I think we can have another look at the brief but I also think he is entitled to his opinion, given' (little cough) 'that he's paying for the work.'

And then the Creative Director goes, 'That client wouldn't know how to sit the right way round on a toilet.' And that's just the first item on the work list.

This is how Monday morning at the advertising agency starts. The Account Directors sit around the boardroom table smiling and the Creative Director roars at them like Godzilla and then goes back to drawing little flowers on his page.

Edgy adj. – 1. Nervous and irritable. 2. Having an intense or energetic quality or atmosphere. 3. Unusually smart or stylish.

Email from Jonathan Kirk 9.33 a.m.
To Hope Swann
Subject: Country Fresh Soups Pitch
Hope – Get everyone together in the boardroom at 11 for a brainstorm

Email to everyone 9.34 a.m.
From Hope Swann
Could everyone go to the boardroom at 11 for the soup brainstorm?
Thank you.
Hope.

Email to Accounts 9.36 a.m.
From Hope Swann
Hello, I was wondering if it would it be possible for someone to tell me when I will get paid?
Thanks very much.
Hope.

Email from Jonathan Kirk 9.37 a.m.
To Hope Swann
When I said everyone – I meant the Country Fresh team not the entire agency . . .
Sylvia has the list.

Email to Hope Swann 9.37 a.m.
Re: Payday
From Frankie Preston
Hopeful . . . you accidentally copied that mail to everyone.
Frankie.

Email to Frankie Preston 9.38 a.m.
From Hope Swann
Subject: O Lord
Who is Sylvia? Where is she?
Hopeless.

Email to Hope Swann 9.40 a.m.

From Gunter Van Wildenberg

Greetings from Finland!

Dear Hop,

We are pitching for the Coke account here in Finland and would appreciate the help of our good friends in the Network. We are looking for the following which we are sure you have on file –

Overview of the current soft drinks market in Ireland – Coke brand positioning, previous advertising – print, outdoor and TV – over the last four years and competitive material also. Would also appreciate input of your planner into our strategy document and creative brief attached.

We are having an internal review tomorrow morning so would need this for close of play today.

Thanks very much for help – and welcome on board!

Gunter.

It is 10 a.m. and there are people walking from the kitchen carrying toast and bowls of cornflakes. There is a smell of coffee everywhere and I am wondering if someone is going to start frying bacon and eggs. Someone has left a pair of old shoes under my desk. There is also a small plastic frog carrying a sign that says 'Good Luck'. The office is like a ship inside; there are high wooden decks and mezzanines and every office has a little porthole. There are four levels rising upward and red and white flags hang down from the glass roof, like sails. Larry has made me a sandwich and I keep looking at it and wondering if it is too early to have my lunch. When I peep inside my lunchbox I see he has also included a bar of Turkish Delight and a little note.

I love you. You'll be great.
Larry xx.

Frankie is supposed to be explaining 'office procedures' – there are things called 'status reports', 'contacts reports' and 'critical paths'. Instead he sits at my desk and asks if I have any chocolate and then he begins to go through everyone on the telephone list. He says that people with names beginning or ending in vowels are basically '*OK*'.

'You're fine,' he says. 'Now . . . *Jonathan* . . . for example . . . is not.' Then he hums the tune for *Countdown*.

'Vowel or consonant?' he asks. When I show him the email from our friends in the 'network' he barely glances at it and then he asks, 'Are you aware there is a Malteser rolling across your floor?'

Email to everyone 10 a.m.
From Jonathan Kirk.
The idea of people having various forms of breakfast i.e. croissants, toast, scones and in some cases porridge in the office – as late as 10 a.m. – strikes me as ridiculous.
That's because it is ridiculous.
Jonathan.

Email to everyone 10.01 a.m.
From John Paul
The tuck shop is open.

Email to everyone 10.02 a.m.
From Sandra
Will the person who is scraping their cornflakes into the sink in the upstairs bathroom please stop.

Email to Stephen Hanson 10.10 a.m.
cc Joe Fagin, Tony Macken, Frankie Preston, David Williams,
Jonathan Kirk
Re: Country Fresh pitch (brainstorm)
From Hope Swann
Hi Steve,
Jonathan would like everyone to meet in the boardroom at
eleven for a brainstorm.
Thanks,
Hope.

Email to everyone 10.20 a.m.
From Jonathan Kirk
Will the people who are parking in the client spaces go out
and move their cars – before I kill someone.
Jonathan.

Email to Hope Swann 10.16 a.m.
From Stephen Hanson
Hope – I don't mind at all that you call me Steve in person –
but I would prefer if you would refer to me as Stephen on
emails especially those copied to clients and staff.
Thank you,
Stephen.

Email to everyone 10.16 a.m.
From Frankie Preston
Who is whistling the theme tune from *Glenroe*? Please stop.
You're giving me distemper.

Email from Hope Swann 10.17 a.m.
To Stephen Hanson.
Hi Stephen. Sorry!! No problem at all. See you at 11!
Hope.

Brainstorm n. – 1. (informal) A sudden exciting idea. Also called brainwave. 2. A momentary psychological disturbance. To generate creative ideas spontaneously for problem-solving, and especially in an intensive group discussion that does not allow time for reflection.

The Director of Client Service gives me some advice. His name is Joe Fagin and he is dark and sleek and wearing a black linen suit. He stands inside the boardroom and we are looking out the window over the car park as the creative people drift into work.

'Look at these monkeys,' he says and he is smiling. Then he tells me that it is very important to find a good position in any meeting room.

'Watch,' he says and he takes a place near the centre of the table. 'Now,' he continues and he is speaking very slowly, 'I have positioned myself in the middle – so I am involved and central to everything that is being said.'

'Thank you, Joe,' I reply and I take a seat somewhere down near the end.

The rest of the brainstorm team comes into the room and they sit down and talk about rugby, cricket and golf.

Then Joe says, 'Why don't we do a survey of supermarket customers around the country . . . ? Hope . . . you could do it . . . you know . . . get out there and interview people at shops and ask them what they like and dislike about Country Fresh Soup.'

Then Jonathan asks, 'How many Spar shops are there?'

'More than three hundred,' says Frankie.

'Great . . . let's do a cross-section. Cork. Galway. Dublin. Donegal. Great stuff.'

And Joe says, 'Why don't we do a vox-pop as well and we'll have a more informed creative brief?'

'Good idea, Joe.'

And everyone is nodding and the creative team is looking relieved.

'So,' the Art Director says, 'we can't start work until we get the brief.'

And the Planner says, 'And we can't write the brief until we do the research.' And now everyone is looking at me.

Then they all get up and begin to file out the door.

'We'll need to play out of our skins to win this,' Jonathan says but my skin is already falling off me on to the floor.

At 7 p.m. Joe leaves a Four Star Pizza menu on my desk. 'Order yourself a pizza,' he says and his jacket is over his arm.

I don't know how to write a contact report. I am worried I will make a mistake and mix up the alarm code. I don't think I even know how to order a pizza – and then I try to order a 9-inch Hawaiian Special because I think I'm *supposed* to do this.

Email from Jonathan Kirk 7.55 p.m.
To Hope Swann
cc Joe Fagin, Stephen Hanson, Tony Macken, Frankie Preston, David Williams
Subject: Country Fresh Soups
Guys,

The pitch date has been brought forward.

We need to lock horns.

How are you to meet at 8 a.m.?

(I'll bring the croissants)

Jonathan.

Devotion n. – 1. Deep love and commitment. 2. Great dedication and loyalty. 3. Strong enthusiasm and admiration for somebody or something.

Mr Costello thinks that the world is ending. He sits inside the bay window, under the red lamp bought from the Oxfam shop. His wife holds his left hand and cuts his fingernails. He has the biggest hands I have ever seen. Made to build walls. Chop wood. But she tells me he was a great musician before he got old.

'It's Hope!' and she says my name loudly and right down into his ear.

'Floods. Earthquakes. Tornadoes,' he shouts. 'It's the end of the world!' No one answers. Mrs Costello rolls her eyes to heaven. She goes to their kitchenette and stirs the soup, broth made with boiled chicken and pearl barley. She ladles it into three green bowls. She does not speak. We sit near him and I lean down to the coffee table, lift my spoon and think, 'Why me, Lord?'

Their flat is old and creaking. Walls painted red. Dark wooden blinds. Oak chairs. A broken-down yellow couch. There are shelves bending under books, an old record player and hundreds of LPs in tidy rows. Their dog walks across the floor towards me. He is slow and heavy on his feet. His nails tap on the wooden boards. I put my hand on his warm head and he stares at me for a minute, asking for nothing.

Mr Costello slurps his soup and there is a hole in the elbow of his cardigan. His wife sees only one of these things. When the soup is over she makes coffee and points at his elbow and goes for her sewing box. She is a small woman with pale skin. Her grey hair is neatly curled and set. Her cardigan and skirt would fit an eight-year-old. Our landlord says she has a 'dicky heart'.

'Here,' she says to him. 'Here,' and she points at his elbow. The cardigan comes off over his head. He sits there, crunches his oatmeal biscuits and waits.

'We're sorry your husband couldn't make it,' she says and she nods into her needlework.

'He's working late,' I tell them.

'Hard for young couples,' Mr Costello says. 'This city is gone crazy. Rent is crazy. Food is crazy. People . . . they're crazy too.' He points the remote control suddenly and the news flashes on.

'These idiots,' he says, looking at the politicians. 'This one,' and he points, 'he's a boy. No substance. Looks like . . . a damn fish.'

Here his wife surprises me by starting to laugh quietly. She looks over at me and she is suddenly old and pretty at the same time. It's something I have not seen before and this is because her old man can still make her laugh. He sees it too and barely smiles but it is a smile and then he turns the TV off.

'How long do you know Larry?' he asks suddenly. His question sounds angry. Wanting to know. Beginning to like me. Warming to us both. He is beginning to enjoy the company he was sure he didn't want.

'About six months.'

'Ha!' he says and then louder, 'Ha!!!' When he grins he

shows brown medieval teeth. A warm moon face, red with blood pressure. Wispy dandelion-seed hair.

'Fifty-six years,' he shouts. 'Fifty-six years,' and he nods at his wife. She has turned his cardigan inside out and spans her fingers under the elbow.

'I don't know how I stuck her,' he says. 'Must be the soup.'

She ignores this. Not even a flicker. She is not bothered. Used to his ways. And when I look over there are tears in his eyes. Another big old joke used to cover up love.

'How did you meet?' I ask, and he looks away. Ignores me.

'You will have to speak up,' she says quietly. 'He has become very deaf.'

'What are you whispering for?' he shouts then. 'Everyone going around whispering.'

She gets up and helps him back into his cardigan. She rests her hand on his.

'You have cold hands,' she says.

'Cold ham?' he asks.

'I'll put on the heat,' she says.

'What?' he roars.

'Heat!' she shouts back.

'Geese?' he replies.

She watches her husband for a moment and then touches his eyebrow. 'Your skin is very dry,' and when she speaks she uses a soft voice and leans into his face. She dots Vaseline between his eyebrows and then rubs it softly into his forehead. He sits quietly during all of this. Letting his woman take care of him.

'I need to wash those trousers,' she says and then, 'Trousers!' at the top of her voice.

He roars his answer back. 'And what do you expect me to wear? My pyjamas?'

'No,' she says, 'I have a nice pleated skirt for you.'

And here she turns to me and she is really laughing now. Her eyes are bright and she is all beauty again.

She walks to the hall door and into the scullery and turns their boiler on.

'How did you meet?' and I shout it out. 'Mrs Costello!'

He hears me now. Understands that we are two strangers heading into another zone. He locks his wide fingers together and tells me. There are no photographs in their room. No pictures of children in dressed-up outfits. No grandchildren balanced reluctantly on knees. There is one photograph of a man and a woman holding two violins. She wears a full skirt and high heels. He wears a big pinstripe suit and he has slicked back his hair. He is handsome. Eager.

'The first time I saw her . . .' and his eyes take me back with him. He says nothing for a minute but I know he is seeing it all again as if it is right now. 'Boy, she knocked me sideways.'

Mrs Costello comes back in. Her shoulders are hooped now. She walks on matchstick legs but she is smiling and I can see how she might have done that to him.

'I had a flatmate,' she adds quietly, settling into her chair. 'Her name was Elizabeth May. She had red hair. I went to her house one weekend. Her family owned a little country pub. We were in there the first night. Sitting on two stools. Drinking a Coke. He was on tour with the orchestra. He came in. Looked over.'

They don't speak now.

'Later,' she says quietly then, 'he gave us a ride in his taxi to a dance. And afterwards took us home.'

She leans in and pours more coffee. He looks out the window now. Not able to hear what we are saying and losing interest anyway.

'Then I went on holiday, to the seaside . . . and I sent him a postcard.' And here she tells me quietly what she did to hook her man. I like Mrs Costello. Until our wedding she was just the little old lady who lived in the flat downstairs.

'He was always a good timekeeper. Doesn't sound important but it is.' She holds the biscuit tin towards me.

'And he wasn't a drinker. Two very important things . . . does Larry take a drink?'

'Just a beer now and then.'

'And he works hard?'

'He works really hard.'

'Ah, well you found a good man,' and she pats my knee.

'Yes,' I tell her, 'Larry is a good man.'

Mr Costello begins to fall asleep. His chin rests on his chest and he snores softly. She makes no apology for him and his regular old man ways.

'Did he play the violin for you?'

'Oh yes. Many times. He was a very fine musician.'

The plates are cleared and I stand with her in their kitchenette. The dog walks sadly to the end of the room and flops down. Until now, lying in bed, I never knew what that sound was. She hands the wet plates to me and I dry them.

'Where are you both from?' she asks.

'Larry is from the West, Mayo.'

'Ah,' she says, 'friendly people in the West – and you?'

'Oldcastle. In Meath.'

She had knocked on my door on Saturday night.

'On Wednesday,' she said, 'you come down and have some chicken soup. Neighbours . . .' and her voice trailed off. Larry had thanked her. Said he was looking forward to it. Made some joke about her cooking and mine. When Wednesday came he was still in Vertigo and so I went downstairs on my own. I wished he had been here to see the Costellos, to watch how they are now and to see what it is all about, after fifty-six years. She puts her arm kindly around me when I say I must leave.

'Of course,' she says. 'You have your own man to care for now.'

On Thursday Larry makes meatballs with rigatoni. He closes the diner early and walks down the street in his apron and he begins to cook as soon as he gets home. The kitchen is long and narrow. We stand side by side and cook together at the stove. He tells me about his day at the diner and I grind black pepper over his mixing bowl. Then he rolls the meat and the egg mixture in his hands and I roll them in flour and toss them on to the pan. At times like this we are never more than a few inches away from each other. He tells me everything about his day and I tell him about 'Hell' – which is my new name for 'work'.

'We had a nice time in Alcatraz today, Larry,' I say.

'Did you, darling?' he replies.

'Yes . . . the inmates were a little restless but otherwise it was fine.'

Today Larry made eighteen euros in profit at the diner and no one at work will tell me when I'll get paid. There is a drawer full of unpaid bills in the kitchen and we jump every time the doorbell rings.

Yesterday the debt collector called again and he didn't use the doorbell at all. Instead he picked up a garden gnome and sent it through the sitting-room window.

'Larry . . . there's a gnome in the sitting room,' Doreen said and then she went back to watching *Coronation Street* on TV.

Then Larry went downstairs and when he came back up, eventually, he was very pale and his bottom lip was bleeding and his only shirt was split all the way down the front.

We eat the meatballs and the rigatoni and we try to think of ways to get the money, and people we could ask for help. But after each suggestion we look at each other and shake our heads.

Juna

The Costellos

Larry's dad

Jack

The Indians

Larry opens a beer for me. He says he's sorry about everything and especially sorry that he wasn't able to buy me an engagement ring.

'What do we want an engagement ring for?' I ask. 'We're married now,' and he looks at me and starts to laugh.

He puts one hand up to my cheek and when he looks into my eyes he can still make me blush right up to my ears. We never bother saying 'I love you' or any of that old stuff. Before Larry, there was no one else. After Larry, there is no one else. It was always straightforward and kind of simple for us.

Pitch v. – 1. To throw or hurl something. 2. To fall or stumble, or cause somebody to fall, especially headfirst. 3. To try to sell or promote something such as a product, personal viewpoint or potential business venture often in an aggressive way.

There are fifteen cars in the car park, and a bubble car sleeping behind a jeep. Inside there are people like me, wondering if

we will ever breathe fresh air again or smell the summer sea.
Two weeks now we have worked on the pitch and the circus
people gather in the early hours to rehearse. The boardroom
is like a trampoline. We bounce out our slides and bow and
step back into our place. It is my first time to attend a pitch
and I even own a suit. Today the Creative Director is wearing
converse runners with a bright red Hawaiian shirt. He says
the creative brief is like a bowl of spaghetti flung in the air and
then caught on a plate.

'OK, Hope – you're on,' Jonathan says.

The only reason I am here is because the Account Director
keeps calling in sick. Last week he came to a shoot by ambu-
lance, just to make his point. Last night at ten o'clock they
decided I should present the research and the creative brief.

'I want them to hear from you,' Jonathan said as I tried to
stay awake. 'I want them to see you up on your hind legs.'

Then Frankie comes in.

'*Bonjour*,' he says and he winks at me and slides into a chair
and then the laptop which carries everyone's presentations
gives a little sigh and goes completely black. Someone asks if
there is a spare laptop anywhere and Jonathan keeps his eyes
fixed on me. He is just staring at me really calmly and he
seems to be breathing in and out through his teeth.

'Where are the laptops kept, Hope?' he asks.

'At Brendan's desk.'

'Why are the laptops kept at Brendan's desk, Hope?'

'Because Brendan looks after the laptops.'

'Why does Brendan look after the laptops, Hope?'

'Because that's his job, Jonathan.'

'How many laptops do we have, Hope?'

'I'm not sure, Jonathan. Fifteen or sixteen.'

Somewhere in my head there is a huge grey cobweb brought

on by my lack of sleep. I have been here until nine every night and so far I have worked every weekend. I miss my husband and I miss getting drunk with Doreen and I miss my grandmother's voice. In two hours the soup people will be here and if things don't improve I'm out of a job.

'So, Hope, are all the laptops at Brendan's desk?'

'Possibly not.'

'So back to my original question, where are the laptops, Hope?'

'In people's cars? Maybe.'

There is a part of me that wants to tell my boss something about this laptop and his arse. It's 7.15 a.m. I am supposed to be asleep.

'Let's move on,' Jonathan says. He is watching a spot on the table and breathing slowly, in and out, and I realize that he is more nervous than me.

After the rehearsal he gives the team a pep talk.

'We better win this,' he says.

Then a very tall girl holds her arms out to me.

'Come here,' she says. 'Come here . . . you look like you need a hug,' and she pulls me into her arms and just holds me there – and I hardly know her. If I was a hedgehog, this is the point in my life when I would roll into a ball.

Email to Accounts 7.45 a.m.
From Hope Swann
Hi, would it be possible for someone to tell me when I will get paid?
Thank you very much.
Hope.

Email to everyone 8.05 a.m.

From Jonathan Kirk

The Country Fresh Soup people will be here at 9 a.m. and afterwards Hope will be giving the agency tour. Please tidy your desk areas. Best bib and tucker please.

Email to the Creative Dept 8.20 a.m.

cc client service

Re: New wastepaper baskets

From Stephen Hanson

Troops,

I have left a new wastepaper basket beside each of your desks. That's where anything less than a 'Shark' goes. If the idea is not jumping, it's not alive. If it's not alive, it's dead. If it's not on fire – I'm not interested.

Mucho gracias,

Stephen.

The Marketing Director begins to speak. He thanks us for our presentation and then he says the brief has actually changed. What he really wants is to promote a new range of French bread with a new range of Mediterranean tomato soup. We are not expecting this so everyone is scratching their heads and wondering about it – and I have an idea but I am afraid to speak. Then I begin to wonder if this could be my big career break – and what a fool I would be not to speak up. But I'm too afraid.

So then I write it on a note and pass it to Jonathan who looks completely horrified and I can feel the colour rise to my cheeks. He glances at it and says nothing and then asks a question about 'competitor market share'.

The note says, *'Fancy a dip in the Med?'* – and I am beginning to think of going in under the table for the rest of my natural life. On the tour of the agency, we meet the IT guy who is wearing a one-piece cycling suit. Then we find a Finished Artist who is arguing with an Account Director and it ends with 'Fuck off and do it yourself.' And then someone's toast sets the fire alarm off.

In the car park the Marketing Director asks about my car.

'Who owns the Messerschmitt?' he asks, and we are both glad to be off the ship.

'It's mine,' I tell him, and when we walk towards it Jonathan watches, with his hands in his pockets, from the door.

'It's a beauty,' he says, and I blush and smile up at him.

I open the doors. Even now I love that faint leather smell.

'Do you look after your clients this well?' he asks and we both laugh. I keep my eyes on him and tell him that 'yes, yes', and 'please, please, yes, I do'.

He walks to his car, smiling, and he gives me a little wave.

One by one the other workers leave. Desk lamps are switched off and it's just me sitting inside my window under the single lamp's glow. There are invoices piled up around me. Emails that are not cleared – and silence now as everyone else leaves to go home. The men in suits swing their briefcases and run through the door. They have wives, and casseroles to eat, and laughing babies sitting in high chairs.

There are footsteps on the wooden stairs and Jonathan appears. His hands are in his pockets. He gives me a small, tight smile. He is not very tall. Just a little bit taller than me. His hair is blond and it is brushed back over his ears. His tan says golf and sailing and money and a second home in the South of France.

'I'm sorry, Hope,' he says simply and I can feel myself blush warm red. He is so sudden and clear and honest about it. My boss wanting to say 'Sorry' before he says 'Goodnight'.

'Things were a bit tense this morning.' He is awkward now and more embarrassed than me. I swallow and say, 'That's all right.'

Until now he has terrified me. He wears a black suit and a grey silk shirt. He is thirty-four. He has already told me. He folds his arms and watches me carefully.

'By the way . . . are you anything to Edmund Swann . . . the artist?'

'Actually . . . I'm his daughter,' and my voice is very quiet.

'Really? . . . My God . . . I love his work . . . I'm a collector anyway . . . but his work is . . . beautiful . . . so you're his daughter,' and he is shaking his head and smiling.

'*Indian Slippers*,' he says and our eyes suddenly meet.

'I'm having a few people over next Friday, how about yourself and Larry come along?' he asks. It does not sound like a question. I have already arranged to meet with Frankie so we can talk about our boss.

'Just a few drinks and some easy food,' he says.

'That would be great,' I tell him, and before he walks away he says, 'By the way, you did well today.'

Outside the stars are brighter. The moon bigger. The wind louder. When I drive along the coast I see the lights dotted around the bay and know that somewhere there is a busy little diner with a tired-out chef.

When the wind blows I open up the windows. I want to drive the Messerschmitt up high now and into the clouds. Because today I did something new and it feels like the very first time 'I did well today'.

Matilda writes about another New Yorker. She says her favourite of all time is Marilyn Monroe. She tells me that she lived at Sutton Place Apartments in 1956 and had her own suite at the Waldorf Astoria in 1955 – and on her birthday and on the day she died, Matilda goes to the front desk at the Waldorf and leaves twenty red roses there.

Email to Brendan Finch 10.05 a.m.
From Sylvia Johnson
cc Hope Swann
Hi Brendan,
Would you mind not wearing your Lycra cycling suit in the office – it caused a slight problem during yesterday's agency tour.
Many thanks,
Sylvia.

Email to everyone 11.12 a.m.
From Hope Swann
Will the people who are eating the M&Ms please stop. These were brought in for a product shoot and I've just checked and they're nearly all gone.
Please. Leave red and yellow alone.
(Thank you very much)
Hope.

Email to Hope Swann 11.13 a.m.
From Frankie Preston
Subject: If it's of any help . . .
I think one of the Finished Artists has gone up a dress size.

Email to Jonathan Kirk 11.15 a.m.
From Hope Swann
Re: Country Fresh Soup
Jonathan, thick country vegetable is in reception.

Temptation n. – 1. A craving or desire for something especially something thought to be wrong. 2. The enticing of desire or craving in somebody. 3. Something or somebody who tempts.

Jonathan lives in a tall red-brick house overlooking the river. The front door is painted black and there is a green and yellow creeper growing up the wall. His garden stretches down to the water and there are three swans standing on his lawn.

Larry is wearing the black tailcoat he had on at our wedding.

'It's the only jacket I have,' he says.

'It's a strange sort of jacket,' I tell him and my voice is low as one hand reaches for the bell.

'You didn't think it was strange a few weeks ago.'

The door swings open and Jonathan appears. He smiles with white teeth and blue eyes like a Californian boy. His hair looks tossed and his shirt is open and hanging loose over his jeans. He looks like he is in the middle of telling a really good story and we have interrupted and still he seems glad, very glad that we are here.

He is carrying a glass of red wine and he uses this to show us inside. When he splashes the cream marble floor he pulls a face.

'Four faults,' he says and he keeps walking. Then he shouts, 'It's Hope and Larry.' He asks Larry all sorts of questions about the diner and then he makes a big fuss about getting him an extra-cold beer from the fridge. Larry stops in the hall and stares up at the chandelier. In here, he seems to be growing bigger and bigger. And then a pretty girl comes down and says, 'Hello.'

Jonathan's wife is called Nina and she comes down the stairs with light bouncing steps. She is wearing white denims and a white t-shirt and when she moves her dark ponytail swings from side to side. Her clothes are dazzling to me, her teeth are sparkling. She is the cleanest, whitest lady I have ever seen. She hugs me and when she moves to hug Larry, he steps back like a horse about to take fright.

The sitting room is at the top of the house and there are fairy lights to guide us up six flights of stairs. On each floor there are coloured snapshots of his home and other clues about Jonathan's real life. The sliced mango on the kitchen counter. The framed photograph of Nina rollerblading in the park. The Knuttel eyes watching us from over a fireplace in his study. His wife's silk robe tossed over a soft bedroom chair. There are light shades like giant cream drums in the centre of every room and somewhere in the distance a woman wearing a long white apron is checking that the asparagus is cooked.

Frankie is sitting next to his wife near a window. He looks up at me sadly and then stares down into his drink.

'*Buenos noches*,' he says and his eyes tell me that he is ready to jump. Behind him there are three tall windows that look out over the water and the swans.

Joe Fagin and his wife are sitting on a small couch between two windows and they have already found themselves a good position in the room. I take Larry's hand and we walk into the room together. We sit on a long green couch, afraid to speak and trying not to spill our drinks. The conversation is about advertising and Larry is looking around as if the subtitles are about to appear.

'The two new creatives are on fire . . .'

'They played out of their skins yesterday.'

'They have their asses in gear,' someone murmurs.

'. . . Absolutely – plugged in and switched on.'

'They've got the smarts . . . I'll give them that.'

'At least there is no chance of being dropped in the proverbial brown stuff.'

'Or up the creek – sans paddle.'

Larry looks out the window and he sends his thoughts in Morse code from his eyes.

'What a bunch of tossers,' he says.

The asparagus is arranged on white oval plates. The wine is poured into each round glass globe. There are candles in the centre and a crystal bowl filled with lemons and limes.

Each person has a place card and I notice that Jonathan's name is next to mine. Larry is down at the other end and when Nina speaks she rests her hand on his arm. Frankie sits quietly and his wife begins to pick at her food. I am beginning to wonder why anyone would want to do this on a Friday night.

'Ha ha ha,' roars Joe Fagin. He is programmed to laugh at all of Jonathan's jokes.

'Ha ha ha,' goes Mrs Fagin. She is programmed to laugh at all of her husband's jokes.

Whenever Jack speaks he seems to repeat whatever Jonathan says but he uses slightly different words.

'Hee hee hee,' and this is my sudden contribution and now everyone is quiet and suddenly looking at me.

'So, Hope,' Nina says, 'Jonathan tells me you're related to Edmund Swann.'

The room is beginning to feel very warm. In my head the words are clear but they sound a bit weird as they come out. I answer very slowly and Larry is watching me from the end of the table and trying not to laugh. Someone keeps filling my glass up and I am too nervous to eat.

'We have two of his paintings,' she says, and she is smiling sweetly and I can see there is only mineral water in her glass. The room is beginning to spin a little and I would like to ask where the bathroom is.

Jonathan starts talking about politics and now Larry joins in. *He* is able to tell them what is happening in the Far East and why oil prices are going up and what that means for all of us. They start to talk about a recession in America and Larry is telling them how long it will take to reach us.

'You should come and work for me,' Jonathan says.

I am wondering if I can walk properly and then I lean a little in my chair. The only part I really remember is the crash when the chair turns over and hits the floor – and there is also a very loud noise as my chin hits the table on the way down. It's not bad under the table. Jonathan is wearing loafers. Nina is moving her bare foot towards Larry's left leg – and there is a dog, a black Labrador, and she looks at me and wags her tail.

'Greetings,' I say, and then there are hands and faces and everyone seems to be involved in getting me back out.

Jonathan makes tea for me in the kitchen.

'Now,' he says, 'sit up on this stool and drink your tea like a good girl.' The dog has followed us down the hallway. She has seen me under the table and wants to bond with me now.

'What's it like to be the boss of a company?' I ask him. He looks at me for a minute and he is trying to keep a straight face. There are two wedding invitations on the windowsill and behind us a long-case clock chimes one.

'Honestly?' he asks and he pulls his stool closer.

I nod.

'Promise you won't tell?'

I nod.

'It's a pain in the ass.'

'Oh!'

And he looks at me and we both start to laugh.

'Actually,' he says then, and now he is serious and somehow young, 'it's kind of . . . *lonely* sometimes . . . now how about some ice for your chin?'

'Goodnight, Hopeful,' Frankie says, and when he kisses my cheek he puts his lips close to my ear.

'Be Careful,' he says.

On the way home Larry is quiet.

'Did it look bad?' I ask him.

'What . . . ?' he asks and he starts to laugh. I look out the window as he drives and think about how the knife sounded when Jonathan buttered my toast.

'I don't like him,' Larry says suddenly.

'I think he's sort of OK actually.'

'I don't like the way he looks at you.'

'He doesn't *look* at me.'

'Yes he does . . . he *looks* at you.'

'He's my boss,' I tell him.

'So . . . ?'

'And he's married.'

He parks the car outside our flat and when he turns off the engine he looks at me. He watches me for a second with his dark eyes blinking and then he replies, 'By the way . . . so are you.'

Trauma n. – 1. An extremely distressing experience that causes severe emotional shock and may have long lasting psychological effects. 2. A physical injury or wound to the body.

Pappy was a heart-breaker. That's what Juna says. When he was younger he was very handsome and he was always surrounded by girls.

Pappy was a heart-breaker.

He still is, I think.

Suddenly I am fourteen again and this morning Pappy is late. I wake up early. I think a little about Daniel and then I go downstairs and open up the shop. The stock is not selling now and the red apples are starting to rot. The bread is not fresh. Yesterday he moved the red chair back and threw out the rusty scissors and took the razor blades. At eight o'clock he is still in his bath. From the shop floor I can hear the squeak of the cold tap. Splash. Splash. He is washing and he does not say a word now, not even to himself.

Tick-tock-tick-tock.

Mrs Deegan crosses the street.

She buys one loaf of stale bread.

This is a sympathy loaf and the shop is empty again.

On days like this I talk to Daniel. There are no angels any-where now and no God either, I think. The world is empty and rattling without him.

Tick-tock-tick-tock.

I look at the payphone in the corner and I want to lift the receiver and dial Juna's number and listen to her voice. Tomorrow she is coming to stay with us and everything will be all right again.

The shop is quiet.

The street is quiet.

Pappy is quiet.

The house behind me seems to be asleep.

And then I walk quickly to the door and turn the sign so the shop is suddenly closed.

'Pappy!' and my voice is suddenly lifted up high in a shout.

'Pappy!' and I shout it out again.

'Pappy!' and I am shouting it out now on every step of the narrow stairs.

The bathroom door is closed.

There is no steam.

No sound of water moving.

No words.

'Leonora,' but it is me that says her name.

Tap-tap – gently – quietly on the door.

Tap-tap – again – again on the door.

It is not locked.

In this house we do not lock the doors.

It swings open easily and without a sound.

White room.

Room white.

Bright tiles.

Tiles bright

No steam.

Cold water.

Water, changing colour.

Tap-tap and my hand is still knocking into space.

The restaurant is painted pistachio-green. The tablecloths and napkins are starched grey and white. The waiters smile at me and they stand in a row in short white aprons and black bow-ties. There is a round walnut table near the window and when I walk inside Jonathan jumps up and says, 'Here's the birthday girl.'

When Frankie mentioned it was my birthday Jonathan called the restaurant and booked the table himself. He sits next to me now and his leg brushes against mine. He even asks about Larry again and what sort of food he likes to cook. He listens to everything I say about my clients and he nods as if it all makes sense. He orders more champagne and as the restaurant becomes quieter he pushes a small parcel over the tablecloth to me.

'Happy birthday,' he says and he is awkward and giving me that little smile. Inside there is a small silver cross which he helps me to put around my neck. He looks at me and says softly, 'Something to keep you safe.' The waiter fills our glasses again and when I look at Jonathan he leans over quickly and kisses me – very gently, just once – on the cheek.

The Costellos' door is closed when I get home and every room is shut up and dark. When I look at the phone there is no message from Larry and just one envelope with a postmark that says 'New York'. I recognize Jack's awkward handwriting. He moved away five years ago and he is married and living in Brooklyn now. Every year he sends me a birthday card. He already owns a house in Cape Cod and I know he makes money putting down hardwood floors for famous people – Sandra Bullock, Billy Crystal, Robert De Niro.

I find Larry standing in the kitchen and the table is set with silver and crystal and a white linen cloth. There is a bottle of champagne in the sink and there are pink tulips wilting in a vase.

'I waited all afternoon,' he says and then he shrugs and holds out his arms.

'Happy birthday,' and he hugs me. 'I wanted to tell you something . . . and then I thought . . . why put that on a card? I should go home and say it myself.'

He kisses me again and smiles into my eyes.

'I love you,' he says and he puts his arms around me. 'Another long client lunch?'

'I guess.'

He kisses the top of my head and rests his chin there – and when he looks down again he says nothing and just touches the silver cross.

Email to Frankie Preston 4.12 p.m.

From Hope Swann

Re: How many Art Directors does it take to change a light bulb?

Email to Hope Swann 4.13 p.m.

From Frankie Preston

Fuck off, I'm not changing a thing.

Larry sleeps and I lie quietly and listen to his breath. It is a light sweeping noise, rhythmic and even, and until now it was the safest sound I knew. Outside the traffic has stopped. The flat is quiet and across the city Jonathan and Nina are getting ready for bed. She is wearing a white cotton nightgown – and he is leaning against the sink in his pale green bath-room cleaning his teeth. In my mind he stops for a moment and looks into his own eyes and tries to see me and then he wishes that his wife was asleep or better still, somewhere else. When I open my eyes wide I can see the green luminous figures on the alarm clock and then the chipped plaster on the ceiling overhead. Every day it makes different shapes for us –

here is a dog – or a horse – whichever Larry can think of as we lie on our backs late in the morning and we are both happy to think about the same things. Now I stretch out and feel alone and in the dark and I wonder why I am thinking like this at all.

Larry turns over in his sleep and I kiss the back of his neck and put my arm around his waist. Still sleeping, he finds my hand and folding it into a small fist inside his, he holds it under his stubbled chin.

And finally I sleep – we both sleep – and begin a dream of different things.

Email to Jonathan Kirk 4.38 p.m.
From Hope Swann
How many client service people does it take to change a light bulb?

Email to Hope Swann 4.40 p.m.
From Jonathan Kirk
Have you nothing else to do, Hope?
P.S. How many?

Email to Jonathan Kirk 4.43 pm
From Hope Swann
How many would the client like it to take?

Frankie talks about Seattle and then Vancouver. Places we could escape to, if only in his mind. He jokes about taking me to St Lucia and how we might run away one Monday morning and forget for ever about work. He tells me that the lifeboat is almost ready. That all his plans to leave advertising are in place.

'I have the gas camper on my desk,' he says, 'the tinned food, the powdered milk, the boiled sweets.' He is ready to escape from his job, to break out, to crawl under the wire ahead of me.

'Does anyone know that you're leaving? Do they suspect?' I ask.

'No, no, Jesus no . . . you are the only one I've told,' and by now the dogs in the streets, the birds in the trees, the clouds in the sky, have it like a jingle: 'Frankie's leaving his job, you see.'

'I have mastered the art of disengagement,' he says with confidence. 'I am there but not really there at all.'

I am smiling at him now, enjoying his company.

He looks into his wine. 'The ship is sinking,' he tells me and we are trying to be serious and not laugh too much at our hopeless careers.

'The thing is . . . I am at my meetings . . . but I am not at my meetings.'

'I can see that,' I reassure him.

'I show up and I'm there – but I'm not really there.'

I tell him I understand.

'I'm at meetings . . . but I'm not at meetings,' and I smile at him again.

'The lifeboat is ready,' he says again sadly, and we both know that it is moored safely and not going anywhere and that Frankie will never leave.

Larry stands behind the counter at Vertigo. He turns the bottle in his hands and pulls the cork. We have decided to get drunk together, slowly, quietly, easily; and then maybe whatever we're looking for will just come back. He is tanned and lovely. His hair is getting long. He looks the way he always looks and

I also look the same. Not any taller. Not any smaller. Not any richer and just slightly different inside.

We say things like 'Wine?' and then, 'OK.'

Or 'Tired?' and then, 'Not really.'

Ask me how it happens – and I can't tell you. He says something about working these long hours and then something about how I'm never at home, and I say something about trying to earn some money and the debt collector and then the next thing is we are standing facing each other and shouting. The first plate flies from me to Larry and then he picks up a loaf of bread and throws it against the wall. Then the cutlery tray goes. He picks up four dinner plates and sends them like frisbees at me. There is a sudden bang of thunder and outside it begins to rain. There are blue cups stacked high over the Gaggia machine and I run for them and throw them at him one at a time. I used to think this diner was our world. That no one existed or even moved outside Larry and Doreen and me.

Larry ducks from each one and gets in under a chair. He throws bread rolls. I throw coffee beans. He opens the fridge and takes out a chocolate cake. Last week he made this for me – for my birthday – and when I came home from work he had flour on his face.

The cake comes half-way across the room and then dies in mid-air and falls flat. He finds sausages and rashers and I find eggs. We throw everything we can find – and then I slide on to my knees and start to laugh – and Larry comes and stands over me and he is not laughing at all. He looks at me and when he turns around again a single dark curl hangs down over one of his eyes.

'I still love you, Larry.' I want to say it – this is the time to say it – but *I can't*.

'Hope . . .' he says and then he stops, and now I am crying and he is crying too.

'Hope,' he says again, 'what is happening to us?'

And there is no answer for this.

'We were fine,' he says. 'We ARE fine.' He puts his face into his hands and drags his fingers back into his hair.

I want to touch him but – *I can't.*

Matilda writes a piece about the Flower District and Verdi Square. She says it is the start point of the Upper West Side. She says it is a place where couples sit and eat bagels and it is oddly romantic that people can screen out the noise of New York and fall in love. She has broken up with her boyfriend but she says deep down she knows that he still cares. She says she is thinking about cutting her hair and then going peroxide blonde.

Jonathan opens the door after one ring. There is an open suitcase in the hall and two books in his hand. His fishing rods are leaning against the wall and next to them there is a tennis racquet, a stack of CDs, his laptop, his mobile phone. He says, 'Well, hello,' as if we are old friends, and then, 'I'm packing, I'm going away for the weekend.'

'Is Nina here?' I ask slowly.

'No,' he replies and now he is smiling and then he glances at the package under my arm. Around us our words are echoing in the white and cream marble and I watch as the fig tree loses one of its leaves. The doors are open on to the hall and a pale yellow lamp from his study sends out its glow. In the background Maria Callas sings and her voice soars over us in Italian – and if the words were translated they would mean 'tragedy' and 'jeopardy' and 'deceit'. 'One week' – that was what the debt collector said. His week ends tomorrow and my new week begins.

'I want you to look at this,' I tell him and I nod towards the package under my arm. It is wet from the rain and even now that I am here I do not want to let it go or even put it down.

'Sure,' he says, and when we walk into his study he turns the music down. His hair is wet from his shower. His shirt is creased. He is like any other boy now that we are not at work. I open up the paper and lay my father's last painting out on the floor. He stands and stares down at it, his eyes fixed, his features perfectly still. I stay on my knees and I am still holding the edges with my hands. I can do this. I can do this. For me and for Larry. I can do this. Say goodbye. Say goodbye. It's time to say goodbye.

Jonathan comes down on one knee and he is staring at the detail and still my fingers are on the canvas. First they are gripping and then just touching with their tips. It is all I have left of Pappy. In the threads of this canvas is his voice. In the paints are his bright days. In the brush strokes, the sound of his breath.

Jonathan walks to his desk and takes a chequebook out.

'Name your price,' he says and his voice is low and smooth.

'Name your price?' I think. 'What price a life and sudden death?'

When the cheque is in my hand, my other hand still holds the corner of the painting.

Three fingers, then two and then one.

'What happened?' Jonathan asks softly. And taking a deep breath, I let the past go and it becomes any other painting on a floor.

'He cut himself . . .' The words come out and Maria Callas sings to them. She raises them up before they land and create some kind of horrible thud. But Jonathan says nothing. He just puts one hand on my shoulder as if to steady himself as he gets up. He walks to the kitchen and I listen as his footsteps echo down the long white hall. When he comes back he is carrying a bottle of red wine and two glasses. We sit on the couch and he pours me a glass of wine and then another and then another after that.

'I'm so sorry,' he says finally and he takes a deep breath, 'and I can't take the painting of course.' He watches my face and then he says, 'But . . . I would very much like to borrow it, so why don't you take the money anyway . . . as a sort of retainer . . . and I'll give the picture back when I'm tired of it . . . which will be . . . in about five years?'

'Thank you, Jonathan,' and he brushes these words away lightly with his hand. When I stand up he stands too and then he leans down to kiss my forehead and as he leans I decide to look up and that is when it happens and the kiss falls like a soft whisper on my lips.

We stop.

Frozen.

No part of us moving.

Just our breath, in and out, to keep our hearts from stopping, and I keep my eyes down and then I look into his – 'Just once,' I am thinking, 'I want to look, just once,' and we kiss again. And one more time, for luck.

'I have to go.'

'Wait . . . Hope . . .'

'I have to go.'

'Hope . . .'

'Larry is waiting . . . I have to go.'

Larry turns the sign on the door. He shoots the bolts and pulls down the blinds. He takes a bottle of beer from the fridge and gives it to me with a smile. Then he slides into the red booth and puts his arm around me.

'How was your day?' he asks kindly.

'Larry – I need to tell you something,' and the words come out slowly. He lifts his eyebrows and the colour of his eyes seems to change a little. Dark brown and then just dark.

'It's about Jonathan.'

'Jonathan?' he says and his voice is confused and full of surprise.

'I've borrowed some money from him.'

'Jesus,' he replies and he is shaking his head and looking at the floor.

'And . . . there's something else.'

Outside the rain pounds down on the street. It makes little rivers and puddles and the cars splash through. There is no easy way to say it, so the words just have to be pushed out.

'We kissed . . .'

'What . . . ?'

'It was nothing,' I tell him.

'Nothing? . . . nothing? . . . oh, Hope . . .' and I can't look at him so I just keep staring straight ahead.

'What happened . . . after you kissed?' he asks and his voice is shaking.

'We kissed again,' and I whisper these words and I still can't look at him.

'How did it feel . . . to kiss him?' and his voice is low and sad and he also looks away now when he speaks.

And I can hardly answer him because I am beginning to cry now.

'It felt . . . I don't know . . . sort of nice . . . I suppose.'

He doesn't say a word to me. He doesn't even breathe. He just stands up and not seeing the downpour and without thinking about a coat or his keys or even looking back at me, Larry turns quickly and walks out into the street and the rain.

Email to Jonathan Kirk 8.05 a.m.

From Hope Swann

Re: Social Committee

Jonathan,

Just to let you know – we've had three committee meetings and I'm ready to present some of our thoughts to you.

Please let me know when you're free.

Thanks,

Hope.

Email to Hope Swann 8.06 a.m.

From Jonathan Kirk

Re: Social Committee

Hope – When I asked you to head up the social committee I expected you to take responsibility. Not hand it back to me.

By the way . . . where is the strategy document for the Heinz pitch?

Jonathan.

Bastard n. – 1. A person born of unmarried parents. 2. (informal) An obnoxious or despicable person. 3. (humorous or affectionate) A person esp. a man, 'you lucky bastard'. 4. (informal) Extremely difficult or unpleasant, 'that job is a real bastard'.

Email to everyone 9.01 a.m.
From Hope Swann
Subject: Glad Tidings Comrades
Hi everyone,
Following a number of social committee meetings we have decided to make the following changes to our work place.
1. From now on everyone will get an extra day off as part of their annual holidays.
2. There will be no production meetings on Monday mornings.
3. The agency will now close an hour earlier on Fridays to give people a chance to beat the traffic.
Hope.

Email from Jonathan Kirk 9.04 a.m.
To Hope Swann
Re: Glad Tidings Comrades
Drop into my office.

Larry puts two t-shirts into a bag. He finds his toothbrush and taps it on the side of the sink. The bed is not made, the sheets are twisted and the pillows are flat. Last night we could not sleep. When we tried to make love, it felt desolate and cold. His eyes are bloodshot. He is quiet and I cannot seem to help him. He seems so sad and he still wears his wedding ring on his thumb. He pulls the zip up on his bag. He sits on the bed and takes my hand.

'I gave the keys of the diner to the debt collector . . . we don't owe him anything any more.'

'Larry . . .'

'I need to be on my own, Hope,' and I turn towards him again.

'And this is the part when you beg me to stay,' he says and he gives a dry little laugh. Then the silence fills up the room. He smiles at me. He puts one hand on my forehead. Taking my temperature. He should. I am not well.

'What a strange girl,' he says and he has said this before. 'Of all the strange girls, in this strange world, I had to meet and fall in love with you.'

I pull my knees into my chest and hug them to me now. I want to be smaller than I am. I want to sink and become invisible to him and to myself.

'So,' he says and he sniffs suddenly and then sighs. Two different ways he has to cover up tears. He stands and picks up his bag.

'Hope,' he says sadly and when he leans down he kisses the top of my head.

'We both need to be free,' he says simply, 'and if we are meant to be together, we'll find our way back.'

And I answer, 'Regular people who are married don't do that.'

The bag on his shoulder seems to move a little. It seems to beat, and breathe slowly, in and out. Inside he has packed up his bones, his favourite facial expressions, all his different little smiles, his scar and his beating heart. He smiles then, and one tear suddenly falls down his cheek. I put my hands over my eyes and then I put them over my ears.

Anything – but not the sound of his footsteps walking away, and not the sound of the closing door. And not the idea that our love has failed. And not the usual mundane sounds that signify the end of the world.

Under the pillows there might be feathers, white, light and floating, and Juna always said that feathers were a sign that there was an angel in the room. And Larry's answer sums up our lives, as broken and as mixed up as they are.

'We are not regular people,' he says.

And his feet begin to move. He is wearing his favourite black Converse runners and they walk one behind the other and leave me in our empty bedroom.

Email to everyone 10.10 p.m.
From Hope Swann
Subject: Hello? . . .
Is there anyone else left in the building? . . . is there anyone there . . . hello? . . . hello?
Thanks very much,
Hope Swann.

9 At the New York Public Library

Glassman would have to explain that he had broken up with Matilda. At his age he wondered when he would be done with love and especially the embarrassment of it. He said 'Yes' to the invitation to Trudy's first book reading – and he knew that Matilda would be there too because Trudy was a mutual friend – and she would see this as an opportunity to make another little mark. The letters went into the trash and his finger continued to press the delete button, but she would not understand. She saw their love as something real and alive and she was Brutus with it one day, and Woody Woodpecker the next.

That morning in March the NYU students rushed past him on the street. They were young and used furry boots and bright parkas to cut through the wind chill and the late flakes of snow. He stood for a moment and remembered he was one of them once and now they walked past him, without a glance or a second thought. He would have preferred to be extremely old and he held on to this thought as he walked towards Washington Square with his head down into the wind. Old age was noticed. Someone with snow-white hair and a hunch – but he was middle-aged and he had never wanted to be in the middle place. He could not bear to be 'not one thing or another' and he hated the idea of waiting with a thousand others in this beige waiting room.

Recently Glassman had begun looking for his third place in the city and he especially liked to look for it at night. Some nights he would walk to the deli on the corner and buy a cup of chicken noodle soup and he would sit then, with his hands wrapped around it, watching the world from a cold park bench. So far his third place was a different place every evening. A park bench with soup. The theatre on West Houston where he watched a documentary about Russian ballet dancers, and last night, he found it standing outside Mark Twain's house.

Then he would walk down W9th to Fifth Avenue, and sometimes he would go sit in the church, but usually by then the cold would send him into Barnes and Noble or to SoHo and home.

The first time it happened he was in Canada, standing in the middle of Reindeer Lake and listening to his best friend describe his own death. The light was fading and Glassman could feel the air cold in his nose and chest and it was beginning to eat into the soles of his feet – but still they stood and he would remember the red sunset and the cold and the beauty of Manitoba on the other side.

Tom spoke without looking at him and told him evenly and with a strange sense of calm that he was going to die. Not that he was sick or planning to take his own life – but that he was going to take a knife wound, he was certain of it, and because of that he would die. He didn't know when but he believed it would happen, and Glassman of course could not agree. He listened and nodded and acknowledged his friend's premonition by touching his elbow and leading him slowly off the frozen lake. And two years later when they had both forgotten, Glassman went to visit Tom late one night as he closed his restaurant up and the next morning Tom was dead. He had died in the alleyway carrying that night's takings under his apron. Someone had been watching and Tom did not know it. The last face he saw before he died was Glassman's, and the knife went into his kidneys from behind.

On the F train he saw Matilda. She looked beautiful and as if she had just got out of bed. She was wearing a black raincoat and Chuck Taylors and her hair was pulled into a long ponytail at one side. She saw him and pretended to read at first and then he said 'Hi' to her with a little wave. He made his way up the train to see her and to be polite and to be kind.

'Hi,' she said in that bright breezy way of hers and then she shrugged up at him and smiled.

'Matilda . . .' and he stopped for a second, not sure how to continue, and then he smiled and said, 'You look . . . good.'

'I'm sorry for calling you,' she said simply. 'I just really missed you . . . but I understand now . . . I'm OK.'

'I'm glad you're OK,' he said. 'I want you to be OK,' and she looked up at him and smiled.

He felt the need to get off the subway earlier at 34th Street, and when he looked back she was still turning the pages of *Time Out* and pretending to read. He wanted to feel a pang of something for her and he almost did. He had no love for her but he did feel the loss of another person he knew. At times like this he missed Tom too. He missed that day on the lake and the sound of a friend's laugh and his voice.

He waited on the steps for Trudy and she came, natural blonde, in itself a wonder – and with fresh Scandinavian skin. They had dated a long time ago and they had broken up when he discovered she enjoyed pain. Now, after Matilda's cloying, she was like a fresh wind sent up from Norway, and he noted with some mild amusement that her teeth had been whitened and she had had her breasts *'uplifted'* . . . again.

'Hey, Glassman' she said and she punched him on the shoulder and he stood still for this and laughed down into his shoes. Some women became children around him. They loafed around like puppies, and others, like Matilda, became more motherly and old. Even now Trudy would flirt with him and he would politely flirt back. Sometimes a normal conversation about Hillary Clinton or what the multinationals were doing or the weather, for Godsakes, would be just fine.

She was worried about her reading. Held the book forward as they walked up the steps and they were both shouting now. On the steps he turned, and the wind full of new snow made his eyes water and pinched his red ears and cheeks.

And he shouted back at her, 'Trudy – honey, calm down,' and he steadied her with one hand on her shoulder. That was how New Yorkers comforted one another. Shouting over the noise of the city and giving a minimalist touch. She blushed and turned and he followed her Labrador lopes up the steps.

In the line and while the security man checked her purse, Glassman told her that he and Matilda had broken up, and she turned in silence, with raised eyebrows and the corners of her mouth pulled dramatically down. He could almost feel the glee from her and the details talked out later with her girlfriends at Balthazar. It made him smile, just the thought of it, and how he would be spread out and pinned down like poor old Gulliver – with inaccurate statements like 'Of course, Glassman can't commit' and 'Poor Matilda, she really loved him, you know', and he hoped Trudy would at least add in that he had been great in bed. They would say he couldn't commit but there were other reasons why relationships came to an end. There were married men all over the city. Men who had gone down on bended knee and bought the special roses in the Flower District, and met her parents, and purchased the Tiffany ring.

Men could commit when they wanted to. And they gave reasons for walking away, and women talked it over, and covered it up with female theories, all designed to block out the fact that he just didn't want to be with *her*.

Glassman liked honesty. When he broke up with women he was clear and honest now. When he said, 'I can't.' It was hurtful but it was true.

Matilda was standing at the lunch buffet. She was talking to James Marshall, the academic who would introduce Trudy's book. She would have seen him coming up the stairs with Trudy, that was why she was standing there, and now she was laughing a lot and flicking her hair. She had dressed for him and she tried to hide it. Trudy whispered now that she was sorry but that she always thought Matilda was weird – and he took this information in one mouthful and swallowed it with a little smile. 'Women' – and how he loved their low-down double-crossing ways. And then as the coffee scalded his lips she asked, 'Why???' and he shrugged and said, so that his whisper seemed to echo around the high marble domes and his own voice sounded baffled by it, 'I have no *ardour*.'

And she frowned and nodded and a minute later asked, 'Did you say . . . no hard-on?' and he smiled and it seemed easier and would require less explanation to answer 'Yes.'

He walked dutifully to Matilda and they spoke again. She looked good. Fresh-faced and like she had been getting a lot of good sleep. They talked about Trudy and her book and the snow and how cold it was again, and duty done, he smiled and was about to turn and run.

'Hey,' she said, 'did you find my diaphragm? . . . I can't seem to find it anywhere . . .'

In his mind Glassman could see it in a blue dish beside the cream cheese and the leftover anchovies.

'In the refrigerator,' he said.

'Oh, man. Look, I'll come back with you and get it.'

Glassman wanted to say he would post it to her but he did not have the heart. He became silent and they both knew the game. How she would walk back with him and talk the way they always did. How she would shrug and laugh and put it into her purse. She wanted him to see and feel that she had used this birth-control device for him. That she had protected them from a baby and to remind him that they had had sex. He knew that she was hoping to excavate some old feelings with that. And he wanted to tell her that it was over. He wanted to look into her eyes and say, 'Really, sweetheart, completely and utterly . . . you are mining' . . . and he meant . . . *mining* . . . 'the bottom of the feelings barrel,' and really he wished she would direct her energy towards someone else.

The bell rang and everyone sat and he sat as far away from Matilda as he could. As Trudy read he remembered dating her and how she had taken him to her place at Columbia where there were wide sweeping maple floors and a horseshoe kitchen and a view over the Hudson and even the elevator seemed to gleam. They drank wine and ate a platter of cheese on the long cream couches and she pointed out her framed photographs of children in Vietnam. And how they had walked into her bedroom then, more maple and cream. How beautiful it all seemed to him now. That was before he became ill and everything she did, every little smile, every glance, even the apartment tour could turn him on. He wanted the kind of frenzied love-making that would leave them gasping, damp and embarrassed by it, and Trudy, his then Norwegian Princess, would give him all of that.

Later he would discover a closet full of whips and nipple

clamps and chains and he would instantly lose his lust for her. He did not like any sort of pain. And when she called him later that week, he told her too.

'I can't.'

Glassman would never know why Elsa Graham looked at him. He only knew that she came to class late and when she smiled at him and looked away, there was a soft rose blush on her face. He also remembered that she wore a cotton dress – primrose colour – and that it was the last day of the summer term – 16 June 1966.

Elsa was the prettiest girl in Nauset High and she was somehow always on her own. On that morning he had said goodbye to his mother. He remembered leaving her at the kitchen table and how she was drinking a milky coffee from a small pink cup. He did not kiss her goodbye because at sixteen he felt too old now and too proud for that. That morning she wore a fresh white cotton nightdress and her shoulders were already darkly tanned. Her cup rested on a pretty floral table-cloth and behind her, the remnants of pancake ingredients – eggshells, batter, a jug of milk – stood in a little circle around the stove. When her only son walked around the table behind her, she lifted one hand and he caught it, cool and soft, as she waved.

He walked into the barn to fill the watering can and, still carrying his schoolbooks, he watered the wisteria on the porch. There were three chickens on the back lawn then – black with white speckles, and their red combs were bright in the morning sun. From time to time, they flew over the wire fence and into the meadows and surprised themselves by landing on the beach. Mrs Glassman loved her chickens. She liked free-range eggs and Arthur was used to bright yellow pancakes now. Every morning he watered the plants and then he dropped sunflower seeds into the parrot's cage. He listened to the thud of the *Boston Globe* on the front lawn and inside he felt the weight of Mrs Glassman's *Vogue*.

Today was the beginning of his summer and his last day ever at high school. He would read at the final assembly. He would find a quiet moment to stand still in an empty classroom and say goodbye. As the sun hit the waves in the distance, Arthur picked up his speech, folded it into a book, and walked, and even though he was not late for his bus, but because he felt his whole life suddenly stretch out beautifully in front of him, he began to run and run.

When Elsa came in she was behind the others. She was smiling and flushed and her golden hair was in a high ponytail. She always sat in the desk at the top of the room – near the map of the world and the glass-panelled door. She did not put her hand up ever but he knew her scores were always good. At lunchtime she would take herself away and eat her fruit silently, looking beautiful and a little lonely under some big green tree.

Arthur did not know then that he was good-looking. He only knew that he loved words and that he was a good swimmer and captain of the football team. But on that day Elsa came in and looked straight at him and then moved down and took a desk next to his. She did not look at him again, but when they walked down the corridor together, he felt her arm brush gently – and it felt cool – against his. He felt her fine bleached hairs, the short puff sleeve of her dress and her smooth suntanned skin.

The school gathered in the hall at three o'clock and Arthur took his place near the stage. He had chosen Walt Whitman for his reading – when his English teacher would have preferred Robert Frost. But Arthur had already discovered the milkiness of poetry, and how his skin could ripple and bump with its every rhyming and un-rhyming sound. He did not want to read about mending walls or apple picking – he wanted to find words to describe beautiful women, waiting lovers, and a world full of possibilities now.

In Whitman he had found a friend and he chose 'I Hear America Singing' which his voice carried out across the room. And as he read the hall fell silent and the school listened and dreamed of future plans.

Afterwards his classmates got to their feet and clapped. They cheered and the whole school was suddenly swept up in the same bright moment. And as they clapped he smiled, and his eyes moved until he found her – and she was smiling – yes, and still looking up at him shyly – and using a small white notebook to gently fan her neck.

Arthur delayed and shook his English teacher's hand and when the room was almost silent, he stood on the creaking wooden floor, in long shafts of sunshine, and said goodbye to his school. When the door flapped open a young boy came in and ran to pick up a forgotten book, and as the door opened again he saw Elsa sitting waiting on a bench in the hall. He steeled himself then and walked over to her, and she was just sitting, with her long ponytail down over one shoulder, and studying her white tennis shoes.

'Hi, Elsa,' he said and he felt his chest tighten with the words. She had become another person to him. Someone who was very beautiful and made of yellow and gold.

'Want to walk me home?' she replied, and when he smiled and said, 'Sure, Elsa, I'd like that,' she got up and gave him her hand. The other kids saw them leave and Arthur began to make deadpan small talk. But inside he was puffing himself up like a parrot and he felt like John Wayne bringing his bride back home.

She told him about her brother who had gotten into Harvard and how she was planning on going to a Cordon Bleu cookery school. She said this and looked away blushing and the idea of her in a polka dot apron joined them in the school hall. It was Elsa who suggested the forest trail and as they walked they turned over the usual ordinary things.

Did his mom make him help at the church fête?

Which beach did she like to swim at?

Would he go to NYU or Yale?

Did he want to leave Cape Cod for good?

Would he be here for the summer?

Would she like to meet him tomorrow afternoon?

And the last question hung for a moment in the air, the air that was free now of school and full of new ideas and plans. Her left tennis shoe was scuffed. She had a small pink plaster on her knee. He noticed how the skin on the inside of her wrist was very smooth and pale. When she said 'Yes' and smiled again, her ponytail nodded at him and he did not realize that women could be so beautiful until then.

In the forest he kissed her – and it was a sudden gesture that surprised him more than her. She seemed very calm though, as if she was waiting for it, and Arthur put his arms around her feeling first her lips, moist and warm, the stiff cotton of her dress and then the rugged bark of a tall slender pine.

The forest trail was silent.

Around the next bend they would find Herman's Cottage, an old stone house where no one lived now. He had planned to walk her there and then sit with her on the swing on the back porch. But instead she pulled him closer and they slid down on to the forest floor.

He did not know how to make love to a woman. He did not even know that this was what they were doing now. He did not know that she was going to give him three memories that would stay with him for ever. That after this day he would spend his life looking for a grown-up woman who was still somehow young and innocent like her.

First she gave him the picture of her face and how her blonde hair was full of pine needles. Then she gave him a sound, it was the light little sigh she made – of surprise – of joy – of hurt – of pain, when he entered her. And lastly he would remember how their hands were, joined together, in a small circle of sunlight that had speared its way through the trees and lay with them on the forest floor.

Because of a girl he felt new and different and yet he was somehow still the same. It was as if making love had rearranged all his thought patterns and brain waves and then gave them back to him again. He did not remember taking the bus home. He only remembered finally reaching his house and that the screen door gave the same little creak. He wandered into the kitchen and ate a red plum looking out the window behind the kitchen sink. He turned the dial on the radio and stopped when the Monkees came on. He did not know anything then except that this one moment in his life was perfect. He could still feel Elsa. He could smell her all over his skin. The next day was a Saturday and every day would be a Saturday from now on.

He noticed that the coffee pot had not been refilled then. He saw the pancake ingredients, still gathered at the stove, and then he heard a fly buzz, caught, snared inside a spider's web. His mother would usually meet him in the hallway or come in from the garden or the porch. She would be wearing one of her lovely cool summer dresses and carrying a jug of iced tea or homemade lemonade.

The house was too warm. The windows were closed and the fresh breeze from the beach was locked outdoors. As he picked out words from the song on the radio, he noticed the drip from the kitchen tap and he could hear the fly twisting and dying in its grave.

He walked up the white painted steps and noticed how the net curtains on the landing moved in the wind. He saw how his bedroom door was closed, and how hers was open and that she was still in her white nightgown and lying near the stairs.

And Arthur stood for a moment and checked himself. He saw how she lay on her side as if she was sleeping. How her left hand seemed to wave. How there was no breath or movement or warmth around her, and he did not know if he would rush towards her or begin to cry like a little boy and run back down the stairs.

Glassman left the library without Matilda and in his mind he hurried home and put her diaphragm into the trash. Instead he went to Fifth Avenue at 27th Street and visited the Museum of Sex. Inside he shared the darkness with a middle-aged couple and he let the images dance and wash over him. His favourite porn movie was *The Yum-Yum Girl*. An Indian girl offering herself up in black and white, over and over, all innocence and warmth and without any logic or sense. She wore flowers around her neck and seemed to smile a lot. The old movies jumped and jerked so it was like Mickey Mouse doing Minnie for porn. He liked to go here once a year to see this movie and feel that he would be warm and safe in this girl's arms and that with her, things would be simple and he would just feel something again.

A man in a raincoat sat on a bench and studied it. And Glassman was glad that he was here. Someone needed to point out the fine line between art and pornography, after all.

He avoided the room full of plastic breasts and machinery and walked out into the snow. The sign at the door said, 'Please do not touch, lick or mount the exhibits', and there was a quote from *Hamlet* about men which he liked and he was glad it was still there.

A normal man would leave the museum and want to call an ex-girlfriend and book into a seedy hotel room. A younger man would come out and feel ready to mount a lamp-post. And again Glassman mourned the loss and the losing of himself. He did not use the payphone on the corner. He went into Harry's diner on W30th and ordered fruit salad even though he felt cold. He met Alan Alda at the bar and spoke to him. He told him, unselfconsciously, that he loved *MASH* and had seen every episode and they both agreed that Loretta Swift was a love-her, hate-her kind of girl, and on days like that Glassman knew he should feel real love for New York.

At home he found Matilda sitting on his steps waiting and she said 'Hey' and 'Hi' as if this was all perfectly OK. He stood and towered over her and somewhere deep inside he began to hate her now.

'I need you to stop calling me,' he said gently, and he watched her face change and he saw in brief little flashes, love, hurt, anger and pain.

'I'm pregnant,' she said and the lie lifted up over both of

them and laughed out over the street. During their first week together she had told him. '*Reproductively challenged*' were the words that she used but she had said them very softly and as if they were an apology for something he could not have. And even so they were careful. Somehow even then the idea of making children with Matilda did not seem like a sensible plan.

Lately he had a strange feeling of being watched by someone. He had felt a new presence in the subway. On Fifth Avenue and standing in line at Starbucks, he always wanted to look around. And when he did he felt foolish as there was just the next person asking for a double cream chocolate latte, as alive and as ordinary as himself.

On Saturday mornings he liked to sit in Washington Square. It had become a small ritual of his, like his whisky at Michael's and a movie on Thursdays at Angelika. He would sit and look at the Vietnam vets busking, enjoying their long loose hair over weathered faces, and how they passed the drum and tambourine, like food to be shared, and sang out Simon and Garfunkel as if it was the word of God. And then he would walk to the Farmers' Market near Union Square and buy something ridiculous. Holly berry and pine cones and once something exotic called Kangaroo's Paw. He shopped at the deli on Canal Street and once a month he walked into an expensive hair salon and asked the most beautiful woman there to cut his hair.

But Glassman always looked over his shoulder now, for Matilda or for the person who he felt was following him, or for the next hint at death or a sign that might warn him in advance.

Instead now he saw Matilda and she was smiling and walking away from him and still wearing the black raincoat and Chucks – and she looked more beautiful than ever – because she was still in love with him and she had convinced herself that she was carrying his child, a tiny foetus, created by him for her.

Sugar Boy (May 2001)

Discretion n. – 1. The good judgment and sensitivity needed to avoid embarrassing or upsetting others. 2. The freedom or authority to judge something or make a decision about it. 3. The ability to keep sensitive information a secret.

There is a bowl of red cherries on the table. The black Labrador sleeping at his feet. Apart from that, and Jonathan's blue shirt, everything else is heavenly white. It is almost summer now and the afternoon sun moves in long shadows across the bare wooden floor.

He is in bare feet and I am fascinated by this. The shape of his toes. His heels. The cream corduroys turned up at the ends. He has been on holiday here for two weeks. He has stayed on the lake, fishing and swimming, and today he is somehow a new, more natural man.

'You found me,' he says. He meets me on the wooden deck in these bare feet and smoke curls slowly from his cigarette. His hands are not busy here. His smile is easy. He looks amused and as if he has never even owned a suit. Any minute and he might laugh at me. That is the expression on his face. When he turns there is a waft of aftershave and it is something light and fresh.

Inside there is very little furniture. A patch of sunlight on the gable. A wooden house painted white and, it seems, touched by God. A couch covered in a white sheet. Worn sea grass on the floor. Books filling every wall. An old gramophone. A hand-carved flying bird. And my father's painting on his wall. 'What are you doing?' I asked myself in the mirror and the girl looked back at me and shrugged. She was silent then and blinking and did not offer any words. She was still cloaked by Larry but 'He's gone now', she said – out loud and into the universe and then she put her suitcase into the car.

The dog stirs and gets up and flops down in the shade.

'Some guard dog,' Jonathan says. He has planned every detail. Even what he is wearing. The blue shirt open and his cream cords. In the distance there is an open bedroom door, with sheets thrown back and dangling to the floor.

'This way,' he says. He is more than ten years older than me and beside him I feel like a little girl.

The bedrooms are at each end of the house. So we have the wide bright sitting room in between.

'Her name is Florence,' he says and he nods towards the Labrador. He gives half a smile and here his eyes rest on mine for a second longer than they should.

'Did you bring your bathing costume?' he asks. Even the words are embarrassing. It feels like a 1940s movie now.

Outside the summer light is beginning to fade. He knows the answers to every question – to all my questions. So I would like to ask, why am I here?

There is an Aston Martin parked outside. The leather seats are saddle tan. He owns a house in Ely Place. Another one on the Green. 'Windsor Terrace was my first house,' he says. He has a place in Mayfair. A yacht. A *gîte* in France. And this.

'This is my bolt-hole,' he says. 'I don't bring anyone down here.'

The house is white and made of wood. The double doors lead on to another deck that sits up over the lake.

He cooks lemon sole and we eat. In my mind there is a list of things I could say. I have never had to plan our conversations before. I read the newspaper this morning. I listened to the radio on the drive down. And now that I'm here – he talks about fish – and the sun – how it will rain – and how good the swans look on the lake.

When the rain falls it makes a gentle sound on the water, like rain falling into rain. He carries the wine out and we sit on two wicker chairs. He smokes. His shirt is still open. I can see a silver chain from here. There is something disturbing about this.

I look back at him and he looks at me. The rain gets heavier.

'Would you like to swim?'

'In the rain?'

'Why not?'

'I'm not a good swimmer. I don't like water.'

'Hmm,' he says. 'Something else I didn't know.'

'It will get easier,' he says and he is watching me all the time.

'The separation,' he adds and then, 'You deserve to have a happy life.'

'I had a happy life,' I tell him and then I say 'Goodnight' and go to bed.

The bedroom is almost empty. There is a double bed with a white spread and a folded-up patchwork quilt. There is an old pine chest of drawers. A wooden fan on the roof. An old mirror leans on the wall. A picture of a ship. It has four red sails beginning to set sail. There is an embroidered cushion and three wooden elephants walk along the mantelpiece. I watch how they lift their heavy feet and I would like to follow them out the door. Why am I here? In the room across the sitting room he might be taking his trousers off. His shirt. His underpants. My boss. The silver chain bumping a little on his chest. My suitcase is still packed and I can see the Messerschmitt from here.

'Save me,' I whisper to it. 'You've saved me before.'

I pick up the case and open the bedroom door and he is standing at the doorway in the hall.

'Taking Florence out,' he says. The sound of freeform jazz comes from the CD player.

'Just looking for the bathroom,' I reply.

'Right there,' he says and I walk towards it carrying my case. And of course he sees this. He has invited me to his house and now at night I am still carrying my suitcase around.

In the bathroom I check the window and it will open easily. Another white room. Another perfect white space. The porcelain bath. The new Jo Malone soap. The yellow and white candles. Everything smelling of lemon and lime. The towels are white. He has left a new robe hanging behind the door. Outside the rain has stopped and I try to pee silently into the bowl. Somewhere in my head, I thought this would be a good career move. In the room across the living room, he is curling up in bed and then stretching himself out. He is not able to sleep while this weird girl prowls around his house. The taps squeak. My suitcase opens with a loud snap. Deep breath.

And then I try to unlock the door – and try to unlock the door – and try to unlock the door.

Deep breath again.

The big key won't turn.

The lock is jammed and suddenly I feel like crying. I want Larry back. I can't be in a world where everything costs money and keys don't turn. Somewhere I am telling Doreen about this and she is lying flat on the floor and laughing right up to the roof. I can hear Florence walk across the sitting-room floor. I am in hell. I wish I was dead. I wish I was the dog. The key is jammed. Give up. Look for another way.

'Think,' as Jonathan would say, 'outside the box.' I sit on the toilet and look at my case and I begin to think myself out of the room. Calling out is not an option. He is still awake now and wondering why I have not come out.

The windowsill is covered in tiny glass bottles. There are about a thousand of them. Each one has to be lifted down and put into the bath. Then the window opens easily. First the case goes out and then me. Dropping down into the rose bushes and shrubs. Now the prowling houseguest person is outside the house. And then I do what any normal person would do. I walk around to the front door and ring on the bell. And wait then and I am even whistling a little tune, with the suitcase on the wooden porch.

Florence gives one deep woof and I stand very still and wait. My life is leaving me out through my pores. The lake is on the other side. Calm and still.

I wish I was the lake.

I wish I was the car.

I wish I had never come here.

There are stars in the sky, that don't have problems.

I wish I was the majestic moon.

I wish I was a star.

'Who is it?' he asks. He sounds older than before.

'It's me.' My words are tiny, and posted in under the door.

Silence.

He is *surprised* of course.

'Hope,' I add then, as if there could be any doubt.

The door opens and he is wearing boxer shorts and a blue robe.

He looks confused. There is a quizzical look on his face. An all-round awkward moment I would say. Even the dog has to look away.

'I got locked in the bathroom.'

'Ah' and 'Oh' he says and then we both laugh. And the suitcase, which has grown to three times its usual size, is carried inside – again.

'I see,' he says.

'Did you bring the key?'

'The key?'

And the tenth little Indian is ready to die.

The dog walks away. Then she turns back and just looks at me. The moon fades and the wind drops. He goes to his room. I go to mine. The night sky rests and it is safe to sleep.

There are birds singing outside. A long shaft of light, warm across my bed. Whenever we lose a pitch he says, 'Tomorrow we start again.' Whenever we win a pitch he says, 'Tomorrow we start again.' The dress is white cotton with red roses along the hem. I walk into the kitchen, ready to meet him and start again. He is reading his paper and when he sees me he looks up and smiles. It is the kind of smile that says we're in a new kind of day. It is late morning. He has stayed inside and kept the dog quiet so I could sleep. He stands at the kitchen, and begins to turn the little knobs on his stove.

'We have eggs,' he says and, 'We have ham,' and suddenly from nowhere I can feel myself start to cry.

He frowns. Says nothing, gets busy with his apron string. He makes coffee, sits with his arms on the table talking about all sorts of things. The lake is good for fishing. He has a boat. 'There is a canoe,' he says and then he points it out. This makes me want to laugh. It is an Indian canoe, with the ends turned up.

'We could go out,' he says and he smiles at me suddenly

and looks right into my eyes – and on a day like this one, with the sun shining on the water, he makes all things possible now.

He scratches his face, grins at me, watches my every gesture. Then he takes me out in his car. We let the roof down and the wind lifts my hair. Florence yowls from the back. He takes me to a craft shop and when we stand side by side and look into the jewellery case I can feel his breath near my neck. Behind us the designer is busy at her work. We walk around the room. We walk up white wooden stairs. There are collars and breastplates on display. He stands close to me and we look into the glass case. Then he puts one hand on my waist and when I look up he kisses my bare shoulder and moves on. We stop for tea in a little hotel and he asks me about growing up in a country town. He listens to everything and tells me with an apology that he is a city boy. His nails are white and his hands must be soft. He always smells good. He cooks. His fridge is full. There is nothing to worry about. We drink. He lights a fire. It rains again and we stay inside.

'You're very beautiful,' he says. His voice is level. He is certain of everything and I don't know what to say.

These words are difficult for him now. From nowhere he is uncomfortable too. Saying words because he is compelled to. He sighs. Turns the wine in his glass and he runs one hand back through his hair.

'I'm afraid to say . . .' he begins and then he smiles because he is hanging on a ledge. He is standing on the top of a building and will not look down.

'I'm falling for you,' and the words come out quietly one by one.

Outside the moon moves from behind a cloud. We have the orange light from the fire and silver moonlight now.

He reaches out for my hand and I let him take it.

I can feel it all around me, how easily his power slips from him to me, and I love him for letting it all go so easily.

He lifts a strand of hair back from my face and kisses me. It is as if we are behind warm velvet curtains now and when we kiss – I want it to be slow – so when I inhale I just breathe him in.

Jonathan kisses my cheek and then he strokes it with his hand. Then he moves closer and his lips touch mine again. He puts his arms around me. The fire sparks and sends a red ember out on to the rug. And then it happens again. My eyes are filling up with tears and I am still kissing him and trying to swallow them back.

I close my eyes and when I do, I see the white scar. The Cupid bow laughing up from the pillows on a Sunday afternoon. Jonathan is kissing me but I am kissing someone else. I can never remember the hours without him. Only the time when he was near and that I have lost him for ever now.

So I cling to the man beside me.

He is the only man I have.

I have lost the one I want.

My whole world went crazy and sent him away from me.

Jonathan is breathing steadily at first and then he starts to kiss me harder, his hands running over my dress. He finds the zip and he is actually panting a little – and I never wanted my boss to get this out of control.

'Let's go to bed,' he whispers into my ear and behind us Florence lets out a big sigh. Everything about him is powerful again. He is not afraid of taking a risk and he seems to have that sparkly aura again.

He takes my hand and pulls me gently to my feet and I follow him into the other bedroom like a little lamb.

The wallpaper is pale taupe and apple green. The cushions on the white bedspread are designed to match. They sit neatly side by side and then he lifts them and puts them on the chair. He pulls a cord and the blind drops down. He unties the tiebacks and the curtains begin to close.

And I am standing there and seeing the boardroom and wondering if the projector and laptop are turned on.

He begins to unbutton his shirt. His Filofax is open beside the bed.

Next to it his mobile phone.

His keys.

His Mont Blanc pen.

The flowers on the wallpaper turn into faces, creative teams and prospective clients sitting around the room.

'Do you have an agenda?'

'Of course I do.'

The first item on our agenda is called 'Getting undressed' and the second item is called 'Going to bed'.

Jonathan smiles softly and moves towards me. He lets my shoulder straps down and puts the sheets back and we get in.

'Lights on or off?' he asks.

We will never win the business if he is going to say things like that.

In my mind the bed begins to lift off the ground and I lie back and think of *Star Trek* and Captain Kirk. Where are we going? I would like to know. He begins to make love to me and the bed is setting sail. Up into the night sky and over the lake. I can feel nothing and hear nothing as we glide and fly up through white puffy clouds.

Somewhere down there is the blue house where Juna lives and over to the right, my pappy's red shop.

Jonathan is breathing like a long-distance runner. I am quiet and very calm. My legs curl tightly around him and I feel his skin, taut and smooth, on his back. My nails go in and he stretches his neck and laughs.

Then I start to think about the time he told me off for being late . . . and I let them go in further now.

'I like you, Jonathan, and you know I sort of hate you too.'

There was the time he cut across me at that meeting and my nails drag a little on his skin.

'Easy, tiger,' he says and then he begins to kiss my neck. He is leaning on his elbows and looking up to see where the bed is going now. He keeps a look out and steers the ship and all the time the headboard goes bump-bump-bump against the bedroom wall.

He has done this before.

Many times I think.

Sugar Daddy.

He can hurt me.

Sugar Boy.

Afterwards I wonder if he will say he loves me. He said he was 'falling for me' and now that it is over, he has fallen and crumbled in a heap. He dozes and there are words that need to come out like –

Darling

So special

Need

We
Love
To be
Meant
Care
So much
Watch over
Can't live without

He turns on to his side and faces me. He looks like a sleepy little boy. We lie on our sides facing each other. He swallows and smiles and his eyes are still closed. Jonathan has the answers for everything. He can always find the right words. I am lying beside him, confused and feeling broken – and here they come. The words of love, spoken like a real lover and a man.

Sugar Boy.

'We'll need to be discreet,' he says.

Juna stands on the first hill in the lower meadow. Her hair is like a stiff white cloud and her apron flaps in the wind. She stands here as if she is searching for something and she cannot see it from this meadow or this hilltop or anywhere in this world. What was she like when she was young? Smooth-skinned, dark-eyed . . . proud? On Tuesday Juna put her swim-suit on and walked around the house. It was the postman who found her. And now she cannot bear to be indoors. It is as if she is being led away by something and there is nothing anyone can do to stop it. She is old now and moving to another place.

The worst part is that she knows she is leaving me. She has begun to map out her days with Post-it notes. The kitchen is full of them. Juna who was always so organized and sharp. The Post-its on the fridge tell her own name and her date of birth – and then on another yellow sticker our names are written neatly together – 'Larry' first and then 'My Hope'.

Through the window I watch as she turns from the hilltop and begins to walk back down. She is still agile and wearing a smile like any young girl. Wherever she is going she is happy about it and somehow looking forward to her trip. This is Juna who plaited my hair – and today when she looks at me she doesn't know my name. When she stands up her stockings fall in circles around her ankles. Her cardigan is buttoned the wrong way up. When she walks around the kitchen she lets her heels make a little clip-clop clip-clop.

She stands inside the kitchen window and once again she is looking out. She is watching the door and I see now that she is still trying to escape.

Later, when I put her into bed, she sits up again and takes my wrist. 'Elvis,' she says, 'let's get off this island tonight.'

Email to Hope Swann 22 May 5 p.m.
From Matilda Vaughan
Hope,
Here's the thing with men. First of all they never know what they want and it's up to us to educate them. Your husband left you . . . so let him go. I left my boyfriend. That's a completely different thing. I was the one who got up and left his apartment. I did it because I know he loves me – he just doesn't know it himself yet. Now what I'm doing is making sure he doesn't forget about me and it's only a matter of time before he begs me to come back. You should have seen the way he looked at me yesterday. He's just frightened that's all.

Jonathan is clearly besotted by you. The main thing is to make
sure he sees you.

Men are very visual.

Matilda.

There is a red Georgian door and a small brass key. When I
open my fingers it lies there, flat and warm in my hand. There
is no address and no key ring. It was placed on my desk at the
end of a busy day. The weather is hot. It is June.

The key slides into the lock and turns.

The key has been here before.

How many different turns?

He says, 'I am the only one.'

Through the first doorway a girl with long black hair is
practising the cello. Her hair hangs in a single braid over one
shoulder. Because it is hot she has left her door open – so we
get Beethoven and she gets air. A couple pass me on the stairs.
They are wearing shorts and carrying bags of shopping. I can
see cherry tomatoes, iceberg lettuce, a newspaper under one
arm, and their keys fall with a jangle on the floor. Someone
laughs on the next level and I climb up two more flights of stairs.

The flat is on Kildare Street. It is a simple square room.
There are polished floorboards and a white bed against the
wall. There is an antique wardrobe, an old chintz couch at an
angle, a white marble fireplace, and more elephants . . . walking beside the wall. This time it is a father, a mother and a
little child elephant at the end.

Over the mantelpiece another of Pappy's paintings hangs,
and underneath it Jonathan stands, looking cool and fresh in
all this sticky heat. He is wearing his black jacket, a white
t-shirt and a pair of faded jeans.

The flat – 'the love place' I call it – looks into the Shelbourne Hotel. There are chambermaids and room service waiters with white jackets and trays.

'Shouldn't we be over there?' I ask. There is a bottle of wine and a corkscrew in the tiny kitchen and a red and white checkered floor. Two paper cups stand waiting. At least my pappy would have liked that.

The other room is a bathroom where the shower still drips and Jonathan's towel hangs over the door. At work there are moments, a raised eyebrow in the corridor, a wink at the end of a meeting, a special little smile in the kitchen over the microwave.

He begins to undress me. Button by button and I am not used to this. The dress does not fall. He lifts it gently over my head and then puts it on a hanger on the wardrobe door. Inside I am sure there are only wooden hangers with all the hooks facing the same way. What now? A walk to the bed? Which way to happiness? Straight on, left or right? He is wearing his jeans when he kisses me. His t-shirt and jacket are on the chair.

Upstairs someone makes a sound like marbles being scattered on the floor.

The sheets are crisp and white. The same little blue stripe around the edge. The couple are on the stairs again. They are dragging out the rubbish bags. They meet someone else on the stairs and there is some chat then and a muffled laugh. Jonathan is on his way somewhere and I am trying to keep up. As soon as he kisses my lips, I am lost in the world and out of place. His skin tastes good, his hair smells like rosemary and mint shampoo, he is silent and like a cat burglar, he doesn't make a sound. His aura is still blue and sparkling and when we make love I open my lips and try to swallow his aura in. We are good like this, under the covers, the sex gets better and better, because neither one of us really cares. Downstairs the cellist practises scales, up and down, up and down. The heat is unbearable now. Outside there are faraway traffic sounds – on three levels of this building, three different lives – the cellist's bow, the couple and the lovers at three o'clock.

Juna is in room 106. She is wearing the same dressing gown she has had all her life and crying. She has faded in here. She does not belong in a place like this. She needs to hear music and be surrounded by her family and the smell of home cooking and fresh green fields. I hold her hand now while she cries. I hug her. There is nothing else for it. She is smaller than me now and so broken up, and down – I want to pick her up and cover her in love.

She begins to list out the food she has been given.

'Porridge, for breakfast. Tea. Brown bread and toast.'

She thinks she will never get home. She has never been in hospital before.

'Potatoes . . . chicken . . . and peas.'

A nurse with red hair comes in.

'Yes. She has an appointment with a specialist,' she says. 'It is with a Mr Stafford and he will see you on Tuesday at nine o'clock.

'They might keep her in and it is unlikely that they will operate straight away . . . but it is possible though.'

And I listen to my grandmother's questions now.

'How will she get to Mr Stafford?'

'Can she wear her own clothes and when can she go home?' More than anything she wants to go home.

'No one wants to be in hospital,' I tell her, 'but you have to be here to get well.' I am trying to keep the ship afloat but when Juna becomes lonesome again I struggle not to cry.

We are facing it at last. The inevitability of it, and yet why does everyone have to get old and die? Did I not realize that this was coming? She was always the leader and when I see her fear and confusion now I am frightened and unhinged by it as well.

'You will need to leave here at seven,' the nurse says. 'The traffic will be bad.'

'Will I be able to wear my own clothes?' she asks again. Juna is like a child who had left her coat at school.

'The traffic will be terrible,' the nurse says, 'and your clothes won't make any difference to that.' And here she smiles and it is the smile of an angel with crooked teeth, but an angel. We both look up at her. We stare her out of it. Needing answers. Needing hope.

'Well, thank you,' Juna says and now she is smiling up at her. 'Thank you for bringing some humour to the situation.'

And the nurse is lit up then. She likes my grandmother's weathered face and her nice old-fashioned charm.

Juna tells me about being on the ward with three other old women.

'Those inhalers – you might as well have a lawnmower in the room with you,' she says. 'And there was a woman in the bed opposite . . . never took her eyes off me . . . not once . . . even when she had the oxygen mask on . . . it was very provocative.'

'Will I be able to go home?' she asks when the nurse comes back again. And the nurse sighs, but in a good-natured way.

'I'm in the wrong job,' she says kindly. 'I can't give you definite answers to anything. But I know you want to go home. I'm aware of your desires – and everyone's are the same. Everyone wants to go home,' she says and with this she leaves, probably going to say the same kind words to the elderly lady in the room across the hall.

For a minute or two Juna has hope and today her mind is very clear. She gets up to walk around and she is almost light on her feet.

'That's better,' she says. 'At least there is something happening. I'll be ready to leave at seven and I'll able to put my own skirt back on again.'

Her clothes – the cardigan I bought her at Christmas – her cream pleated skirt – her blue blouse – her shoes – have become armour. Cotton and wool that in the brief seconds after she puts them on, make her believe she can be well again.

When the nurse comes back it is dark and I am curled up beside Juna on her bed. I don't want to leave her on her own tonight and so I stay and know she will wake up with something to look at other than the wooden crucifix on the wall.

I do not know how to tell her that I love her and the air is thick with it. I would like to say 'Thank you' to her, for everything, and yet I can't. I wish I could just say it to her now or at least open the window and let it out. When someone is eighty-four and not feeling brilliant, it's time to stop kidding around.

Email to Hope Swann 22 June 3.02 p.m.
From Matilda Vaughan
Re: Men.
Hope,
I know it feels like you don't know what you're doing. That's

my whole point. None of us know what we're doing. Love is irrational. It's a yearning. An ache.

That's what love is like, Hope . . . it's a runaway train . . . and we're on it.

Matilda.

We drink wine from paper cups. We do not talk after the deed is done. There is nothing to say. We are not like normal lovers and we do not need to hear each other's stories now. He does not need to tell me about his old girlfriends and how and why they broke his heart. And I do not need to tell him about my last boyfriend and besides there was only ever one. We are quiet. We are discreet. After this I will go home to the flat in Bray. And Jonathan will call Nina and go back to the office and work late.

Her breath becomes weaker and I am at her side. Even a small signal of weakness is frightening and the great white tornado is losing strength. It is as if the house and all the trees around it are bending and, one by one, they begin to crack and break. The doctors come in. The nurses smile kindly. They say things like 'She's more comfortable now'. In the middle of the night she sits bolt upright and her eyes are bright and clear. She was young once like me. She fell in love and probably made a fool of herself over some stupid guy. Why can't things stay the way they are and where do dead people go? She knows me in that last hour. Just when she sat up in bed. I lie on the bed beside her, her hand in mine. Her blue veins laced underneath her skin. Her breath rattling, like a great old train.

The sun begins to come up at 4.15 and it fills the hospital room with a pale orange and pink glow. It moves upwards on the white wall, up and up until it sits like a coloured cloud over the bed. 'It is the start of another perfect June day,' I tell her and I want her to wake up and look at the light.

I keep my arms around her and I lie there looking up at this strange coloured cloud. The nurse comes in and lifts her wrist gently. She looks at us without speaking and then she closes the blinds. All the usual blood pressure checks are not necessary and there is no need for food and water now.

Today Juna is free from all of that. She has no need for material things. She does not need baby food and vitamins to keep her alive. Juna is free and it's time, but I lie here not able to bear it, and know that for the first time, she will not be a part of a clear June day.

The ashes are scattered over the green hill in the lower meadow. I try to see Juna's face and imagine her smile and her laugh. I wonder where she is. There are things I wanted to ask her before she died but I was afraid. I wanted to ask if she could come back in some little way and tell me what it is like. If there are angels and if there is any God and if my brother Daniel is there and if he is as happy now as he was in his life. I would like her to check in on my pappy too and tell me that he's happy and smiling there. I want to believe in something. More than anything I want to believe in something other than a man I meet in a square room with four white walls.

Yesterday I asked Doreen if she would measure me because I feel as if I'm getting smaller now.

Most of all I want to ask Juna if she can see Larry anywhere because for the first time ever I really don't know where he's gone. I try to talk to her about it and I ask her if she can stand up on the clouds with a giant white telescope and just try to spot him on Planet Earth. I imagine he would be a bright red spot moving silently like a plane on a long-distance flight. I ask these questions but there is no answer, not from the sky or the clouds or the waving beech trees. When the casket opens the ashes are swept away. A life that was full and plenty. One grey puff and Juna is gone.

Mrs Kirk is standing at the door. She has turned the key and has walked up the two flights of stairs. She turns the handle and taps on the door jamb. Nina is wearing expensive perfume and she is tall and beautiful and polite.

Jonathan is stretched out on the couch. He is not wearing a shirt but he is reading his newspaper and looking very relaxed. I am in the bathroom and I am looking through a crack in the door.

Jonathan looks at her and he is very quiet and calm.

'Johnny,' she says, and he says, 'Hello, darling.'

She is carrying a Burberry clutch and her hair is shiny and black. She looks like she goes to the gym every day and in my mind I see her lifting weights and then lifting me up and throwing me against a wall. She is the kind of woman who could leave a lot of bruises or maybe drown me in a barrel.

'Who is it this time?' she asks and she walks into the room and looks around. Jonathan does not speak. Instead he shakes his head and smiles.

The bed is not made. It never is. We do not bother to change the sheets. They are twisted and turned and the pillows have fallen on the floor. There are empty wine bottles in the kitchen and the floor is covered in paper cups and take-out bags. I am wondering if I could step out into the room and reason with her. Just introduce myself and say 'Hello'. And then there is the sound of glass breaking and she has picked up an empty wine bottle and flung it across the room.

'Sweetheart,' Johnny says, 'be reasonable . . .' and then, 'She means nothing to me,' and I step back from the bathroom door and when I turn, I see the sink is full of flowers – tulips, delphiniums and roses – that he brought here for me. The curtain flaps a little in the wind and the tiles are gleaming white.

But Mrs Kirk is screaming at him now and a chair goes flying across the room and then she picks up one of the wooden elephants – the papa elephant, I think – and she aims it at his head.

She is not someone who would welcome a friendly conversation. There is a loud crash, a thud, and Jonathan is behind the couch. I give up the idea of reasoning with her and do what any sensible person would do. I find the open window and begin to climb down the fire escape instead.

Doreen is on the couch in the flat. She is eating a pizza and watching a keep-fit video on the TV. I am soaked from the rain and the heel has broken on my shoe.

'Let me guess,' she says after a minute. 'You were chased by a dog.'

'Mrs Kirk,' I tell her, and she opens her mouth and turns and stares.

'What happened?'

'I didn't wait to find out.'

'What's she like?'

'Stronger than me.'

'What did she do?'

'She threw an elephant at Jonathan.'

'Wow,' Doreen says. 'She *is* strong.'

'Let's cool it for a little while,' Jonathan says. He is sitting at his desk and I am sitting opposite on the low red couch. The door is closed and he is frowning, with his tie off and hanging over the back of his chair.

'I'm sorry she did that,' he says, 'but don't worry, it will all be fine . . . Hope . . . it will be fine . . . we just need to cool it for a little while,' and as I sit there I can feel icicles beginning to form under my nose.

'It's fine,' he says and he is shaking his head and smiling. 'We just need to be more discreet.'

When I go back to my desk he has sent me an email.

Email from Jonathan Kirk 9.36 a.m.

To Hope Swann

Subject: Don't worry!

By the way . . . you look lovely today . . . x

Juna is smiling, I am sure of it. Sometimes you need to push the boundaries a little. That's what Jonathan always says. 'Hope . . . sometimes you need to take a little risk.' I don't mean to send the email but then my hand slips and I do.

Forward email 9.40 a.m.

To everyone

From Jonathan Kirk

To Hope Swann

By the way . . . you look lovely today . . . x

11 *Arthur and Marilyn*

Because it was Friday, Chief Gallagher left Manhattan early and as he headed towards Brooklyn and his third wife, he listened to the *Laurie Roth* show. It was too hot even for July and the radio irritated him. 'What a turkey,' he murmured. He always said that to Laurie Roth and even now he could not get used to the sudden heat of the city and he seemed to have been fighting against it all his life. He had married a woman from the force two years ago but he had already known her for several years. The Brooklyn boys usually knew the Brooklyn girls and this time he was forty-nine and this wife was thirty-three.

He had listened to her complain at dinner on Sunday. How she came home from work as tired as he was and then fell into the sea of laundry at her feet. He had four boys. Their football vests and shorts clogged her housekeeping system up and every second Sunday they had to take his mother out. They fought over it and lots of other things – but more than anything they argued over sex. He wanted more than she did and when he took a beer from the refrigerator and sat on the porch, he thought about this briefly – men wanted it more than women – and he shrugged as the first bubbles hit his throat and he guessed there was nothing unusual or revolutionary about this.

When the doorbell rang he was wearing a NYPD t-shirt and shorts and as he walked down the hall, his hot feet sticking a little, he noticed that the houseplants were leaning and that the goldfish bowl looked too warm. When he opened the door there was another wave of heat and then he saw his friend Arthur Glassman standing looking up at him from the bottom step.

They embraced with a smile and from The Chief, 'Hey, man.' The heat from Gallagher was obvious because in his arms Glassman felt chilled and almost cold. He smiled up at him and Gallagher, in spite of his bad mood, could only smile back. He wanted to slap him hard on the back but he was afraid he would knock him down the steps. He had been like a boy in Vietnam. Smaller than the other troops but somehow he had more life and spirit than the rest of the men.

The Chief had not wanted to see anyone that evening. Not even his sons or his wife – and yet here he was, unexpected and uninvited, and with him a gentle bright calm came into his life. Suddenly his warm house was better now and he was proud and when they walked through the hall, he pointed out trophies and photographs of his sons and his wife. He smiled when he opened the kitchen door and he went to the yard for more beer and some ice.

'I'd prefer some hot chocolate,' Glassman said.

'Man, in this heat,' and he laughed and shook his head.

He found another photo of his wife and handed it to his friend and watched his face.

'She's a looker,' Glassman said

'And . . . Matilda?' The Chief asked and he smiled as an image of her formed in his mind.

'Matilda,' came the reply and the voice was low and level with just a hint of humour behind it. 'As it happens. She's quite a piece of work.'

Here there was silence and only the kettle began to hum and whistle and neither man spoke as Gallagher whisked the hot chocolate up.

'Are you in some kind of trouble?' he asked.

'You could say that,' and here The Chief put one hot bear paw on his old friend's shoulder and walking him out on to the high back porch he told him to 'spit it out'.

So Glassman spat. He told him about the letters and the phone calls, every day and every night.

'And what does she say?'

'That she loves me.'

'She's only human, Arthur.'

But Glassman couldn't manage a smile.

'That I still love her.'

Here The Chief barely nodded. So far this was no good.

'Anything else?'

'I come home from work and she's sitting on my steps.'

'Every evening?'

'Most evenings.'

The Chief lit a cigarette and they both fell silent and outside the small dogs of Brooklyn began to bark.

'Those fuckin' dogs,' he murmured.

'She's actually beginning to scare me,' and Glassman's voice was slow and careful and there was no hint of embarrassment in it.

The Chief nodded.

'She says she's pregnant.'

'Is she?'

'No.'

'You sure?'

'It's a fantasy. Before me she had three miscarriages. We were careful and she told me herself . . . she's *reproductively challenged* – go figure.'

Here The Chief lifted his eyebrows and took a long swallow of beer.

Glassman told him that she had been into his apartment even though he had changed the locks.

'Maybe I'm being paranoid,' he said quietly and he looked out over the trees to the church.

The Chief's face was without any expression.

'She's blowing the Super,' he said.

'It's breaking and entering,' Glassman said.

'Not if you have a key. And besides we need to catch her doing it.'

And Glassman told him about the perfume which he believed she was spraying around every room. And there was no response at all now and he felt mildly humiliated by that.

They fell silent then and this was only because The Chief did not want to tell him what he already knew. They waited and they were both deaf to the sirens and the barking dogs now.

Then Glassman took a deep breath and laid out the contents of his pockets. There were all gold-trimmed letters. Each one carried a quote and was written in black ink with a red lipstick kiss at the end.

'I don't understand why people aren't a little nicer to each other.' Marilyn

and

'All little girls should be told they are beautiful, even if they aren't.' Marilyn

and

'I don't mind making jokes, but I don't want to be one.' Marilyn

The Chief read each one with a look of concentration on his face. Then Glassman handed him another. 'This one came this morning,' he said.

'*A career is wonderful, but it won't keep you warm on a cold night.*' Marilyn

Arthur could still remember the night he told her about it. How he had noticed her that first day in the swimming pool and how she had reminded him of Marilyn Monroe and how he then foolishly, romantically told her and how she had held on to it. How it had become their thing and in her head their 'raison d'être'. How they had drunk and got a little high and made love to the thought of it. Those first weeks were like going back in time. When women wore felt hats and heels and skirts that fell below the knee but also had real breasts and an ass. And her lips were beautiful, always beautiful, and Glassman, even now on The Chief's back porch, could give her that.

'You see,' he said to The Chief, and here he turned his cup in his hands, 'I was Arthur and she was Marilyn.'

His friend took this piece of information, not handed over easily, and with some degree of shame. And because he thought until then that he had seen everything, he saw the funny side first and had no mercy for his friend's pain.

'Some people dress up as doctors and nurses . . . and you play Miller and Monroe?'

And here both men managed a laugh and then The Chief got up and walked out to the yard. When he came back he was carrying two more beers. 'You're having a beer,' he said to Glassman and then he told him what he knew all along.

'She's not breaking the law,' he said, 'but we could have a friendly chat with her. It might aggravate her . . .'

'It might help,' his friend replied.

And then The Chief gave him some friendly advice.

'She thinks she's Marilyn Monroe – do you really think this

woman is going to see sense? This is my advice. Give her time
to cool off and in the meantime go home and pack a bag.'

'So,' Glassman said quietly, 'I have to run away.'

'You still got the house on the Cape?' The Chief asked.

'Sure – and she doesn't know about that,' Glassman replied.

'You're not running away from her,' The Chief said. 'You're
taking a vacation – go down to the Cape – a few weeks out of
the picture and she'll calm down.'

At home Glassman cleaned the apartment again. He wanted
to smell floor wax as soon as he opened his front door. He
replaced the security chain and shot the small brass bolts and
then stood facing his own world again. The locksmith had left
a small splinter of wood on the rug and he picked it up and
twirled it between his fingers before putting it into the trash.
Otherwise the parquet floor was gleaming and the sunlight
landed on it in long golden shadows and then bounced off it
again. On days like this he used to feel elated. The summer
sun lighting up the street and every corner of Central Park.
He ran his fingers along the long narrow mahogany table, the
telephone, the olive-green bowl where he kept his keys, and
there was no dust. It was as if everything had been replaced
with identical items so his home was suddenly clean and new.
And everything else was exactly as he had left it. The soft
French cheese in the refrigerator. The toilet seat standing up.
The small pea of toothpaste in the sink. The kitchen mat
kicked with his feet. He could still taste The Chief's hot
chocolate and how kind his voice had been when he told him
in a roundabout way that he could not help.

But really he had given Glassman something he did not
have before, he had given him permission to leave.

He could be replaced at the hospital. Since he became ill he could only work the shorter shifts. He wanted to get out of this city soon before it kicked him until he turned green.

He pulled his t-shirt off over his head and dropped it on the hall floor. He caught sight of his slight frame in the mirror and as usual he did not know for sure now if he was sick or well.

He stopped for a moment then and told himself to breathe slowly. He was suddenly afraid again. He could get it, the smell, he was sure of it. Last week he had called Trudy early on a Saturday morning and asked her to come over.

'Glassman, can't it wait?' she asked and then, guessing that he was in real trouble, she pulled a coat on over her night-clothes and jumped in a cab in the rain. When she came in, she was fresh-faced and smiling and he just loved her then. Her hair soaked and how she shook it out, not really caring, and said in a voice full of humour, 'Arthur – what gives?'

He said he needed her help. He needed her to explain the smell. He needed her to tell him in clear simple language that he was not imagining it. He needed Trudy to tell him that he was not losing his mind. And she pulled a dramatic face and then walked through his apartment and said, 'Sure I get it' and then in a completely casual way, 'I think it's . . . Chanel No 5.'

The traffic from Prince Street seemed to be inside the room today and he hated the noise and how it seemed to fill and buzz inside his head. He turned on the shower and then he stopped for a moment and listened again.

'No,' he told himself and then he said it out loud to remind himself one more time. He needed to deal with this. He needed to get a grip on himself. He had to stop coming home at night and checking every room. But tomorrow he knew he would change the locks again and hire someone else to clean.

The sound of the cold water calmed him. He stood under the water and leaned his head back so that the water bounced a little off his face. And when he looked down he saw with some satisfaction his feet still slightly tanned and standing firm on the green tiles. She was still sending notes to him. One said she was walking out on her contract with 20th Century Fox. He had no idea what she meant. But she was getting into his apartment and moving things around. He was sure of it and yet it was something he could not fully prove. 'We need to catch her in the act,' that was what The Chief said. These days after work at the hospital Glassman liked to take long walks through the city at night. He kept himself busy without explaining it. The real reason was that he felt he was living with a ghost.

He adjusted the showerhead and the water pounded over his back and it was only when he was finished that he heard the sound.

It sounded like a door, the bathroom door, he thought, being gently closed. And in sequence he swallowed and his mouth went suddenly dry and then he knew that the noise from the traffic was coming through the open bedroom window and that he never left the windows open, and that that was something only she liked to do.

He did not need to turn around so he calmly reached backwards for his towel and waited as he wrapped it around his waist, and then he turned, knowing that the bathroom door had opened and closed and that he would see her standing there.

'You better start talking to me,' she said and her voice was without any emotion and it was low as if she did not want someone to overhear them arguing in the next room.

Glassman twisted the towel around his waist and used his hand to take the drops from his mouth and nose.

'OK,' he said and he followed her down the landing and into his bedroom. The bed was covered in pale taupe silk. The cream headboard pressed against an exposed brick wall. His jeans were slung over the armchair and he noticed that his belt had uncurled itself on the floor. Matilda walked towards the bed and waited for a moment. 'Quite a performance,' he thought.

She wanted to stand and face him from his bed and to remind him of what he had taken from her there.

'So how is The Chief and his young bride?' she asked. She was speaking in a light whispering voice and he no longer knew if she was high or insane.

'I know everything you do,' she said simply. 'I know where you go. I know who you meet. I know who you see. And I will keep following you until you listen and understand me,' and her eyes were boring into him now. 'We're meant to be. I know it. And you know it too.' He could smell her heavy scent from here. She was wearing black stilettos and when she sat suddenly on the end of the bed he noted with some strange throwback affection that they had red leather soles.

'Matilda . . .' and even now his voice was gentle, 'I don't love you,' and she stared back defiantly.

'I don't believe you,' she whispered back. And then, 'Glassman, there's no need to be so afraid.'

'I don't believe I ever did,' he said and this was the first time he deliberately hurt her and he marvelled at it. How deep and hurtful and powerful those few words were.

When Matilda walked towards him, she was swallowing and big tears were beginning to roll down her cheeks. Even her tear-ducts were dramatic and pouring out small rivers of black mascara now.

'I curse you,' she said simply and in the sweetest voice he

had ever heard. And then she blinked, closing both eyes for a second, taking her keys from the table as she always did, and as she left she buttoned her coat carefully as if against the cold. And what she said had almost made him grin and her last words to him showed up his life in a sudden jagged flash.

'Don't bother,' he wanted to say because Glassman felt quite sure he was already cursed. And the next day Matilda wrote an article about famous suicides – Mark Antony, Adolf Hitler and Marilyn Monroe.

The Chief wanted to help him. Not only because he cared about him but because in Vietnam he had saved The Chief's life. He had held him when blood ran out of him and he knew by the look on Glassman's face that as they held each other close one of them might die. But he couldn't help now. The problem was big inside his friend's head – but after one busy day at the Precinct it was really way too small in his. Men and women and the world wars they caused for one another – sometimes it would be better if everyone just lived apart.

That night he put his hand against his wife's back and felt her breathe in and out and he could almost hear her thoughts, the internal debate, the reminders of what she should be punishing him for now – how he had promised to stop smoking and now because he hadn't quit she might withhold sex. But it was Friday night and the boys were with their mother and so she turned and quietly sighed as he put his hands on her breasts. She smelt like soap and water and her hair somehow had the aroma of freshly baked bread. She was Irish too, somewhere along the line. She had that distracting look of fresh health around her and even now, as she made love to him in her sighing, lamenting way, he rode the 1916 Rising and then he went into her and rose again. Her name was Maggie and when he came he groaned it into her ear. She was not the type to make phone calls and sneak around his house if he ever left her.

In quiet whispers then, they did something they had not done for months. Instead of fading off into noisy hot sleep, they talked. She listened as he told her about his friend's trouble and she said that the woman was wasting her time and that if it was her – Maggie – she would go around there once with a shotgun and blow off his balls and Gallagher smiled into the dark. And it was the first real smile that day – and he loved her, for her brutality, for her own version of love and for the sweet simplicity of it.

12 *Love, Loyalty and Friendship (September 2001)*

Experiment n. – 1. A test carried out in order to discover whether a theory is correct or what the results of a particular course of action would be. 2. An attempt to do something new, or a trying out of something to see what will happen.

The red dress is a mistake. It is a 1950s shirtdress that is strangely demure but still shows off my figure and it is a mixture of raspberry-red and pink. He looks relaxed and I know that living on the boat gives him that. That he is happiest on his own, free from other people and me. I am wearing pink amethyst earrings with one matching bracelet and when he walks in I notice that he does not see any of this. When he looks at me he just looks into my eyes and I cannot decide if this is good or bad. We sit on two high stools at the bar and in between drinks we tell each other about our lives.

He tells me he works for a record label and I tell him I help to make the ads that run on TV.

'Do you know the story about the young bull and the old bull?' he asks. 'No,' I tell him and I am leaning forward and smiling. I am trying. Every time I meet a new guy I try again. Every time it doesn't work I say I am finished with men – and then another one comes along. And every time another one comes along he is always different and he seems like 'big game' compared to the one before. When we sit facing each other we pretend it is all perfectly normal and that meeting like this is an everyday thing, and that neither of us wonders if our second date could be magical and the start of . . . something.

He notices how I fold my arms and then unfold them again. That my dress is red and that it shows off my ass. That I am a little nervous when I speak and that my breasts are small.

I notice that he is five minutes late. That he is freshly shaved and smells of soap. That when he speaks it is as if he is holding a watermelon in his hands. That he is wearing a Claddagh ring and that his heart is turned in and that something has changed since we last met.

'The young bull says let's run down the hill and fuck a cow,' he says. 'The old bull says let's walk down the hill and fuck them all.' He says this sitting on a high stool and then he nods at me and smiles. I do not know if I should be frightened or turned on by this.

He tells me about the woman who broke his heart and I wish he would stop all this. How they fought and how he couldn't let her go and how they got back together for a one-night fling.

'You should never go back for a second look,' I say wisely and I am thinking about the night I booked a room in the Burlington because I was too drunk to go home and how a married man I know peeled my stockings off and then fell asleep, as if exhausted by them.

The old bull touches the waiter's sleeve and asks for more drink. I think he is an old goat to say what he said, that he is probably a tiger under the sheets, and where are all these animals coming from anyway?

'Yes, but I was in love,' he says. 'It was what I wanted.' He says it has taken him ten years to forget this girl. He holds up ten fingers to mark the years and all I can see is the Claddagh ring. He wonders if I will sleep with him. I wonder if it is too soon to leave. The radio behind the bar is playing 'Stay' (I missed you). When he asks me if I want another drink I think about my empty life and hear myself say, 'Yes.'

'A lot of women fancy me,' he says.

'Oh,' I reply and here I cause the conversation to stop.

I wait a moment then, before tapping a little nail into his hand.

'Sometimes,' I begin, 'men think I fancy them but really I am just taking a look.' I hope this will knock him back but it doesn't work.

'No,' he says and he is firm now, 'I have had three stalkers. I mean three serious stalkers and one woman who said I was the father of her child.' Here he holds his hands over an imaginary bump on his stomach.

I try to put in another nail.

'You must have got worried when I called you,' I say and I am smiling for what seems like the first time in about ten years.

'Now, Hope . . .' he says and he grins at me and looks into my eyes. It is the first time he has said my name tonight. It is the first time I think about going to bed with him but it is still only a thought.

I try to look concerned then and I am. I have no idea why three women would want to stalk this man. I wonder if it is a lie and why most men don't have any stalkers and why he has had a batch of three.

I go to the bathroom and ask my reflection how our date is. My reflection looks nice in the red dress that he isn't able to see. Then the girl in the mirror says it might not be a date actually but I am not able to hear that.

In the bar he is probably checking for messages from women on his mobile phone.

He seems to find me interesting in little flashes but sometimes I seem to fade and bore him. He tells me this by checking his mobile phone again, by yawning (twice), by sending a text to someone as I speak.

He tells me more about his life. How his parents separated. How he is fine with that. How he does not want to get married. That he does not want to have children. How making these decisions was like losing a monkey on his back. He tells me he is fine. I tell myself he is not. He says he is not sure about relationships, that he does not like the rules.

'What rules?' I ask. 'There are no rules.'

'Rules,' he says. 'Like it's a Tuesday night and she says . . . let's go to a concert at the weekend.'

'Oh,' I say, 'that rule.'

'I don't like to think beyond today,' he says.

We talk about going out with people and how everyone starts off well and then you start to notice things.

'Ah yes,' he says good-naturedly and here we share a little joke. We both understand the disappointment of it. The day we find out that our lovers are human and real.

'You see her in a particular light,' he offers. 'Or you don't like what she's cooked for you . . .' and we both warm to the point and then it comes out, real easy and slow. Timber.

'There's this girl I'm seeing at the moment,' and he thinks for a minute to get his words in order and it is something else about how disappointing real people are and I understand this point too well now. I imagine his girlfriend is tall and standing in a window and that when he looks at her he cannot see how she is.

'I'm not in love with her, but it's nice,' he says and the word 'nice' comes out as if he has invented it. I imagine nice mashed potatoes and nice pyjamas when he speaks.

'It's nice,' he says again as if he is forcing the thought upon me. He wants me to say that nice is good. I want to say that I really don't care.

'She's twenty-nine,' he says. 'She's an artist and she has lots of ideas.' I listen as he destroys his girl. I imagine how she would feel to hear this and what it is like to be noticed now in a particular kind of light. How he only thinks she is nice and has sex with her anyway. I wonder how his girl would feel about all of this.

'Are you seeing anyone?' he asks then.

'I thought I might be seeing you,' I want to answer but instead I shake my head.

'What age are you?' he asks.

'Twenty-three,' and I look into my drink to tell him that he is rude.

'How many in your family?' and for a moment I want to ask if this is an interview for a job.

'Just me,' I tell him.

He says nothing and then, 'That's a surprise', and I begin to hate him then but I cannot leave because he has only just mentioned his girl.

We talk about our work again and he asks me if I am an 'Accounts Executive'.

'No,' I say and I explain that in advertising Account Executives work for people like me. I am weakened and Lenin deserts me and I pretend now that I am top of the heap.

'Oh,' he says and his voice is dry, 'I didn't know there was such a hierarchy,' and in that moment I think he might jeer me. I wait and watch as he takes another tack.

Now he tells me that I am amazing. That I am inspirational. That I am an incredible girl, and I look back at him and each compliment floats back over my head and I am happy to let them just fade away. I do not know if he likes my dress or why we are meeting or what he really thinks about anything, especially me.

Then he pays me a compliment and it is in Irish.

He says each word out slowly as if this will help and then translates carefully.

'Quiet but guilty,' he says and he is much more pleased about this than I could ever be. Then he explains the English version as well.

'Quiet but a lot going on inside,' but I already know that about myself.

I imagine what it would be like to do a two-hand reel with him.

'I didn't speak English until I was eight,' he says.

I want to tell him that he is still not speaking English but I no longer have the heart.

When he spoke in Irish I imagined how he would herd sheep and hurry them around a crawling Japanese car and how 'Hup hup' is the same in any language and anyway sheep don't really care.

'I have a very high sex drive,' the bull says then and this comes from nowhere of course.

'Sorry,' I say, 'what did you say?' I had heard him very well but I would also like the other people in the bar to hear.

'I have a very high sex drive,' he says again. He has folded his arms which I know now is a sign he is handing over a hidden part of himself.

'I've tried celibacy but that's just repressing your needs,' and now I look at him and try not to laugh.

'I am a man with needs . . . cravings,' he says.

I smile at him and think he is a small man in a sports jacket.

'I was in Cannes recently,' he says, then, 'I got out of the helicopter and I was surrounded by girls. Beautiful girls. I have cravings. Such cravings. I have written poetry about the cravings I've had.'

When he comes back from the bathroom I am wearing my coat.

He says, 'Yes, I have to go too.'

'Come on,' I think as I pick up my bag. 'At least give me this, at least let me be the one to say goodbye first.' I walk ahead of him. I breeze along and feel careless and slightly drunk. I do not care if he is behind me or not. I do not care if I see him again. I do not care that he is going to his girlfriend's flat now, after me, where they will have a bad dinner followed by unusual sex.

He hugs me as my taxi pulls up to the kerb and I feel like an ironing board in his arms. He would not know that I made a face over his shoulder. He would not know that I had pinned some fine hopes to this meeting and to him.

He does not need to know that.

'So let's keep the communication going,' he says and he is being warm and friendly now.

'Sure, sure,' I say and I kiss him on the cheek. He is chewing spearmint gum and he looks older under the streetlights.

He would like to see me again but he does not know how to express this or what we are supposed to be when we meet.

'Don't think too much about anything that was said tonight,' he says, and I do not understand this but I do understand that for the first time tonight he is trying now too. In the taxi he sends me a text and pays me that Irish compliment again. 'Oh fuck off,' I whisper quietly to my phone.

Claddagh ring n. An elaborate ring originally given in Ireland as a token of affection. Symbol: Love, loyalty and friendship.

At home I sit on the floor of the flat and pick small flecks of wool from the carpet and I light three white candles instead of the light. The bull said he was romantic but I could see no evidence of that. I would not have met him if I'd known he had a girlfriend and I preferred the young bull anyway. He seemed more honest or something. I stretch out on the floor and think about nothing. I feel alone and so alone that I am conscious of my own edges inside this room. I do not want to feel like this any more. For once I would like to wake up feeling happy and warm and with fuck-knots in my hair.

'I need to change my life,' I say out loud and into the dark to no one at all.

At 4 a.m. I look for my vibrator. The batteries are dead so I take two from the remote control and use these instead. I make myself come just to forget about him and about me and after coming I think about Larry and I cry.

'Look, a rainbow,' Doreen says. She is sitting inside the kitchen window in her favourite white dressing gown and looking out across the overgrown grass. When we both watch, it seems to dissolve and then run away in different colours with the fresh drops of rain. She puts her chin in her hands and rests her forehead on the glass.

Mr Costello taps once on the door and waits until Doreen calls out to him. He brings us our post in the morning and stands in our kitchen with his braces hanging down. Two weeks ago his wife died. She was watching *EastEnders* in her favourite chair and now we can both see that her death has left a new kind of mark.

'Come in, Mr Costello,' Doreen says and she gets up and pulls back a chair. We take turns at cooking. On Mondays

I roast a chicken. I make homemade gravy with sage and thyme stuffing and Doreen waits quietly at her place. She always sits at the end of the table with her back to the window and I always sit at the side.

Last week a down-and-out lady moved into the garden. So far no one has had the heart to ask her to leave. 'It seems rude,' Doreen says and Mr Costello says nothing in response to this. It is another thing in life that seems pointless to him now.

Without his wife he has become a shadow man. Someone who stands behind other people, looking out – there and not there – at the same time.

On Tuesdays Doreen will make the exact same dinner as me. Roast chicken again. On Wednesdays I make spaghetti and on Thursdays she makes spaghetti too. When I ask her to stop doing this she says, 'Stop doing what?' and the next night for dinner she gives me toast and scrambled eggs.

Last night Mr Costello sat on the stairs and cried. No matter what we did, we couldn't make him stop. Eventually Doreen put her hand on his shoulder and said, 'Excuse me, Mr Costello, but you need to get a grip.' At night he sits in our sitting room and within minutes he falls asleep. His chin rests on his chest and the corners of his mouth turn down and then one leg kicks out suddenly and his foot shoots into the air.

'That's restless leg syndrome,' Doreen says calmly. The last tenant was a doctor and now she reads his monthly copy of *Medical Review*. When I am having my breakfast she tries to make me look at a picture of an ingrown toenail.

'Look,' she says, 'please look at it.' We go through this almost every day.

The first flatmate lasted a week but we only liked her because of her microwave and her little radio that you could hang in the shower. The second one worked in another ad agency and she left a trail of false nails behind her and used the breadbasket for her contraceptive pills. Then there was Liz, who left long black hairs on the sofa and smelt of TCP.

'I miss Larry,' Doreen says suddenly out through the window and then, 'Sorry' as if the words had come flying out by themselves.

The bull has golden hair. It is cut neatly into his head and when he runs his hand back over it he makes a little quiff. We take deep breaths before we speak and try hard not to look too deeply at ourselves. It is our third date and we're tired of each other already. The wine bar is almost empty and he steers me towards a wide table meant for four under the archway and I know now that he has some more secrets to tell me about himself.

He is still wearing the Claddagh ring too except now his heart is pointing out.

'So what's been happening?' I ask and my voice is easy and light.

'What's been happening?' he asks back and then waits.

'Let's see . . . when did I see you last? I've had a lot of new work on. I've probably been in and out of a relationship . . .' and here he stops and I know that I am here to talk about men and women again.

'Oh,' I say and then, 'Did she dump you?' and my voice is very gentle but there is a little laugh behind it.

He smiles up at me for a second.

'Things were going really well,' he says calmly. 'We got on well together. My family loved her. We went away for weekends. We just got on well, you know, but she was planning for next year . . .' and he trails off and looks at the menu. Somehow when I think about his girl I see her in a hard hat on the building site of their lives. But he's not finished yet.

'She said she loved me – and this became everything to her.'

'Why?'

'Because I couldn't say it back.'

The waitress comes over. She is a tall girl with brown eyes and a soft easy smile. She stands with folded arms and he orders bangers and mash 'with mustard' and he adds this as if it is of great importance.

'I'll have the salmon,' I say.

'With mustard,' he says again and when he looks into the waitress's eyes she seems to say, 'OK. I love you too.'

'Once I did tell her I loved her,' he says. 'You know, I love ya, kind of thing, one night . . . and she held on to it.'

And I know this happened right after they made love. It had just come out and his girl had held on to him and it and she had told her friends that he had said 'I love you' and her friends had smiled and said, 'This is it.'

He tells me that they argued and then she ended it.

'She wanted children and I didn't,' he says. 'But I did tell her that at the start,' and here his grey-blue eyes are pleading for forgiveness and he would like me to see that even if he didn't love her at least he had been honest about the children part.

'So anyway,' he adds and he sounds very tired now, 'it's over.'

'What age was she?' I ask and I know that his girl was six years older than me.

'Twenty-nine.'

'Ah,' I say wisely and the sound comes out quiet and

soft as if to comfort him. 'Twenty-nine-year-old girls want husbands.'

I know that he has slept with Twenty-nine. I know that from the first drunken night at her flat when the air was fumy with alcohol and his raggy whisper said something about 'a condom' there was always a question mark getting bogged down in the duvet and lost in the dark.

I understand how Twenty-nine had woken up with the strange warm smell of a man in her bed. And how she had listened in wonder to the noises he could make – breathing in deeply and quickly before he finally woke and how he had probably snored her awake before that. And how she lay there listening to him knock bottles over in her bathroom, and then lift the toilet seat up. She had heard all the scratching and grunting and grinding as the newly evolved man took his first long wee into her toilet, and the tight little fart that escaped and how he gave a long yawn as she waited for the toilet to flush and then she waited for the seat to come back down, and waited.

And she knew then that for happily ever after – the toilet-seat business would be annoying and even with his funny little habits – she was already growing fond of him from the start.

On that first morning together they were like two children who had discovered a new toy to play with. She was happy when she made real coffee and carried it into the bedroom. She was happy when she handed him fresh towels for his shower. She was happy to hear him wash. Just the noise of a new man, getting clean inside her house.

I want to tell him that it is not about 'I love you' and 'I love you too' and that it is nothing to do with what women want when they're twenty or twenty-three or twenty-nine or thirty-two. It is about every time he had slept with her, speared her, flattened her and rolled her out and how in time she had learned to come underneath him without even thinking about it. And every time he did it, she came and gave herself back to him, over and over and over, piece by piece, she opened herself up to him and said, 'Take me' and then 'Have me' and then 'Of course you love me . . . please.'

He eats hungrily, cutting the sausages and then blotting them into the mustard, and I feel for the older woman and in equal measures for the newly evolved man. I would like to take his hand and so far it is just his simple confusion and ignorance that are touching.

'We fought over it,' he said, swallowing. 'She rang me. I could hear her anger,' and he is still surprised by it all. He is intelligent and can't see the damage he has caused.

I know that Twenty-nine was probably crying on the phone to her friends and then on the stairs when she went to bed. That she cried under the sheets, the same sheets she had slept in with him, and then at her desk at work and then in bed again and really anywhere she could.

I wait before I ask my question because it seems important now and I would like to tell my friends about what he has done and what his answer is.

'Are you upset about it?' I ask quietly. 'Are you hurt? You know, do you feel bad about it?'

'No,' he says calmly and his voice is light in the same way mine was at the start. He sees that I am staring at him and waiting for something so he adds more words –

'No,' he says again and this time he shrugs his shoulders, 'I'm not – to be honest.'

And I can see that he is perplexed by it too. That Twenty-nine loved him and that he really didn't care at all. He is just as baffled as she is. All that sex. All that . . . love? Really. Honestly. It's time to find another word.

'Men and women,' I say and I even sigh about it and here our eyes meet and now his eyes give me the soft burn. I will tell Doreen everything tomorrow and she can tell someone else. We all need to know how little men can care – and how kind and honest they are about it – but – just how little they can care.

'That's a very pretty dress you're wearing,' he says, then, 'the colours . . .' and here his words just trail off.

'Men and women.' His voice is soft and he shakes his head.

'I am in wonderment,' he says.

I call Doreen and say, 'There is a Claddagh engagement ring in the window of Rhinestones.'

'The bull should be alerted immediately,' she replies.

The man from the TV Production Department slides into the taxi beside me and tonight we are both very drunk.

'Do you or do you not,' he asks and he is speaking in a highly confidential voice, 'find me attractive?'

'I don't,' I tell him and I have an urgent need to laugh.

'Sorry,' I whisper then to soften the blow. There is a new CD player from the raffle under my arm and so far this is the best thing about my night.

Pixilated adj. – 1. Behaving in a strange or whimsical way. 2. Feeling bewildered because unable to understand what is happening. 3. Drunk (slang).

'I'm a twenty-nine-year-old man,' the bull says. 'Of course I've cheated. I've slept with women, used them, fallen for them and left quietly in the dark without saying goodbye.'

He tells me about his boat and how it feels to glide over deep water. I want to tell him that the worst sound in the world is the sound of your bedroom door closing too quietly. And yet, there is something about him that makes me feel free. He does not want to get married. He does not want to have children. He does not want to – keep me and there is something wonderful in this.

He tells me that he loves his boat. That he has never had a rat or a mink on board but that he has seen slugs. He has woken up in the early morning sunlight and smiled up at their silver trail.

'What?' he asks and he is laughing. 'Would you have a problem with that?' and then, 'Slugs have to live somewhere too.'

'Aren't you worried that you will stand on them? Up on deck?'

'What deck?' he says. 'They're inside.'

He talks about his boat in the feminine and I know once again that it is a slug-out between her and me.

'She was a big old lump,' he says sadly, 'and I wanted to make her better. It wasn't that I wanted to give myself a better place to live. I would sleep on that . . .' and here he holds up a butter knife and runs one finger along the blade.

'I wanted to do it for her. I wanted her to feel better . . . to be better in herself.'

He describes her carefully, like an older woman he is in love with – where he was when he first met her, how he cared for her, how he loved her and brought her back to life. He chose each piece of furniture carefully – a red armchair, an art-deco couch, and a perfect kind of bed.

'So how big is your bed?' I venture for no good reason and I know in the split second that follows we will both see our bodies entwined in it. He gives me the slightest smile and then moves on to tell me how she is as long as Dante's restaurant. I keep trying to catch his eye. I wonder if he notices my figure in this black dress, how my breasts rise and fall and the angles of my collarbones.

Instead he says, 'She's an old hulk,' and there is pure love in his voice and I know I am down one point to her again.

He tells me about sailing her down the Shannon and how he wanted to give her some of what she had given to him.

'There was mist and swans, you know . . . early grey morning light . . . 6 a.m.,' and his eyes are becoming wet.

'I leaned down and kissed her,' he says. 'Can you believe that? I kissed her iron back,' and then he starts to blush and laugh. 'I'm kissing my fucking boat.'

And once again the great old dame in all her ugliness moves between us, cutting us apart and taking him away to another place, and I know I can't compete with that. The old bat gives him freedom in a way I cannot.

After dinner we walk to an old-fashioned bar. It's the kind of place where old ladies and gentlemen line up against the wall and we are no different except that when he speaks he turns one knee towards me and I do the same – and so we touch, at last. I don't love him but I want his warmth. The sensation of his corduroy moving against my dress. That is all. I want him to want me and no part of me can see that he just might not. He asks me about Doreen and Jack and other mutual friends and the little bells dotted behind us are there if we need to call for help.

'Service bells,' he says and then the barman comes over and I move my lips and say a silent 'Help'. We are almost out of time again. The night is slipping from me and he hasn't found me yet.

'Tell me about Larry,' he says and here he introduces another person to keep me at bay.

He smiles slowly at my silence and this triggers a laugh.

'I want to ask you something,' I tell him and at last the words are out.

'What?' he asks and here our knees are still touching. He puts his chin in one hand and waits, never letting me go with his eyes. There is a long pause and he does nothing to hurry me.

'How do you see me?' I ask him slowly.

'As a friend. A woman who is bright, and who is a very good listener as well.'

'Oh,' I reply.

His answer sounds like something he has already written down.

'I need something more from you,' and each word comes out very slowly. 'I want to be with someone . . . but not for ever – and I know you don't . . . can't do that.'

He says nothing and looks away into the distance and my gin and tonic tastes like fear.

He leans in and takes my hand.

'So . . . ?' he offers and he speaks very gently, unsure of his space.

'I want a month of your time.' He frowns for a second and then looks away and now he is thinking about what this month could mean. He is a man who says he loves all women. A man who has run from every solid space. A man who says he has . . . needs, *cravings* . . . to use his own words – so he can see the appeal and yet when he looks at me he sees – in the same brief moment – that I am offering myself to him and he knows that I could easily break.

He doesn't speak.

'I told you it wasn't something small.'

'It's not small,' he agrees.

My hand is warm now and safe inside his.

'I want you to belong to me for a month – and in return I will give you myself – and then we can both just be free . . . again.'

I know he is capable of this and that he is also capable of being a cheat. I know somehow that he is capable of great kindness and love and freedom and that for one month of his year, of his life and mine, he is the only person I could ever ask for this.

'I want to know you,' I say simply, 'and I promise to let you go – and you have to promise the same and nobody will ever say "I love you",' and I try to simplify it for us both.

The old ladies' eyes stare straight ahead as if they can hear and are horrified by my every word.

He looks into my eyes for a moment and then gives the faintest flicker of a smile and then he looks down for a moment and seems to think.

He is going to say 'No' and my stomach is knotting inside.

He will refuse me and I will never be able to face him – or anyone – again.

He finishes his drink and I want to take him home with me.

We walk out on to the street and into the uncertain light of late August. I link his arm but his hand stays stiff in his pocket, not giving me any way in.

'Let's go out,' I say suddenly and by now I am ashamed of myself but when you're so far out of control, why stop now?

'I would love to,' he says, so much quieter in himself, 'but it's late.'

We stand and face each other and when he hugs me I keep

my arms folded across my chest. I am prepared to let him go now and he can sense it. He hails a taxi and watches me turn.

And all I know is that I hurt. From my stomach up and that is where my heart is now, I think.

He looks hurt when I turn towards the taxi. He is confused and watches me turn towards the car with a blurry cast-off goodbye. I am drunk and uncaring. I will go home to my flat and Doreen and he will go home to his boat on the canal. And we begin to leave each other now, in some sort of confusion, both hurt and in pain without really understanding why.

He watches me turn away and in the second before I start to walk he catches my hand.

'Take September,' he says and he smiles.

At the restaurant Frankie buys me a snow globe but he has to barter with the waitress first. There are high-backed Quaker chairs and rows of plates on every wall. I order corn on the cob and half a chicken.

He smiles up at the waitress. 'I'll have the snow globe,' he says, 'and the other half.'

He tells me that he has had his annual review from 'Mr Angry'.

'How was it?'

'Angry,' he replies.

Around us there are businessmen with their ties slung across their shoulders. There are lunch meetings and in the distance one of our clients is meeting a friend.

'What did you do?'

'I became Mr Humble,' he replies.

'And what did he do?'

'He turned into Mr Helpless.'

I smile at him and tell him I have bought him a present for his birthday. It is a miniature lifeboat and when he unwraps it he puts one hand over his mouth and begins to giggle helplessly.

'I will keep this on my desk,' he says in a solemn voice. 'And only you and I will know its meaning.'

He lifts his glass.

'Here's to freedom,' he says.

The waitress arrives with the chicken in two halves. There is a joke to be made but neither one of us can think of it.

'I would prefer to leave on a high,' he says then. 'You know, win a big account and then . . . exit gracefully . . . hand it to them . . . and say, "Now, go fuck yourselves."'

And here we both start to laugh helplessly again.

'We're entitled to some anger,' he says and he is shaking his head and wiping tears of laughter from his eyes.

Behind him an Italian couple sit close together at the bar and I envy them. She is about thirty and he is older than Frankie and me. How lucky they are, to be inside, miles apart in years, and still close together and in love. She is bright-eyed and very pretty and he watches her, like an old tugboat guiding her to shore.

Doreen listens when I tell her about September.

'OK,' she says and she is leaning on the kitchen table and nodding into her shoes. 'This is what I think . . . you have a great husband who you need to find . . . and instead of doing that you are going to do something that will completely derail your life.'

'Not necessarily,' I answer and I have never seen her look this serious before.

'Translation . . .' she says quietly. 'Are you completely insane?'

She shakes her head and looks out at the wet street. Her sudden concern is mixed with frustration.

'You need your head examined,' she says and now there is a small crying person sitting opposite her as well.

'Find Larry,' she says – and I tell her, 'I can't.'

And when she looks at me now I have to look away.

'*Eclaircie*,' he says and he smiles at the sound of it. His true love is named after a break in the clouds. We stand and face each other.

'It's a noun,' he says, still smiling, 'it means the moment when rain stops and the sun comes out . . .' and here he shrugs, 'or a sunny spell in your life.' The barge waits in silence for us, listening quietly under the trees as we talk about her name. Further down the bank, the heat has sent three white cows into the water to drink. When they lift their heads, they watch us with water spilling from their mouths.

The chestnut trees are weighed down with leaves and conkers, and there in the sun-dappled shade *Eclaircie* waits. It is the first week of the month. Our month, the first and last month in our new short life.

His hair is bleached blond from the sun now. His face weathered, his eyes still the same sparkling blue. He is in bare tanned feet with white toenails, faded denims rolled to his knees. His old white shirt has a torn pocket and the tail is hanging out. And he is still wearing the Claddagh – and his heart has turned as promised, for four weeks, for me.

He stops for a moment and watches a jeep drive past. The driver salutes him and he waves back. Then he looks at my luggage. One bag, that is all I am allowed. His eyes are saying, 'What are we doing here?' and mine are answering, 'Don't ask me.'

Eclaircie is painted forest-green, her stern is ivory and she has ample breasts, snow-white in the sun, with a pink stripe on her hull. He tells me that this colour is called Californian Poppy but someone has scrubbed her down and painted those colours and I would never have thought him capable of that.

'So she's French,' I say.

'No, Dutch.'

I might have guessed.

Strong shoulders, stoic, formidable, impervious and moving into battle now.

He tells me that she was built in 1902 and that she was a 'Beutship'. A working vessel carrying passengers or freight.

'Which am I?' I want to ask and as if he can read my mind, he says, 'We need a new name for you.'

He tells me about her curved deck line and her sharp bow and she seems beautiful now. He points to a sky-blue bicycle then. 'That's for you,' he grins. 'For when you cycle to the bakery tomorrow morning. It's a nice Jewish place on the corner. The best bagels ever and it opens at six.'

He takes my bag and holds out his hand and as I step over the water, we can both feel her around us, holding us up, letting our short time together begin. He opens a low door and I follow him, my heart beating in my chest, and when I need to steady myself he takes my hand again. He looks away quickly then and we are both terrified now that the other one is afraid.

We are standing in a small wooden space with a curved tongue-and-groove roof. There are bookshelves crammed wall to wall. There are books on the floor under the shelves and then stacked on top of more books until they reach the roof. The wood is polished beech. The floor is white painted wood. The walls are palest blue. His kitchen is at one end, green louvre doors on every cupboard, red mugs, and a low row of shiny copper pans. There is an old blue sofa under the window covered in a throw, two high-backed chairs, for reading, an old record player, shelves of LPs, jazz and blues. At the moment he is listening to Frank Sinatra singing about the summer wind. And right here at this point I feel so afraid and there is only him now, the bull and me, and I must turn to him for help.

'What is it?' he asks and his eyes are suddenly wide and full of concern. The only answer is my throat making a sudden swallowing sound.

'Hey,' he says and he smiles and steps towards me. It is only one step and I respond by stepping quickly back.

'Look,' he says then, 'we don't have to . . .' He sighs.

'You look really scared,' he says and he begins to smile.

I tell him I don't like the song that he is playing because it is a song that reminds me of someone I used to know really well. He lifts the needle.

'That's what songs do,' he says and he takes the record off. 'Now we're learning something about ourselves.'

He walks through a small arched door behind the kitchen. 'This is the guest bedroom,' he says and he puts my bag down. 'Your own bathroom here.'

Across the sitting room is another arched door; this is the one that leads to his bed. The door is open, and there is a cream jacket hanging on a hook. His sheets are fresh white with one pale green stripe around the edge.

He cooks dinner and we sit out on the deck and watch the sun going down. He puts a lot of food out. Big helpings of everything. Tall glasses of wine. Blue glass tumblers with ice for water. Three different kinds of bread. We eat in silence and there are two mallards watching us. Two males palling around.

'They can't find a mate,' I offer.

'Or maybe they just like it like that.'

'Or maybe they're gay.'

And he looks at me.

'They're ducks,' he says.

And they move away silently with their shiny green heads, their dark earnest eyes, and those comical orange feet.

When the light fades, he brings up a hurricane lamp. He pours more wine and slides down into his chair. The village begins to come to life then and someone whizzes past on an old black bike. Couples appear and sit outside a pub and everyone watches the canal bank. A dog yaps somewhere and small squares of gold appear as kitchen lights are turned on. I try to think of something to say and then I realize that he lives here because he doesn't have to talk. He is different now, as I have never seen him, sitting in peaceful silence and letting everything else wash over him.

And the water is quiet around us. There is no sound at all as we sit in silence and float.

He wakes me by gently tugging my hair. It is cold and dark and there is just the light from the cabin below. We walk down the steps and stand with both doors open now. He is older and stronger than me and I want one of us not to be afraid.

When I turn he sighs and sends his hands down deep into his pockets.

'I would prefer it if you shared my bed,' he says and the words come out, simple and without further complications from me.

There is nothing like fear in his eyes. And I follow him through the doors and we lie side-by-side, facing each other and talking in whispers before we fall asleep.

In the morning the sun has gone and the September sky hangs low into a mist. The water seems darker and the air has a new fresh chill. He is up before me and I lie on and listen to his feet walking across my roof. He makes coffee and he has already been to the bakery and back.

'Good morning,' he says and then he trips over my shoes. He picks up a book I have been reading and puts it back into its place. Then he gets up and closes the door.

'You leave doors open,' he says.

'You snore,' I tell him.

'So do you,' he replies and the two ducks are back and listening in on this. I am beginning to think about the bull now in a different way and imagine what he would be like minus the Claddagh and in a nice black suit.

We are different to last night. We have not touched each other yet and we are colder now in the morning light. When he washes up, I watch. And then he stops what he is doing.

'You like to be waited on,' he says. His voice is firm and matter of fact. He has left the Claddagh ring on the windowsill beside the open window and then I lift my hand and just knock it out. We watch each other closely now. His forehead moves very slowly into a frown and somewhere inside I want to laugh. The worst part is that it makes a tiny splash.

'Why would you do that?' he asks 'Why did you do that?' and he turns around and walks out.

'Where are the angels?' he asks. We are standing in the foyer of the Conrad Hotel ready to attend the Angel Ball. He looks good and he is polite and well-behaved in his tuxedo after all.

'I am sure you will be able to account for two places at the table,' Jonathan said. He came into my office and stood watching my spider plant. He is expecting me to arrive with my husband and now I show up with the bull. We sit in a wide circle. Mrs Kirk is sitting beside him and when her shoulder strap falls, he kisses her shoulder and pulls the strap back up again. We arrange ourselves so it is

– boy – girl – boy – girl – boy – girl – bull.

'What do you do for a living?' Jonathan asks.

'I train racehorses,' the bull says and I suddenly want to laugh. They are all there with their wives and they are trying not to ask who the new man is. Jonathan's wife wears a diamond tiara. The only angel at the table so far. Later I dance with him and the bull waits at the bar. Then I find him sitting on his own in the foyer.

'Those people,' he says, 'are the reason I left my job' – and he hails a taxi and goes back to the barge.

Doreen says that the sex could be amazing. 'It will be completely savage, or great,' and then she says, 'Either way, it will be great.'

The bull talks about his father. He chooses small words to fill up his empty space.

'It was bad,' he says. 'He left,' and then he shrugs.

When *Eclaircie* moves she is quiet and respectful. We pass

quiet streets and sleeping houses and if someone is up as early
as us, we always wave. We leave the city and towns and
villages behind and move from canals to rivers and quite
suddenly there is just sky and a blue horizon ahead. He does
not speak at all and suddenly we move in silence out into an
open lake. The wind lifts and he is calling out orders and
pulling down ropes. I can feel myself panicking already as we
move into the centre and further away from the safety of the
riverbanks and the shore. Then he kills the engine and pulls a
rope and *Eclaircie*, dull Dutch woman that she is, becomes
something completely different as she sets sail.

'I didn't know,' I tell him, breathless, and the wind is
blowing out every other thought.

'She's full of surprises,' he says and he is glowing with pride
and we are moving along at a fair speed.

'And you ask why I want to live like this?' he says. When
we anchor, he stands on the deck in shorts and dives in and I
wait and am silently praying that he will come back up.

He dries off on an old red towel. He rubs it over his hair
until it stands on end.

'Tell me,' he says simply and we drink tea on the deck and
the story of Daniel comes out. Three sentences. That is how
quickly I can tell it now. His face is still damp from the water,
his lips cold when he leans in and kisses my mouth. And then
the clouds turn dark and the only sound is the wind in the
fallen sails, and the noise the rain makes on the lake.

We walk downstairs where we are safe in our watery cave.
He turns on a light and the room is warm and yellow now. I
want to touch his skin and make him warm because he is cold.
I want to pull him inside me because I know nothing about
him except that he is almost always alone. I know what we
promised, there will be no holding and keeping, but we need

to mark each other somehow until we know where we both belong. And *Eclaircie* holds us and each footstep is steady as we walk across her worn sea-grass floor, and each little creak like music, as we move towards his bed.

Outside the rain spills down on to the roof and the sky is lower, pressing down on us now, and there is a roll of thunder and still *Eclaircie* has folded her sails and is discreet and matronly now.

'Music?' he asks and I shake my head.

We stand and face each other and my bare legs are touching his bed. He rests his hands on my shoulders and then tugs my t-shirt so it falls and he kisses my cheekbone and my lips and then my collarbones. His sheets are fresh, the bed neatly made. Everything tidy and in its place in his man's world. He pulls the sheets up over us and we stay there together under the white light. He makes love to me and I make love to him and those feelings crash together somewhere in between. And afterwards we lie in silence and he can never know what I am thinking now.

We promised. We promised we would give it all and then give the other person back.

We eat straight from the omelette pan and he opens a bottle of wine. We have left the ordinary world now and will not talk about ordinary things. He never mentions his work and I never mention mine. Instead we talk about the tides, the boat and the sunset outside.

He tells me that he loves nature, that he believes in living moving trees, the green of the leaves, the sounds the wind makes, and that water for him has always created a special magical place.

After we make love again he sits and watches me, cross-legged at the end of the bed. When I pull the sheets up, he says, 'No' and 'Please' in a very gentle voice.

'Don't move,' he says. 'Please . . . just stay as you are, as you were, because after you've gone I will want to remember this.'

'What happens after I've gone?'

'We go on,' he says, 'like we said, free and on our separate ways.'

'What if it's different?' I ask

'Of course it will be different,' he answers. 'What did you think? – That we would collide like two stars and then just forget?'

I turn on my side and he draws a line with his finger from my shoulder to my hipbone to my knee.

We don't speak for a long time. The little windows are misting and there is a soft orange spot from the sinking sun. I curl up with the sheets around me and listen then as he begins to speak.

'After you've gone, I will still have *Eclaircie*. I will have the clouds and I will have the sun. But everything will be just slightly different. The trees will be another lighter shade of green. The water will be quieter to me and it might move in a slightly different way. And the sun will be different and at night-time, when I'm not able to sleep, because I won't be able to now, I might not be able to find the usual full moon. So maybe you don't believe that I love you. But you see, in my own odd way, I probably do.'

And when I go to him he pulls me on to his knees and holds me tightly there.

'It's only September tenth,' he says and he is grinning at me. 'We still have nineteen days.'

'A lifetime,' I tell him.

'Our life,' he says.

And then something happens in my stomach and then in my heart and I'm suddenly frightened in a way I was one September a long time ago.

In the middle of the night I wake and in the second after waking I think, really believe, that I am back in the flat with Larry – and outside Doreen is rattling in the kitchen as another new day begins. Beside me is the man who can't say 'I love you'. The bull who reluctantly gave me one month of his life – and somewhere in the world is Larry, who is somehow still my husband and I am somehow still his wife.

The bed creaks a little when I sit up and then I creep across the floor on tiptoe. He stirs in his sleep and turns over and I watch him and he doesn't wake. I close his bedroom door quietly and begin putting my clothes into a bag. There is a red lipstick in the pouch pocket, my favourite red shade, one that Matilda recommended called 'Rage'. It writes easily on his shining bathroom mirror and will probably be difficult to wash off.

'I want you to stay with me.' That was the last thing he said before he drifted off to sleep – and now – while carrying my shoes in one hand, I give him my best answer.

'I'm sorry,' I whisper into the mirror and then I write the words

I can't.

'On days like this,' Frankie says, 'you go home and hug someone you love.' He is standing on the street outside the agency and there are real tears in his eyes. His briefcase is held like a shield across his chest and at three in the afternoon he says he needs to see his wife and his boys. Beside us a girl with blonde hair flies past on rollerblades. She laughs when she sees us and calls, 'Watch out!'

It is a hot day in September and the news from America is breaking through.

When I pass Jonathan's office everyone is inside, lining the walls, and sitting in silence like Indians on the floor. The TV is on and everyone is watching. I can see through the wooden blinds, the half-open door and past the sea of faces to a small TV screen . . . and then I watch, with everyone else, as the first tower comes down. I can feel it fall, I can almost hear it – and with it, a soft ripple of goose bumps moves across my skin.

Our receptionist sits on the floor at Jonathan's feet and the telephones don't ring.

I don't wait to see the rest. It feels like a new kind of world to me – a new world that has just begun – and so I go down to my office and work quietly until it is time to go home.

At home Doreen sits beside me and we watch, terrified, from the couch.

'This will be like the day they shot JFK,' Mr Costello says. 'We will ask each other, years from now, over and over . . . where were you and what were you doing . . . the day the towers came down?'

The next morning our doorbell rings and the man on the steps is like a bookmark from my old life. He is wearing a wig and polished brown brogues and there is a notebook and pencil in his hand.

Larry's dad.

'Mr Forbes,' I say and he nods and bows slightly and then walks through the door.

He refuses tea.

He refuses food.

He has been driving since early light.

Then he writes down a simple question in his notebook and he hands me the page. When I read it my hand begins to shake and all the fear I have in me is beginning to scream out loud.

'*Do you know where Larry is?*'

I shake my head and then, 'He wanted some time . . . the diner is closed . . .'

He looks at me and wonders how someone like me could be a wife. He writes quickly, it takes about two seconds to send my world falling, and my stomach turns inside out.

'*New York.*'

THREE

13   *The Last Man to Die*

Glassman did not know what to pack the day he decided to run away. He stood in his apartment in the warm afternoon sunlight and waited for something to call his name. He waited for the solid tick from the clock in the dining room, or the pale green flowers on the wallpaper in his bedroom to move, or for each well-thumbed book to flap a memory towards him. But his apartment and all its contents seemed frozen and outside the street was quieter than usual and as he waited the only sound was his own breath, in and out. And the closet door did not swing open as he had hoped and it did not offer any practical advice.

'It's cold on the Cape' – that was his first real thought and somewhere was the idea of folding his burgundy sweater and his hands pulling a suitcase down from the closet in the hall.

On the saddest day in New York City, Glassman knew he had found his chance to leave. In a few days he would be able to walk through SoHo again and hire a car in Midtown and begin his drive to the Cape. There was no electricity. The telephone lines were down. The streets were blocked off. No one could get in and out of Downtown Manhattan and somewhere on the Upper West Side Matilda did not know if he was alive or dead. He knew that he had seen his last dying face – and that he was no longer a prisoner and that he could in some strange way rejoice and be free. He went to his physician's house in the Village and he told him to go. He said if ever he had a chance for recovery it was in fresh air and near the sea.

'We've done everything we can,' he said. 'It's over to you and your body now.'

So Glassman did not need to think about it. Not any more. He went to the basement and took down two fishing rods. Two sweaters. One that was old and grey to work in and the burgundy with its two rows of cable stitch. He did not take the black cashmere – the warmest one he had – because it was a Christmas present from Matilda last year – and he felt just the thought of this leave a small mark on him. But he told himself to get busy now and he left those old thoughts folded with the sweater in his bureau drawer.

He packed jeans. Fawn-coloured corduroys. One pair of old green Converse sneakers and then he looked at his two crates, one full of books and the other full of broken glass. He had packed them the last night he found her inside his apartment, the same night she had threatened to kill herself.

He walked through his rooms and he was careful to leave his toaster plugged in and not switched on. He left his bed slightly tossed. He put some laundry into the dryer and turned it on. He made it all look as if he was a normal living working person going out to work on September 11th and with every intention of coming home. He even left his kitchen window open an inch and he put some music on and left with it playing on a loop – the way he often did when he ran to the deli on the corner or walked for some air to the Park.

He called his dealer and organized some pot and this went into plastic bubble wrapping with the broken glass. He pasted the 'Fragile' sticker on the yellow splintered wood and smiled at the joke in it.

As he packed each item he decided that he would be well again. That he had been saved and that it was for a reason.

He would go to the cottage and be well and happy and just
... *be*.

The boy who died had not felt pain.

On the morning of September 11th Glassman had finished
a shift at St Vincent's and then without knowing what had
happened he worked on one of the first bodies to come in.
There was an elderly woman first and then a handsome young
man. Only one had died. The boy – but there was no pain.
Glassman could not explain the medical reasons for that. His
face was grey with dust and the first thing Glassman did was
wipe his eyes. He could tell that he was good-looking. His
eyes were a beautiful dark shape and he had long dark lashes
and black eyebrows slanting back. His face was not bruised
and even though he was breathing, Glassman knew he was
going to die. He had been crushed by something, inside and
out, everywhere except his left arm and his face. But there
was no pain and no fear. There was no look of it in his eyes
and when he began to lose him, for the first time, and he knew
now, for the last time, Glassman gave his own version of the
last rites.

He held the boy's hand and whispered into his ear, 'I'm
sorry for any hurt that I have caused,' and then after a moment
as he felt the boy really slip from him, the boy's eyes opened
for a second and then slid gently sideways and his eyebrows
seemed to lift, and Glassman wondered if he was laughing
at him or if the boy had even heard. Then there was no
breath. No pulse. No heartbeat. He left this life and dragged
Glassman's face and words with him like smudged ink on the
page. He was just another dead boy but Glassman felt as if he
had known him and that he had been a good son, a good
husband, and that because of the faint white circle around

his third finger he had, until recently, worn a wedding band.

He could not feel sadness or any sense of mourning but he did feel that the world had lost someone good. And that this city, this place, this planet would not be the same without this young face. He blessed the boy's forehead with his thumb and then closed his arms around his chest and wiped his face and tried to imagine a smile. And around him the news began to come through and the volunteer doctors began to pour in. They stood and waited in the sunshine for the ambulances and in the eerie waiting quiet they began to wonder if the silence was because there were no survivors, no one left alive, no one left to save.

In the end everything Glassman needed fitted into one small bag. He pressed the delete button on his answering machine and deleted away the last unheard messages from Matilda and then he lifted the phone gently and left it off the hook. He opened his mailbox and he put her latest love words, in a handful of cream and gold envelopes, straight into the trash. He turned the keys twice and listened to the sound of his double locks, checked his pocket again for his keys and his wallet. And then Glassman picked up his one suitcase and walked down the two flights of stairs.

On the street he turned and looked up at his own windows and he could remember taking her there that first afternoon, and now, in his current state of illness and fear, he marvelled at that. How he had been attracted to her and how he had, so willingly then and with such innocence, allowed a lunatic into his home. He stood for a moment and looked at the devastation that surrounded him and the veil of grey dust that seemed to disguise his old life. He lifted his suitcase and turned to look over his shoulder – and in that instant as he felt his neck click he told himself to get moving. He told himself that it was time to stop living his life through his own rear-view mirror and this time, he forced himself to look straight ahead and to walk on.

14   *The Falling Man (October 2001)*

Hope n. – 1. (sometimes plural) A feeling or desire for something and confidence in the possibility of its fulfilment: his hope for peace was justified; their hopes were dashed. 2. A reasonable ground for this feeling: there is still hope.

The barman can't find the bottle of Bombay Sapphire. 'Not much call for that here,' he says. So I stand up and then up again on the low counter foot rail and point it out to him and the men from Brooklyn join in and help.

'Right – right – right – right,' they say and when they speak they nod under faded baseball caps. The bar is called The Blue Haven, a long tired stretch of mahogany on Berry Street where men smoke a lot and then lean into their drinks. The gin and tonic arrives, big and overflowing and no slice of lemon, but I am afraid to ask. Yesterday I arrived in New York. I emailed Matilda and I telephoned Jack and I told no one where I was going, not even Doreen.

The barman has been in New York for eighteen years and he has the strongest Kerry accent I have ever heard. He has no citizenship and 'I don't want to go there,' he says. 'Afraid of what they might find.' His green card is good until 2011 and he tells us that by then he will be dead.

Jack drinks his beer by the neck and we listen while the barman talks. He stands and drinks with us and now and then he gives a reluctant service at the bar. He tells us that The Blue Haven has been sold and he smokes Dunhill cigarettes and blows their blue smoke at us.

'I don't know where I stand with the new owner,' he says and he is talking to me like we've always been friends. 'All I know is that I still come into work every night. I don't give a fuck. Do I give a fuck? I don't. They could just get rid of me. I see it all. I know everything about this place. I don't want to leave here. It's home. But do I look like I'm panicking? Do I fuck? My wife has a great job. She's making a thousand dollars a week. Do you see tears in my eyes? Am I panicking? I don't give a fuck.'

He is fifty-five and terrified he will lose this job. He buys the *Irish Independent* every morning. His wife listens to Radio One on the Internet when she works. She is his second wife and he's been with her now for twenty-five years. Last week she rang him at work to tell him about something she had heard on the Marian Finucane show. 'There's a lot of VD in Kerry,' she said, and he watches us and waits for a response and really we just want to have a drink and a quiet talk.

'Stay out of Kerry,' Jack offers and then someone else calls for a drink. He tells me that you would need a stick of dynamite to blow the barman and his wife apart but the barman comes back again and he is still talking at us from behind his bar.

Jack looks at me and grins.

'Or maybe just a stick of dynamite,' he says.

In a while the barman is drunker than we are and he comes back carrying the Bombay Sapphire again.

'It's funny but when you're drinking you see everything behind the bar; you've got a better chance of finding the Jack Daniel's or the Kentucky Bourbon or the Jim Beam than me.' He pours another beer for himself and serves another round we have not asked for. I am not sure which side of the bar we are on now. There are no sides in here.

He serves another customer. A lonely-looking man with a

cowboy hat and grey hair and I'm watching my Kerry man and this is my question for and about him just . . . why is he here?

Jack explains that when he came to America he came with 100,000 other Irish people.

'A lot of them don't make it,' he says. And here there is silence.

'He didn't make it,' he says simply. The words are awful as they are, dropped now from a height.

'He can't go home.'

The barman lives in a two-room apartment on 59th Street. There are no Irish left in the area. It's almost empty. Only Chinese and Lebanese.

'So they go home for three weeks in the summer,' Jack continues. 'Throw their money around Kerry and hire a good car and then come back. His wife works in New Jersey and he spends every night in here.'

The Kerry man is getting busier now. He serves two new lonesome soldiers and there are now five customers at the bar. The music comes on and everyone's spirits are lifted for a moment and then they seem to fall back down. But the barman is back and talking about how great his wife is now.

'She plays poker better than any man. She's entering the "Bet 'em or Lose 'em" in Vegas next week.' He tells us that her name is Elizabeth and the sound of her name seems out of place in here. She's known as 'No Face' by the other players and she can talk just like the poker-playing men.

'Fold is it? Listen, dude. I'll fucking fold when I fucking feel like it.' He pretends to be her and we glance at each other and laugh. Then he talks about the Christmas hamper she got and how at the end of the working year this is her reward.

'There was marmalade,' he says and he takes another drink.

And for the first time tonight I feel for him. 'Apples, pears, bananas, every kind of fruit.'

'Keep it healthy,' Jack says and he looks at me, grinning.

'She walked down to get it and had to get a taxi back.'

I can see the barman opening the hamper in their apartment now and passing his hands over all those glistening jars.

'Chocolates. Caviar. You fucking name it,' says the Kerry man who knows better than anyone that he didn't make it in New York.

'She walked down to get it and had to get a fucking taxi back.'

Jack is as I remember him. Brown-armed from the sun with bright questioning eyes. He is the same boy who became friends with my brother Daniel. And after Daniel he became friends with me. He tells me about the landlady in Brooklyn who took him in.

'She was forty-eight,' he says. 'She was my best friend in the world.' In the winter the snow banked up and he shovelled it away and took out the trash.

'I helped her,' he says. 'She needed help.' He makes a life in New York sound simple, and hard. How they laid the markers down, how a friendship grew over trash cans and shovels of snow. He spent most evenings in her kitchen talking to her husband and they were all tired out from work. She gave him his dinner and he gave her rent whenever he could. He says if you can count your friends on one hand then you've been lucky in your life. Now Jack is rich. There are two hundred men who hammer down floors for him.

'All over Manhattan,' he says, 'Staten Island. Chinatown.' He sips his beer and turns the bottle in his hands.

'Doing up two brownstones for a guy in Chinatown right now.'

Then the woman died. He holds up one big hand. Five fingers and now – after Daniel and his old landlady – two friends are already gone.

'She got cancer and it took her,' he says simply.

'They handled it well. She never complained. Then one night I went down to the basement and I found her husband down there, he was really quiet and the room was almost dark and he was working his way through the laundry and just crying there.'

Behind us a hen party walks in. 'Here comes the bride,' Jack says. He always frowns a little as if to think before he smiles.

'I'll never forget that night I found him there,' he says and he takes us, easily, back to a basement in Brooklyn, New York.

'What they had,' he says slowly, 'that was love.'

He holds up one big hand again in front of me.

'Five real friends and you're lucky,' he says and he grins. 'Talk to the hand.'

The last train passes under us and we all wait for a second as if in respect.

'There goes the subway,' Jack says and we listen, not to it, but how it makes the bottles rattle gently behind the bar.

Three pumpkins climb the steps to Jack's house. The American flag waves from the door. There is a log fire burning in the grate and a little Halloween witch stands inside the porch. All around me the brownstones of Brooklyn are getting ready for Thanksgiving. And this year why would anyone say thanks? Everyone I meet is asked about Larry. There are pictures of him all over the city, sellotaped to every lamp-post and covering the subway floor. There is a new language in the city. It comes from the news bulletins and subway flyers and from talking to people on the street. It goes like this and until recently no one ever heard anything like it before –

120 storeys
1500 feet above the ground
At 8.46 a.m. America was wounded by an aeroplane
1000 degrees Celsius
Windows of the World
Pastry chefs and short order cooks
1000 trapped in the North Tower
600 trapped in the South
Nearly 3000 people were missing
'How many of them jumped?'
'No one jumped – they were blown or forced out'
The Falling Man
Some poor soul
Choosing to be seen
The quietness of falling
Nobody wants to know the jumper
There was something 'forever' about him
The grace of falling
Such heat
But to be out in the air
Away from the heat
The final act of control
A lonely ten-second journey
A very public way of dying
A very private way of mourning
No one knew him
No one wanted to know
A text that said, 'I love you, Kate, take care of our son'

No blood. No guts. Just a person falling
'I would recognize my brother's hands and feet'
Landing loudly like stone
The unknown soldiers
A final email that asked, 'Are you there?'

I don't know what any of this means. These words fall and land without any real sense around me.

But where is Larry? These are the only words I need.

New York. Swallow me up. It is a warren of yellow taxis, wooden escalators, skyscrapers and kosher restaurants, Mexicans, Irish, Chinese and blacks. Yesterday an old Jewish man beat a yellow taxi with his umbrella. That's what you get if you don't stop. The manholes puff out great moving clouds of steam. The cops eat doughnuts in their cars. It's like being part of a new TV show. It's better on TV. You can turn the volume down. Nicer without sound. The noise, the hum of it, the blowing, honking, screaming decibels of New York.

'It doesn't matter,' Jack says suddenly and without any reason. And we stand and face each other at the bottom of his steps. 'Nobody cares about anyone here.'

Jack's wife tells me where she was when the towers fell. Her name is Marcia Gallagher and she sits near the fire with her long blonde hair combed loose and falling below her shoulders. She is not what I expected. She is beautiful and soft and welcoming and she says her family, and this must include Jack, are 'her joy'.

'I was at home . . . nursing Adam. I was watching TV and there were two guys in the house, painting downstairs . . . and they came in and we watched it together . . . and I remember they started freaking out . . . they dropped everything and said – "We have to go home" – and I was just staring at the TV and thinking ... *"Oh my God, a plane just flew into the World Trade Center"* ... then my brother Sean called – and he was hysterical – he said something really weird had happened and then I started getting scared. I put Adam into the car and then I drove to my mom's and then Franklin, my brother, got called in and everyone was trying to call The Chief. That's my eldest brother – he heads up the Midtown North Precinct. Everyone calls him The Chief. All the fire-fighters were called in and Franklin was down there a whole week. And then –

'they fell . . .

. . . while we were watching . . .

. . . I'll never forget that . . .

I just got up and ran to the car and went to the school for my kids. The teacher was saying, "They're OK, they're OK," but I just wanted them with me, I wanted my family around me,' and her eyes are wide and frightened now and she scoops the air in around her as she speaks.

'So Mom and Sean were OK. And Franklin. And The Chief. He hadn't been working. Thank God. And the kids were with me. But it's a day I will never forget.'

I want to ask her where Jack was and why she did not mention him in any of this. For me it would have been him before anyone. Jack, hammering on metal somewhere near Battery Park. Not far from it as it happened. He might have gone to get a coffee at the deli. He might have taken the wrong exit and ended up made of dust. I would have called him first and I would have cried just dialling up his number. But she didn't seem to remember doing that.

She tells me that this is a season of funerals, wedding bands buried without any fingers or hands, body parts, whatever they found, are mourned and laid to rest. She looks into the distance and her eyes ache with pain.

'Funeral after funeral after funeral,' she says like a mantra. 'It's like it's never-ending. We all know someone who was taken. It could have been my brother. But you have to move on.' And here she mourns the loss of other people and an America that has been lost. And yet she is calm and gentle around me. Like someone who understands pain and has seen more of life than me. She is sorry that I have lost my husband but she has seen so much of it now, she would be happier if I gave up. At a time like this and after all those funerals, it is uncomfortable to be around Hope.

'The trouble with him,' Marcia says, and she nods her head towards Jack, 'is that he doesn't know when to come home . . . and apparently . . .' and now she looks at me, 'neither do you.' It was 5 a.m. when we left Kitty's and we stood together and waited for our car in the cold. I didn't want to go home then either. I would have gone anywhere else with him. Jack says that New York is the loneliest place in the world but at least we were together and we could have been anywhere if it wasn't for the lights behind us on Brooklyn Bridge.

Thanksgiving dinner. Jack's boys have their hair brushed back and they're wearing little dicky bows. We carry bottles of wine, chocolate cake, and Jack carries the turkey which was put into the oven at 5 a.m. And Marcia walks ahead, her hair blowing backwards, fresh and full of life, and our hangovers follow her through her neighbour's door. There is no real welcome for me. Only her younger brother, the firefighter

called Franklin, asks for my number and says he will take me
to the firehouse so I can talk to the men there.

'Everyone wants to slide down the pole,' he says and I look
back at him.

'I've just lost my husband,' I am thinking, 'I will not want
to slide down the pole.'

The table is set for eighteen and everything is laid out on
paper plates. There is turkey, egg salad, pickled onions and
sweet potato pie. And there are children everywhere, under
the table and jumping on every chair. This is Thanksgiving
and the only time to say thanks is when it is finally over. At
grace most people there are in tears.

I am put sitting beside Marcia's three brothers. Her eldest
brother is Chief Gallagher who is in his fifties, and on the
other side – the last remaining bachelor of New York and in
the next place after that – the younger brother, the firefighter
who has my number in his phone.

Jack owns a green cardigan, bought at the Blarney Woollen
Mills, and I look at it hanging on the stairs, and when it gets
cold and that New York wind blows I want to put it on and in
some way wrap a piece of him around me and feel safe and
warm. But I can't because it would look weird – and so I sit
there, chewing on cold turkey and watching how his wife
walks behind him and touches his shoulder with her hand.

The bachelor looks like Jack Lemmon and he sits in close
to me and tells us what he knows about women in New York.

'The women are different in all the boroughs,' he says. 'In
Brooklyn it's all family. Having babies. Making a home. The
Manhattans are different. Harder. The city makes you hard.'

He watches me carefully. And when I look away I know he
is staring at the side of my head. He is mentally undressing
me and I am mentally dressing myself again.

'What's the beef?' he asks quickly. 'Do you have children?'

'No.'

'Are you married?'

Silence.

'Is there a man in your life?'

Silence again.

And then Jack walks past and puts one hand on my shoulder and Marcia looks up at him and then looks away. We make four pots of tea and then the table is covered with every kind of dessert. The people around the table begin to relax now and one by one they open up and talk.

The Chief's wife is called Maggie and she tells me about the subway people – the people who live in the underground city of New York.

There is a man living under Greenwich Village. He has his own green couch. He carried it down the stairs and on to the tracks, in between trains and into subway land. He has a TV connected into the subway system. He has a favourite TV show. He has a woman. They live underground. They carried the couch between them. They know the trains. They've got the timetable down. They watch TV and there are rats. They don't know or care about the dirt and the steel dust that they breathe. They can't hear the noise any more. Without it the world would be a strange silent place. They're together. In the dark. A subway couple. And if they can make it work, why can't everyone else?

'So there's a whole world down there?' I say.

'A whole world,' she says. 'They've even elected their own mayor.'

'What you need,' the Lemon says suddenly, 'is a man to keep you warm at night.'

'Great . . . do you know any?' I reply.

Then they talk about relationships and Maggie and the Lemon have a lot to say about this.

'Men and women fight about such stupid shit,' he says. 'Like who made the mess. If the mess bothers you, clean it up.'

'Why should one person have to clean up after someone else all the time?' Maggie asks.

'I think the thing men and women fight most about is sex,' she adds. 'Men can never get enough. Never enough, and if you don't give it to them – they sulk.'

'I never sulk,' he adds here, 'and some women want sex all the time. Everyone knows women want to at more times than others depending on their cycle. Some men don't want to have sex during a woman's period – what do you think?' he asks.

'You're putting me off my turkey,' I tell him.

And Maggie looks at her husband and smiles and then she takes another slice of apple pie.

Later in the kitchen, in between scraping plates, the Lemon explains marriage to me.

'When you're single,' he says, 'you get a jar, and every time you get laid you put a peanut in the jar, and pretty soon your jar is full. When you get married,' he continues, 'you take a peanut out of the jar every time you get laid . . . when you get married you never have an empty jar.'

Jack smiles at me from the sofa. He winks and holds one hand up. Five fingers and they're like a secret code between us now. Around me everyone seems to be drunk from eating all that food.

The firefighter's girlfriend arrives. Her name is Caitlin and she is wearing a new outfit because she is meeting her boyfriend's family today. She smiles brightly and nods at everyone and then she puts down a cake that looks like a chocolate hedgehog. And when they walk out into the kitchen someone whispers that 'She is the one.'

The Lemon is worried because he is losing his hair and Maggie tells him that 'Baldness is a sign of virility in a man,' and he says, 'Any more virile and I'll go mad.'

We eat more dessert and I discover Snicker Doodle Cookies and then The Chief pulls up a chair.

'Tell me about your husband,' he says, and as the voices around me grow louder and the wind keeps howling outside the door, I tell a complete stranger everything I know. The date he got here. The last telephone call he made and how we think he was working near the World Trade Center but no one is really sure and how his family tried to find him but gave up quickly and went home. I tell him I believe that he is still alive and asked what did The Chief think – really? And he tells me the truth, like a good doctor would, that he really doesn't know. Then he looks at me again and asks me a final question: 'His name is engraved on his wedding ring?' and I tell him 'No', that Larry put my name inside his and I took his for mine. And he nods here and his face is expressionless like a man who has seen it all before. And then he tells me he will do what he can to speed things up. I give him a photograph of Larry from my wallet and he tells me he will keep it safe. He takes out a cigar and moves towards the kitchen door and then he turns for a second.

'Hope . . . right?' he says and then he leaves without waiting for an answer and I watch as he sits outside on his own and smokes.

Willow Street is quiet and it feels like Christmas night. I step outside and wonder where the rest of the world is. The shops and diners are closed and behind every window families sit around tables and give thanks. My head is aching and my throat is sore and when I stood up to leave, the room was spinning around.

'Do you know what they are doing there?' Frankie had asked. 'They're giving girls wedding rings and zip-lock bags of dust.' I didn't even tell him that I had booked my flight.

Recently I've got it into my head that Larry might have jumped.

I think, knowing him, that he would have wanted the last ten seconds of life to himself.

And he would have fallen with grace, and landed silently, like a single white feather on the ground.

I leave the Thanksgiving dinner and walk towards the bridge. The lights are on and it makes me feel less alone. Across the river there is the Manhattan skyline and then I look towards Jack's house and nothing will persuade me to go in.

I walk to the payphone and I am thinking about the only other person I know on Thanksgiving Day in New York. And I begin to push the numbers slowly and carefully and somewhere on the Upper West Side a telephone begins to ring. It rings eight times, long shrill bells, and my heart is suddenly beating fast. Then there is a click and the receiver is lifted up. There is a delay before she speaks as if she can't quite find the word. She might have been sleeping or having a long soak in the tub. A cat miaows beside her and after that I can hear the sound of freeform jazz. When she speaks her voice is smooth and quiet and as if she has spent many years just practising each and every word. I am not able to speak at all then and when I finally manage to say her name her voice comes back like music and Matilda is smiling and saying, 'Hello.'

Parallax n. The angle between two imaginary lines from two different observation points meeting at a star or celestial body that is used to measure its distance from the earth.

Matilda sits at the piano. There is a cigarette between her lips and the smoke moves in a curl over her nose. In between talk of men and mortality, the piano has been nudging at us all afternoon. Three Slowballs later and she is sliding her fingers over the lid and then lifting it up as she gently touches the keys.

The little sign says 'Please do not play the piano' – it is the one Cole Porter played after all. Around us there are photographs of Grace Kelly and John F. Kennedy but she seems to be completely at ease. She leans back a little then, her back slightly hooped and swaying, and she begins to play some far-off old-fashioned tune. Her cocktail is resting on some sheet music – just to show she is in no hurry at all – and beside her chair, her handbag has turned over and three bottles of pills have rolled out on to the floor.

'Uppers and downers,' she said casually as she broke one into her gin. She doesn't care what people think and I already love her for this. Grief picks at us in different ways. There have been tears all over the city and now there are no more tears left. The businessmen walk through dust on Wall Street but up on Park Avenue, at the Waldorf Astoria, everything is art deco and covered in cream and gold.

When Matilda called the waiter over and asked for afternoon tea it was as if nothing bad had ever happened in the world. She orders food in odd numbers.

'Five tea sandwiches. Three pastries. One savoury tea pie. Three scones with Mascarpone and please – no Chantilly cream.'

She says she likes odd numbers, she likes that they have pointed edges whereas even numbers are round. And the waiters tiptoe around us walking a fine line between humour and respect.

When she orders tea she asks for 'One silvertip' and 'One Darjeeling' and I have no idea what any of this means.

In the city there is talk about hedonism. She wrote about it yesterday in the *New York Post*. And how those who are alive suddenly want to live, and live and live. There is a new tolerance in New York, Matilda wrote – but when she sits at Cole Porter's piano the waiters' eyes are suddenly full of fear. They stand in twos and confer with their silver trays balanced casually on their hands. They could be talking about the weather but they are looking at my Converse runners with the hole in the toe, the rucksack, the black beret. The hat was a find this morning at her favourite thrift store on Angel Street – and this is the only sign of mourning she will allow.

Beneath the palm trees and at white linen tables, the Manhattan girls have afternoon tea and cocktails and talk. They drift in and out of conversations and when Matilda starts to sing their words begin to slow down and finally stop.

She is wearing a tight lilac cashmere sweater, a pale lemon pleated skirt and white high-heeled shoes. I have never seen anything like her. Her earrings are like pink seashells, angel wings or slipper shells. I can't remember which. Her hair in a blonde bouffant style.

'We are all misfits,' I said after the third cocktail and she laughed and for some reason she seemed to really like that. The head waiter walks towards her but her voice, tiny and tired and without any real tune, begins bravely to come through.

'As I lie in my bed in the morning, without you, without you,' and around us in a matter of seconds there are eyes filling up with tears. When the maître d' appears he signals to the waiters to leave her be. 'Let her sing,' someone says and her voice begins to ring out into the carpet and chandeliers. And around us people are beginning to join in and sing. When Matilda sings she is lost to the world, she seems to lift herself up into the sky and float, and everything I have ever been sad about, in all my life, comes out in her soft voice. And when she finishes there is a round of applause and she beams at her audience and bows. Then she lifts her glass and empties it and bows again before stepping away.

'I lost someone too,' she says and her voice is tragic and full of pride and pain.

After tea we walk together from the hotel and the doorman rushes to the door and bows. And she links my arm and we walk down Park Avenue, in the still warm autumn sunshine, in a ladylike and old-fashioned way. We browse in shops. She buys a pretzel and insists I have a real hotdog. We call into a small boutique on Broadway that only sells hats and gloves. She buys her Christmas cards. Small and with a simple black and white photograph, showing a couple holding hands and walking over Gapstow Bridge in the snow.

'Isn't that the most romantic thing you have ever seen?' she whispers. And I nod and turn away because her eyes are filling with tears. Then we take a cab to Barneys where she has an appointment at Robert Sweet William. 'My brows,' she says as if they are a matter of life and death, and I wait like a child while they work on her and when she sits up, her face breaks into a beautiful smile and there is no trace of tears.

On Madison Avenue she calls a cab and takes me to Grand Central and we stand there on the steps and watch as everyone rushes for their trains. One of her favourite places in New York is Whispering Gallery and she even gets me to stand in one corner and she runs to the far end and whispers something to me. I will never know what she said but already she is the kind of woman I would hate to disappoint, so when she waves I just smile and wave back.

Her apartment is on the second floor in a tall brownstone on W78th and Columbus. Inside there is a narrow mosaic hallway and a tiny kitchen and a new red pullout couch under a bay window. Even now in the almost winter she has left the window open and the white curtains float back into the room. The cat glares at me from under a radiator and I envy him his simple life and how he greets her, lazy with his manners and himself. She has a small spare bedroom and in here she has already made up the single bed.

'It's actually a closet,' she says, 'but there's a window and it's cosy and warm.' And around the walls there are pictures of old movie stars – Rock Hudson, Cary Grant and Marilyn Monroe.

She makes tea in the kitchen and we sit on two blue-painted stools at its old-fashioned stove. She tells me what she has in New York and what matters to people here – the black and white floor tiles in the kitchen, the exposed brick wall in her bedroom, a cat that does not ask for much, a nice neighbour downstairs, and because of him, she tries not to make noise, and because of him she has put down rugs. She has a Steinway piano, inherited from her mother, a proper bathtub, and a bay window in her living room that gives good light. 'I have a good life,' she says, and as I look through her stack of sheet music I think she must be one of the loneliest women in the world.

When she sits on the red couch, the autumn sun begins to
go down behind the brownstones across the street and it is
red and gold. She says she loves the Fall and that tomorrow
she will take me to Central Park to see the leaves. She curls
one leg under her then and says –

'I became an orphan when they put my momma away,'
and this is offered up with a sad little smile.

'I was angry . . . bereft,' she whispers and there is silence in
the room and it is just us in the small apartment that is growing
colder now and losing the light from the sun.

'It is difficult for me to talk about *him*,' she says then, and I
am looking around the room for a prompt. I can only presume
she is talking about the man she loved and lost. And then she
begins to talk quickly and the words spill out and embarrass
us both. At first he was like a father to her. A very attractive
older man. He was the first man that she trusted. 'The first
man ever in the world.'

And every day something new happened, something that
made her want to say, 'Thank you, God.'

'Every day – there was another joy. It was love – one big
love –' she says. 'That's what everyone gets. And to remember
each day that he gave to me – I would make a little mark – it
was like keeping a diary about a woman and a man – one big
love,' and she says it again.

And I nod and listen and I am beginning to feel cold and
sad inside.

'What sort of mark?' I ask.

'On my skin,' she answers simply.

She reminds me of a broken bird, hopping around, trying
to live and eat with one wing hanging down.

'And he's not dead. I know that,' she says quietly.

'How do you know?' and my voice is gentle.

'He's pretending,' she says and she smiles at me.

'Why would he do that?'

'It's a little game,' she says and she is still smiling.

The marmalade cat gets up and walks across the room and his tail is held high and proud.

'He was the kind of person that could walk into a room and everyone just wanted to stand near him,' she says and then, 'Sometimes I think he was an angel. You know, not quite real.'

That night I hear the sirens of New York inside my head and now and then the door opens and Matilda floats towards me wearing a pink negligee. She says I have flu and that my temperature is 103. She makes green tea and honey and she finds fresh cotton pyjamas. She makes toast and gets up in the middle of the night to find a deli that is open and selling chicken soup. And when she leaves I find myself repeating the names of all the buildings I know in New York. The Empire State – the Chrysler Building – America International – the Flatiron – the Woolworth Building – 53rd and 3rd – the Waldorf Astoria – and the next time she comes in I am hallucinating that there is an ostrich wearing glasses in my room. She takes the next day off work and we watch old movies in bed. My favourite is *The Odd Couple* and hers is *Some Like It Hot*.

On Tuesday Matilda takes me to the wall at St Vincent's. We stand side by side and find Larry a space. And here he is now, in the middle of a thousand other smiling faces – Larry's eyes, his smile, and when I lean in closer, I can see his faded-out scar. I miss him so much now that I can hardly breathe and somehow Matilda instinctively puts one hand on the small of my back and I need her now, to protect me and to hold me up.

The photo was taken outside Vertigo. He is wearing his chalk-stripe apron and a reluctant smile. He liked that photo best. He has his hands in his pockets and there is some ketchup on his apron and a cigarette behind his ear. 'Go on . . . get it over with,' his face says. The day we took that photo there was an east wind coming up from the beach. I can remember the sound the camera made and how it felt cold against my cheek. How I wish for it now. Why did I not run towards him and give him a hug? Just one more, to have an extra memory now, and for luck.

'Larry,' the words say. 'My husband. He might be wearing his wedding band. My name is inscribed inside, Hope.

He has a scar across his top lip.'

The girl is crying as she pins her flyer. 'I spent my whole life looking for him,' she says and she is crying harder now. 'My whole life – and I just don't know how to start again – without him and without our life.' Her flyer shows a boy in a graduation cap and gown. His parents on either side, flanking him. And now I go here almost every evening. There is something about being here, in this quiet, sad, mourning space – where people feel what the bereaved feel and silently move on. I don't know why I want to read the flyers. I only know that I do. When I see a face taped to a lamp-post or in a phone booth or in the subway window I stop and understand that this face is here because there is someone else behind it who is in an awful lot of pain.

'Caesarean scar.'

'Wedding band engraved "Nick".'

A watch 'Truly madly passionately T'.

That night my mobile rings at 4 a.m.

'Is that Hope?'

'Yes.'

'Is that Hope?'

'Yes.'

'This is Caitlin.'

'Who?'

'Caitlin.'

'Caitlin who?'

'Caitlin. I'm Franklin's girlfriend.'

'Who is Franklin?'

'He's a firefighter.'

'A firefighter?'

'Yes.'

'Why are you calling me?'

'I'm calling you because I've just found out that my boyfriend is cheating on me and your number is in his phone.'

'Who is your boyfriend?'

'Franklin Gallagher – he's a firefighter.'

And now I remember this is the man who wanted me to slide down the pole.

'I'm really sorry to hear that he's cheating – but he's not cheating with me.'

'OK.'

'Do you know that it's four in the morning?'

'Yes. Goodnight.'

'Goodnight.'

Then I hang up and lie back on my pillow and I think about

how things used to be before it all got this crazy on me. I turn on the light and take out my wallet but there are no pictures of Larry left. I work my way through it. There are till receipts. A subway ticket. Eighteen dollars. A photo of me and Juna and Daniel in the garden and it seems like a hundred years ago. And then I find something I didn't even know I had. It is a note from Larry written with his favourite black fountain pen and hidden in there for me to find. He liked to sketch a little heart in pencil and put our names on either side. It was usually something like 'Dinner is in the oven, xx Larry'. Or 'I miss you, Larry'.

It was supposed to fall out in the supermarket. Or in our flat. Or at my desk. But this one didn't work out like that.

Our days were long, I really believe that now. Bright bands of happiness stretched out smooth and sweet. And I can only remember the best of us and that the weather was always fine. The first regret is that I didn't know what I had then. That I took him and me and what we had for granted, because I didn't know then that he was – that we were – the one. It is a note that tells me how much he loves me – and because there is no date I have no way of knowing when.

Matilda sits in her green armchair and the air conditioner buzzes over her head. Outside the traffic is backed up on Broadway and the whole world has been shrunk down into this one warm place.

The summer has appeared again briefly and only the nights are cold. 'An Indian summer,' she says quietly, as if this should comfort me. But I want to say, 'Let's walk. Let's run. Let's take this problem outside.'

It is nearly three months now. And I don't want to but I

have to ask someone when I should begin to let go. And how can I anyway? It is like slipping under water, fingers losing their grip on a raft. Sliding down into deep water and beginning to drown. And lastly, I remember and regret that I didn't say 'I love you' to him that day he left – and because I was so sure he would be back again soon, I didn't even say goodbye.

'Where are you?' I ask as I look out the window over Columbus but there is no response from the yellow taxis, and the leaves that are changing colour fall silently from the trees.

Hope,
      You know what's great about being married to you?
      . . . Being married to you.
      Love you always.
      Larry x.

It is noon when my mobile rings. It rings once and I look at it from across the room. The apartment is empty and Matilda has gone to work. It is the middle of the day and the sun is high over Broadway and today the cabs are flying and glowing on the Upper West Side. The phone rings and I sit on the red couch under the bay window and watch it. The phone rings and I know it is not Matilda or Jack or Marcia or anyone else I know.

The phone rings and in two steps my hand reaches for it and I can hear the voice of The Chief.

Today he has news and he says it out to me, one word holding the next word's hand, so they are joined together and making sense, and the voice he uses is that of a tired old man.

He has seen everything before and still he waits quietly for the words to fall into place.

And inside my head, the building is suddenly tumbling

downwards and the top floor slides down into the next, and that floor slides down into the one below. There are rafters and floorboards and clouds of snow-white dust. People dropping downwards, floating, falling, gliding and without any noise at all. We are all floating and falling together and now and then I hold on to another word. The Chief tells me that they have found Larry's wedding ring and that my name is inside and the date we got married – 4 January 2001.

Goodbye to New York City. I have one small rucksack and my husband's ring on a chain around my neck. Jack sits with me on the steps and we wait for a cab. The house in Cape Cod is his idea. He bought it last year and he understands that I need to escape.

'I'll come down and check in on you,' he says and I know he needs to escape sometimes too. 'It's going to be very quiet down there. No one goes to Truro at this time of the year – but there's a phone – and email – so you'll be fine.'

He puts one large hand around my shoulders and then he turns my face into his chest. A small dog starts to bark in the distance and a bum begins to work his way through the trash.

The bus leaves from 41st Street and 8th and the traffic holds us up. The city wants to hold on to me and it will not say goodbye. Soon there will be a freeway lined with red and gold trees. Then there will be small towns with white fences and porches and swings that move in the wind. 'Goodbye,' I whisper out to the yellow taxis, and the bus moves – one inch towards the coast and New England and one inch further away from New York. I am not ready to say goodbye to Larry. Everyone says I have to but maybe I never will. I take the notebook from my rucksack and I ask the lady beside me if

I can borrow her pen. There is a new word inside me and I have to write it down. I will never forget this one though and I know exactly what it means.

Heartbroken

And beside it I write his name.

15 Wellfleet, Cape Cod

Dawson Cottage was hidden by trees. It was built back near the forest away from the sand dunes and the lonely sound from the sea. Glassman would learn that as much as his mother loved the ocean she had also heard the stories about dangerous tides and New England winters and of children and sailors and even houses that were swept away by the sea. He would also learn that Dawson was the name of the man who had never been her husband but had fathered him and then went his own way. He was not hurt by either of these things. His mother and father lived apart but they had really loved each other once which was more than a lot of people could say.

Whenever he thought about the cottage in New York, he remembered how happy they were there and he could only see the wooden porch at the back and the stonework dappled by summer sun coming in through the leaves. He could remember how dark the kitchen became in a deep summer afternoon and how cool and welcoming the floor was under hot running feet. He remembered very clearly the dog that sat at the front door and never moved as if he was being paid to keep the ghosts of dead sailors away. Glassman kept this picture in his mind when he handed his credit card over the counter in Hertz and as the car swung out on to W29th and Broadway he put dark glasses on and glanced with a small tingle of pleasure at the suitcase on the back seat.

He kept the picture in his mind as he left the city on Route 95 North to Providence in Rhode Island. It was 245 miles and it would take him five hours with one stop for coffee and gas.

He hoped that this stop would be in Barnstable and that it would be at three in the afternoon and after that he would take Exit 20 for 1–195 East in Providence and then continue deeper and further east to Cape Cod.

Now, in mid-September, when the New England leaves would soon lose their red fever and begin to shrivel up and give in, he preferred the freeway and to only imagine the cottage and the warm summer sea of old. He had no illusions about winter there either but it was the memory of summer that prevented him from thinking about his Manhattan loft and its advanced thermostats – and from turning around again.

He had always felt safe at the cottage but three years ago he had ploughed $30,000 into it and now there was a new boiler, proper insulation, security alarms, fitted shutters, and everything that would warm the impractical and hopelessly romantic holiday home. He remembered the old stories about the cruel winters there too and people who had died in houses banked up with ice and snow, and sailors and lighthouse keepers who had frozen to death or drowned. He also re-membered reading about this in the warm library in Wellfleet when the sun shone from the bluest American sky and it was hot and the idea of death and cold and drowning seemed impossible to the boy.

But it was to New England he went now. Ashamed of his retreat but less ashamed than afraid. He worried that he might have a breakdown and went here now to make something as he had promised – and to be alone. As he drove he had to beat back a worry that for some reason he would get there and the cottage would be gone. That the sea would have risen up in its highest possible tide and covered the shore and crept up over the sand dunes and back into the meadows and ponds to wipe out his home.

He leaned against his car as he drank bitter black coffee from a paper cup. He leaned and watched as people walked forward into the autumn wind to begin their working day. How welcome it was, a place where people had no affectation. 'They take you as you come,' he said to himself. And around him the shop windows were almost bare and the handwritten chalk signs were like something from another century now. Everything arranged for honesty and openness, rather than display.

He told himself to rest from driving but three mouthfuls of coffee and he was back in the car and driving away. He suddenly needed to get there before the sun disappeared. And all around him the first raggy leaves were falling and he wanted the colours of autumn to hurry themselves and give way to something simple and more pure, like snow. He hoped the house would be covered in it, and anyone looking for him – and here he grinned at the thought of it – would have to be extremely determined and armed with an ice pick and travel by snowplough.

Wellfleet had not changed at all over the years and he found himself warm and smiling at the dashboard because Mr Huckstable who owned the hardware store was standing inside the window and putting a log on the stove. If Glassman had not been hurrying he would have liked to park and run inside and embrace him, just for still being there.

The Congregational church was still there as he remembered it, with the steeple clock that chimed the hours in eight bells, according to ship's time. He followed the signs for Newcomb Hollow although he did not need them and eventually, after more than five hours, he turned off the engine and took a deep breath and said, 'Home.' The dog was still there. He could see his head over the long grass that had come up in the yard. There were no leaves on the trees and there was a sharp salted wind whipping up from the beach when he opened the car door – but the dog made from stone whom Glassman and his mother named 'The Invincible Dog' was still there, barking at evil spirits or, as Glassman thought then, 'baying at the moon'.

He had left things as if he had expected to arrive here at the end of summer, worried about illness and cold. The barn was full of driftwood and coal for the stove. There were maple, ash and sycamore logs piled high to the roof and the new shiny boiler gave an easy click and buzz and came on.

He lifted the dustsheets one by one and remembered everything – here was the old table they had always used in the kitchen; it was so well worn now that the corners were soft and round. Here was the old stove, still black and shining, which he could occasionally use, and under another cover, the ice-cream parlour chairs. And in the pantry, the ceramic tins he had labelled 'Organic' and 'Non-disposable' waste. He was neater in Wellfleet. He was somehow more well behaved and he had a conscience as if Wellfleet made him a better man. He would shower as soon as he got out of bed. He would eat better food. He would exercise every day by walking on the beach. If he was to recover, ever, it would be in Wellfleet, and he promised himself that he would on his first day there.

Glassman unpacked slowly and cleaned away dust as he moved. The house began to warm up and he opened the door out into the barn again. He had known that some day he would work here and after he made his first simple meal of cornbread and cheese and a bottle of Heineken, he set up the diamond burrs under the skylight there.

Tomorrow the crates would be delivered and the next day

he would begin to work. He did not know yet what he would make as he hid in Wellfleet but he told himself that he would sleep eight hours every night. That he would keep a journal. That he would eat fresh organic food bought at the Saturday market. That he would walk for hours on the beach and he would fill his lungs with the freshest of air. That he would not think about New York or Matilda or any other woman until he reclaimed his body and won back his strength.

He knew he would not always use the bedroom at the top of the white-painted stairs and that there would be nights when he would leave his shoes on the first step and take a newspaper and then fold himself into the little cot low down and near the stove.

He knew that some days he would feel the cold regardless of his new boiler and that his stomach would reject any kind of food and that his courage would desert him and that on days like that he would not want to climb the stairs.

He would make chicken soup and eat it with parsley and in the mornings he would eat oatmeal and drink hot chocolate and he would drive into Wellfleet in the hope of some sort of chat. And when the weather became warmer again, he would do something he loved; he would take his boat and paddle through Gull Pond or Higgins Pond and see them in summer as they were then, like precious jewels, and then he would visit the harbour and buy lobsters and the famous oysters from Wellfleet.

The barn which became his studio was at the end of a short cobbled path and on the first dark October morning he went to the fuel shed and gathered logs and coal and lit a fire in the grate. He liked the flaky whitewashed walls and how his fishing rods looked against them. His crates had arrived and he had opened them up and spread his life on a canvas sheet across the floor.

He adjusted the diamond burrs again and he set up his table and chair. Then he put on the old grey sweater and noted the red splash of paint on the neck. That was the day he helped Matilda to paint her kitchen door. But he let the thought go quickly and then he sat at his work desk and held a piece of glass in his hands and began to shape it. He knew that outside those wide double doors there were other people like him, that there were wet yellow meadows, and he worked on without knowing what would become of him.

Later he hunkered down and ran his hands over the pieces, each one already smooth from the sea, each one already touched by some drinking sailor's hands. Pale blue, turquoise, opaque, white, but for him he saw the different shades of darkness. He saw illness and he saw his own plight. Blue blood vessels. A girl's face on a gurney as she struggled for air.

He wanted to move on but first he had to give something back.

He wanted to hand something out into the cosmos and for all the people who had died – and as he slowly cut each piece, it became something else and it wanted to attach itself to another, and yet neither piece had any idea of who or what they were.

He wanted to be strong again and yet that night and for many nights after, when the wind picked up and the hurricane lamp flickered, he hunkered down on the Shaker stool and did not know where in hell he was.

And there were nights when he felt really sick – and alone.

So when a song from *Westside Story* came out on the radio, 'There's a place for us', Glassman gave in to it and he put his face into his hands and he cried, and when he cried he coughed and then he cursed the air because it was already full of glass dust. And then he had to open the door and as the wind, already threatening snow, came in, he was not only miserable and sick, he was also very cold and he could see himself as he was – with warm snot on his face from crying – and his last remaining option then was to take a beer from the fridge and laugh.

The low moment was now complete.

It had passed.

The idea of not having a TV had seemed worthy. He practically ate the words from his newspapers now. He had not wanted to be polluted by the media, he did not want the extra noise – and yet on a night like this, with only the wind for company, he would have been grateful to have been corrupted and polluted and infected by thirty minutes of *Frasier* or *Ally McBeal* or *Friends*.

16 Where Are You, When You're Not With Me?

At first Matilda thought he was dead. She was sure of it and reported him missing to the police. Then she went to her closet and took down her favourite picture of him. She stopped then for a moment and sat with it and Godot came and lay beside her before turning on to his back. She placed two fingers on Glassman's forehead and prayed that she was wrong and then she wrote out his details with her special black fountain pen.

'Arthur Glassman. 5ft 9 inches. Hair turning grey. Blue-blue eyes. Beautiful hands'. And here she stopped and could not go on. And so she simply wrote in her phone numbers, her apartment, her office and her cell and finished, 'Please send him home.'

And Godot turned over and looked up at her. He seemed surprised by it, taken aback. But she covered her picture in plastic and went first to The Armory at Lexington and 26th Street and then to Union Square and St Vincent's Wall. And there were all the others. The faces lost perhaps for ever now and Glassman joining them, smiling and eating Ben and Jerry's ice cream from the tub.

'He hated broccoli,' she told the woman who was crying beside her, and the woman replied, 'We had an argument on our last night.'

It was only when she reported him missing that the police went to his home. They arrived with a carpenter and she watched – with a key in her pocket – as the door was lifted and left leaning against a wall. Now that he was missing she was not able to come here alone. And how they stood – the door gone and the sunlight coming in through his windows and all his things as he had left them. No one wanted to be the one to walk in so it was Matilda who stepped forward easily, into a world where she had always believed she belonged.

First she saw the telephone taken off the hook and this created a small pinprick of anger somewhere towards the back of her head. And the two officers watched her and one of them seemed amused by it. The other, a young Italian man called Nardoni, seemed embarrassed and afraid. They checked the closets and there were no clothes missing. Just one or two items that he could have been wearing on any given day.

'His green sneakers are missing,' she told them and everyone present presumed he had died in those shoes. When they lifted the lid of the trash, she saw the cream and gold envelopes with some coffee grits thrown over them and she blinked and swallowed in her pain. And then in the upstairs studio she found the emptiness she had wished for. The small glass ice mountain was packed up and gone.

'Thank you, officers,' she said quietly and she smiled sweetly up at them as she walked across the bedroom floor. Her legs were extended by stilettos and fishnet stockings and then she turned and said, 'I'm sorry for wasting your time.'

The next day she called a friend in Queens and asked him if he knew where she could buy a gun. And he, who had lost a college friend in the World Trade Center, said he understood why she was frightened and asked, 'Where were you when it happened?' and this was how everyone began their conversations now.

Early on the morning of 9/11 Matilda had felt a new wind on Broadway. It lasted a few seconds and there was no hint of summer in it. The heat had stayed on into September but on this day, it carried a chill and she thought suddenly of wet red leaves from New England and freshly fallen Nova Scotia snow. Another New York fall. And soon the leaves would turn and turn, and fall and fall, a monsoon, a flood, a blizzard of red and yellow and gold, and all – without him to hold. 'What was different?' she would ask herself later, 'different to the September mornings that followed,' and she would answer, 'I wasn't afraid.'

She fed her cat and he turned away as she cleaned his litter tray. Then she took her dry-cleaning over her arm and a subway map and she guessed that Godot went back to sleep.

'When I go out,' she told her friends in a hushed voice, 'I am sure Godot turns on the TV, and sleeps on my bed, and does not put the CDs back into the correct cases, and I know he borrows my clothes and shoes, which he wears when he visits his private cat club on 72nd Street – and I'm sure he has other cats round,' and here her friends would laugh and inside think, 'She's been on her own for too long.'

But each evening when Matilda came home, he was always there to welcome her, curled, and rolling over to greet her, from a single patch of sunlight on her floor.

On that day Mrs Schwartz said, 'Good morning, Matilda' and she was wearing her white Persian cat like a stole. She was also polishing the number on her apartment door and she was wearing her cultured pearls. She did not tell Matilda that she had an appointment with her optician that morning and because she was going downtown for it, she would also meet her daughter for lunch. She did not know then that her train would get in earlier and that she would wait at a diner on Wall Street, looking up at the office where her youngest daughter worked. She did not tell Matilda any of it. It was all so important but how could she have known? Now that she was gone Matilda could not stop thinking about her. At night when she closed her eyes she could still see those pearls and her smile. Before 9/11 fear had not moved into her. It did not belong inside her. It did not take over her space, sit on her couch, eat her food and refuse to get out.

In the same way Matilda did not tell anyone that she took the elevator instead of the stairs. That the fire extinguisher had fallen on its side and that she put it right. That she bought her newspaper from a vendor and her coffee at Starbucks on Broadway, instead of on Amsterdam. How all of these small details combined to weave and map out *her* day. Did the flower-sellers notice that she wore a new navy dress on September 11th and that she had not washed her hair?

The girl in Starbucks gave her a mocha in a hot orange cup and when she smiled she said, 'Have a nice day, ma'am.'

She did not know that it was a day to stay at home – under the bedclothes, or in a closet under coats or in an apartment under the floorboards.

And when her friend in Queens told her that he was washing his car when the news came through on the radio, it sounded strangely American and therefore more noble and patriotic than the story she had to tell. As he spoke, his voice breaking with emotion, she lost any real will to explain – that as the first tower fell she was pushing a $20 bill into a tipping envelope in a hair salon in the Village after having her black hair dyed peroxide blonde.

One week later when she rode the subway to Brooklyn Matilda wanted to talk out loud. She wanted to be one of those blonde crazies who carried a shopping bag filled with old newspapers and made other people look around. On 20 September she ran down the steps as the heavens opened and heard the other feet rattling in behind. It was so New York – for everyone to have the same sort of problems, like losing a love or getting caught in the rain, and no one would ever say a word to the same suffering citizen at their side. The train began to move and Matilda felt that she was going backwards and moving away into a deeper, darker place. She was going to Brooklyn and she was suddenly frightened and confused by it.

'What have you done with Manhattan?' she wanted to ask.

When Matilda thought about Manhattan, she thought about bright yellow taxis that could float through the air. And the green leaves of early summer, and people who always re-membered to carry umbrellas and still dashed like rabbits into the subways at the first sign of rain. She thought about doughnuts from a vendor in Washington Square, yoga mats and a little hat shop in SoHo where the hats in the window looked like iced cupcakes. When Matilda thought about Brooklyn, the only colour she could think of was 'brown'.

She knew the A train and C, the D and the F . . . but take her out of Manhattan and Matilda felt like a child who did not know where she was going. She opened a copy of *Time Out* and looked again for the bar called Madisons. It was close to midnight and she did not know where she was going and as fewer passengers got on and more and more got off, she found herself in an empty dripping station deep in a foreign borough and she wondered quite seriously if she would lose her life.

She wore a pair of high heels and a white belted mac, and her scarf, a red and pink Hermes, was pulled up loosely to cover her hair. Yes, it was different to be blonde. It was simple; men always looked at her now. When she stepped into a room it was as if a light bulb had gone on. They saw her and she liked it – except that in Brooklyn she did not want to be seen. She followed the map along Atlantic Avenue and of course no yellow cab in its right mind would cross the Brooklyn Bridge. She stopped and asked directions from a young couple who were walking and sharing a pizza slice. It smelt warm and good but now when she saw a couple in love she always felt a pang of jealous pain.

The bar was closing by the time she got there and she had to plead gently with the bartender to let her come inside, and she found him then, as agreed, sitting in the second booth. She began by smiling at him and he responded by looking away. Then she apologized for being late and he raised his hand and asked for a tequila. So she stopped speaking then and nodded at the bartender to say she would have the same.

He was Mexican and she did not know his name but when she handed the envelope towards him under the table, she could not avoid touching his thigh and the denim felt greasy and warm. He took his tequila and gave her the *Village Voice* and then he got up and left.

Matilda felt a gentle buzz of excitement and she knew it was there in her hand and that it was done. In the end her friend in Queens had agreed to help her but he had only offered when she told him she would do it by mail order instead. She took the newspaper and went into the restroom. How many times, she asked herself in the mirror, had a woman done this before? She stood and remembered her friend's words.

'Don't try getting a gun by mail order, honey, that will only bring you all sorts of trouble,' and 'The gun that you choose should feel comfortable in your hand.'

She sat on the toilet and took it from the newspaper. It was heavier than she expected and when her red nails wrapped around it, she felt a sudden sexual thrill. She curled her long slim finger around the trigger and said in a whisper, 'This is what it's like to be a man.' She put it into her purse and closed it with a little snap and then walked back and instead of leaving she took a stool at the bar. The gun had calmed her and she was no longer feeling abandoned and afraid. Her friend had recommended a handgun that would fire a .38 calibre bullet or bigger – because anything smaller, he said, would 'not reliably stop a large violent man'.

The man at the bar looked sadly into his drink. He was going a little bald and he was younger than her. She wanted to sleep with him. She wanted to take him outside against a brick wall, surrounded by trashcans and squalling alley cats. He looked up at her and then took a second longer to look deep into her eyes. And he saw it all, the hurt and the damage and the pain.

'I like your hair,' he said simply.

'My name's Matilda,' she replied and she offered him her hand. He said nothing for a minute and then said, 'There are two reasons why a woman like you comes into a bar like this.'

And she raised her eyebrows at him.

'You want to fuck someone and don't want your husband to catch you. Or you want to buy a gun.'

'Maybe it's both,' she answered and she leaned in and took a sip of his beer.

'Lady,' he replied, 'I'm married.'

The bartender watched them for a second and then he turned the sign on the door and said, 'Folks, I really have to close.'

'And there are two reasons why a Manhattan girl wants to buy a gun,' he said.

'I need to protect myself,' she said quietly and her eyes were big and dark.

'It's to kill someone or to kill herself.'

And here Matilda changed the subject.

'You know a lot for a young guy.'

'Can't you see I'm going bald?' and he was smiling softly at her now and then he paid for her drink and left a lot of money on the bar.

'Bald men get more head,' she said and he frowned a little and then smiled at her.

'Great,' he replied, 'I've got that to look forward to.' He walked with her to the subway and told her to take the R.

And on the last train into Manhattan, Matilda began talking out loud. And she knew she was different now because other people looked blankly over her head or just looked away.

'I know the A, the D, the E and the F . . . but take me out of Manhattan . . . why have we stopped? . . . why is this train so fucking slow . . . are we going back into Brooklyn? . . . I need to be in Manhattan . . . I have a friend there . . . he promised to meet me in Manhattan . . . why the fuck would anyone want to go to Brooklyn? . . . are we going to Manhattan?' she asked the empty carriage again. And then she took off her scarf and looking into her own face in the black window, she took a comb from her purse and fluffed her hair. Her lipstick was in little smudges and there were tiny red bleed veins at the corners of her mouth.

'Does this train go to Manhattan?' she asked again of the empty carriage. 'I need to get into Manhattan. When I'm in Manhattan I know where I am.'

17   *The Glass Heart (November 2001)*

Heart n. – 1. A hollow muscular organ that pumps blood around the body. 2. The source and centre of emotional life, where the deepest and sincerest feelings are located and an individual is most vulnerable to pain.

Attwoods store is on the corner of Wellfleet's Main Street. The faded-out sign says 'Stoves – Hardware – Paint'. Inside there are boxes of breakfast cereal, red apples in a barrel, loose flour, Ritz crackers, cookies in tall glass jars. On the other side there are white shelves filled with light bulbs, matches, nails, paint – and the owner stands in a starched white apron and glares at me as the bell rings from the door. Any minute now and I'm expecting Nellie Olsen to appear. When the owner sees me, his mouth and the corners of his eyes, in fact his whole face, turn down.

'Ma'am,' he says, and I stand for a moment and look around. This morning I took the bus from Truro and travelled five miles to the nearest town. There's just one food market in Truro and a lighthouse, and a post office and not much else. I wanted to see the library at Wellfleet and after borrowing my first book, I forgot about walking the beach and instead came into the warmth of a hardware store.

There is a man with silver and black hair sitting near the stove. He is drinking hot chocolate and reading a copy of the *New Yorker* and he does not look up when I come in. Outside a school bus turns the corner past the church and the library into Main Street. A woman with a blue muffler takes a child's hand and the child looks up at her, telling her mother everything about school, and she does not want her to miss a word.

The man with the silver hair turns the page and folds the magazine back. His eyebrows are raised and questioning on his weathered face. We are both here for the same reasons, to see other people and to get warm. My hair is too long now and after one day on the beach it became impossible to comb and I have windburn. My skin is on fire even though I am freezing cold. The beach house was a romantic idea but I needed to escape any further madness from Matilda and New York.

I ask the owner for a coffee – and he nods towards a chair and I sit down. There are three chairs around the stove and then another man – I recognize him from the library – comes in and takes off his woollen hat and says, 'Arthur' to the other man. And Arthur puts down his magazine and his face breaks into an easy, happy smile and the room is suddenly full of good humour and charm and he replies, 'Jake.'

But before getting up to speak to him he says, 'Here' to me and puts the *New Yorker* into my hand. It seems he wants me to read a Gary Larson cartoon.

The coffee arrives in a white mug and I put both hands around it and stay near the warmth of the red stove. There is a steel bucket full of split logs and without a word Arthur comes back and opens the little door and throws on a log. We watch together as a shower of red sparks flies up the chimney and are gone.

'You staying long?' Jake asks and he pulls up a chair to mine and I tell him I'm staying in a house near Long Nook beach, near Truro.

'My oh my,' he replies, 'and you know the story of Herman

Dill?' and I look back and for some reason I say 'Nope' instead of 'No'.

'He drowned in a cottage near that beach.'

'He drowned in Wellfleet, in a lighthouse,' Arthur says and he frowns at the other man.

When Jake goes, Arthur sits down again and he looks at me for a minute over his small silver glasses which he has pushed down on his nose. I don't know what he is thinking or if he is taking me in, but when he speaks again his voice is lyrical and warm and what he says is simple and in a voice full of kindness.

'Sweetheart, you're gonna freeze.'

At that moment the winter sun blinks out and the sky – through the vast skylight – is a brilliant cold blue and when the single shaft of sunlight comes in and floats down over me it makes a warm spot on my head. And here we both smile at each other and he holds my gaze and then I look away. Jack's house is made for summer. There is no way to block out draughts. One solid fuel stove. An immersion heater that hisses and threatens to explode. A sofa covered in damp striped ticking. A single lamp. A whistling kettle. A stool covered in chipped white paint. A pirate chest used as a coffee table. A wooden duck inside the door. A picture of a ship about to go under and it is called 'Brig on a Stormy Sea'. A telescope. Why? One blue enamel mug. There is no furniture or TV but I can sit on the floor beside the stove and watch the moon and the stars. The floor is made from wide chestnut boards and the wind blows up under them and this morning there was a small sand dune inside the front door.

The man is right – I will freeze but I am not going back to sympathy and tea and home.

What would Larry do?

And this morning I stood in the middle of the room and

asked this question of the sea and the mug and the single white chair and like me they were silent and sad and did not seem to know.

Arthur gets up then and walks without a word on to the porch and I take my groceries and stand outside with him. There are three identical white painted rocking chairs parked in a row and he is sitting on the edge of one rolling some loose tobacco for a smoke. He turns one shoulder a little to fend away the sea breeze.

'Smoke?' he asks and I find myself saying 'Yes'. He is a stranger to me and yet since I met him I can feel a warm feeling beginning in my chest. He is older than Pappy was but there is something magnetic about him. And he is older than anyone I know and yet with those strange eyes, that seem to keep a big secret, and his lined and weathered face, he is somehow beautiful too.

He wants me to sit beside him now and I recognize the basic primal need from him to me and back. People who find themselves alone and need to hear the sound of another voice. Two people who stand and stare into the rough dashing waves of New England and listen and listen as if the sea could actually keep them company and talk.

He only wants a chat.

That is all and I can give him that.

When he gets up he goes into the shop to buy some matches and I start rocking over and back. I am thinking of old men with raggy beards who spit tobacco and have names like Isaiah and Jethroe. Old-timers and now a young-timer like me. The chair starts to rock faster and then faster again and the next thing I crack my head on the stone wall behind and when he stands over me again there are little silver stars and blue birds circling around my head.

'Wow,' he says and at first he looks shocked and then I can see he is actually trying not to laugh.

'What was that?' he asks.

'That was my head. On the wall.'

And when he comes towards me laughing he puts both hands around my head to nurse it and inside I am thinking, 'All my life. All my damn life. Why does this sort of thing always happen to me?'

And he is still laughing and saying, 'Trust me, I'm a doctor.'

'Here,' he says then and he hands me a neatly rolled cigarette and then he strikes a match. We sit side by side, quietly smoking and looking out towards the beach.

'I'm not able to sleep,' I tell him suddenly and my own voice surprises itself so that there is a tiny upswing at the end.

His voice is cool and easy and he does not look up straight away and when he does it is over his small silver glasses again.

'What's wrong?' he asks simply.

He sits back and waits and then, because it is a difficult question, he says, 'I go for a long walk every evening, right down Newcomb Hollow Beach, if you would like to come with me tomorrow.'

'Great,' I answer – and then I come out with something really dumb.

'Walking is a good idea. It's good for your body . . . and your brain.'

'My brain,' he says with some mild wonder. 'I gave up on that years ago.'

Arthur is waiting for me in Wellfleet. He is leaning on his car with both hands deep in his pockets. The sun is gone and we are surrounded by a misty grey afternoon. When he sees me he pulls on a woollen ski cap and then he opens the car door without any words. He drives towards Newcomb Hollow and then we take the sloping path down through the sea grass meadow and on to the sand – when I pause he points the way.

'I do it in one hour every day,' he says.

His eyes rest on my green army jacket for a second and he asks, 'Will you be warm enough?'

'Yes.'

'Would you like some gum?' and he offers me a Wrigley's Spearmint.

'Thanks.'

And the only sound is the crunch of our boots on the long stretch of shingle and how it slopes down at first and then stretches upwards into more damp mist and wet sea grass.

New York is mentioned early and he says that 9/11 has passed and people need to start rebuilding the city and to try to move on.

'Did you lose anyone?' I ask him.

'Only myself,' he says and when he catches my eye he is smiling and there is no hint of sadness in his voice.

We pass an old beach shack with boarded-up windows and there is mildew covering the outside walls. He tells me that this is what the disease inside him is like and as we fall into step again he talks.

He starts with a nurse holding the first syringe up ('A very attractive woman,' he adds, 'in a low-cut blouse.') and how he looked at her and said, 'Hello, I'm James Bond,' and he ends with the day he looked at himself in his own mirror in Manhattan last January and thought that he was already dead.

When he describes his disease it is like poetry, or some Shakespearean tragedy he has to perform. He plays out each part beautifully. The awfulness of it. The weakness. The fear and the pure comedy that suddenly surrounded him when he thought he might die. And there is nothing even close to sadness or embarrassment in his voice. His spirit seems to crackle inside him. And he is thin. Wan. I hardly know him and *I* am suddenly worried that he might die.

'And are you feeling better?' I ask.

'Yes,' he says and he stops for a moment and smiles at me. 'I am feeling better today.'

He loves New York. He loves everything about his city – and suddenly here on a cold beach in New England his city is so different to mine. There are sticky green buds in springtime, long walks in Central Park, the first fall of snow in November and a date with a woman he later wanted to marry on top of the Empire State.

'What happened?' I ask.

'She had a weak heart, she died.'

And then he says it – bringing us back to real time and bringing us together again.

'Mortality has always been a big part of my life.'

When we pass a house two terriers come tumbling out and they run to him as if they are all old friends. These are his buddies whom he meets every day on his walk – and then we turn and I ask him questions about the Cape and he describes the seasons and the cool blue sky over the ponds at night. And I continue to question him because he seems to be able for it and because it helps me to avoid having to talk about myself.

Wellfleet is his real home and he knows and loves every inch of it.

'Before the pilgrims, there were Punanokanit Indians,' he says and with these words his voice warms with pride and then he says, 'We have sandy soil here . . . sometimes the old bones rise up,' and his eyes are twinkling at me, teasing, and making me laugh.

I notice that he does not mention his family and I do not mention mine. He says he left New York because one day he looked into his bathroom mirror and 'The face looking back was green' and he shakes his head and blows smoke into the wind and laughs again at his own poor health. He was being followed by a woman whose heart he had broken and here his voice is level and without emotion and then he meets my eyes and says, 'She was beginning to frighten me.' We do not talk about my life because he senses that I can't. Then he tosses the cigarette into the wind and we begin to walk again.

We take the road past Gull Pond and then over the long narrow boardwalk and he points out his house to me. It is not made of wood like the others. It is tall and made of cut stone and there is a bright red barn behind it and tall waving trees. He offers to drive me back to Truro and we talk again in the car.

'Did you know anyone when you came to New York?' Arthur asks.

'Only Jack – the guy who owns the beach house – and a woman I met through the Internet and she was nice . . . but a little weird.'

And here Arthur pulls a tired face.

'You were in New York,' he replies and he salutes a woman who stands at a street corner and she smiles back and gives a little wave.

He parks near the post office and we cross a narrow sandy path and then we are walking over the dunes and over soft sliding sand towards the beach. There are three cottages in a row. Two are empty and Jack's cottage is at one end. He walks in and looks around. He knows I have no hope here but he tries to help. He tells me he will bring me fuel from his shed. He points out window shutters that I didn't know I had. He looks at the broken-down couch and tells me I would be better sleeping on that and not to even try going upstairs.

And then his face breaks into a smile and he suddenly looks like a little boy and he is really excited now and pointing to the high shelf and I am looking blankly at the old green box beside the wooden duck.

'You have Scrabble,' he says and it seems really important to him.

'On Friday,' he goes on, 'come to my house for dinner, play Scrabble,' and he shivers in my sitting room. 'Get warm.'

He opens the door and looks up at the sky for a moment, and then without saying goodbye he leaves.

Email to Hope Swann 4.48 p.m.
From Jack Mitchell
Hey, Going to try to get down there at the weekend. Saturday afternoon.
Did you work out how to light the stove OK?
Jack.

Email to Matilda Vaughan 5.02 p.m.
From Hope Swann
Hi Matilda
How are things? Sorry I left in a hurry and without saying goodbye. I just needed to get away and think. I'm in Cape Cod. Truro. In Jack's beach house. Do you know it? It's nice but very cold. I am so mixed up about everything. I just need some time.
There's one interesting person here. An old guy who invited

me to his house for a game of Scrabble!?! Is that a date do you
think?
Anyway, hope things are good with you, and sorry again
I didn't get a chance to say goodbye.
Hope.

The bedroom window faces away from the beach. From here
I think I can see the lights of Wellfleet and in the distance a
single light like a yellow star and that could be from his barn.
When he left I stood in the doorway and watched as his feet
sank a little when he jumped the step on the front porch and
landed in wet sand. He turned the corner without waving and
then he was gone – and somehow he has been with me ever
since. I do not understand this. He seems to have turned into
a hundred different shadows so that he is imagined to be
seated on the white chair, or adding a log to my stove or
stretched out on my bed on a warm June afternoon. And when
his face is gone I stand still for a moment and try to remember
his eyes and his smile and I think I have the memory now and
then it's gone again.

There is a bottle of wine in the bag of groceries and I see that
Mr Huckstable has chosen a Californian Shiraz. I will take the
next bus carrying the bottle and with the box of Scrabble
under my arm. I can remember Frankie's voice as I step out
on to the porch: 'That's like asking someone with dyslexia to
play Scrabble.' Today on the beach Arthur told me about all
sorts of things and there were words shooting in every direction and it was impossible for me to catch them in my net and
pin them down.

There is no one on the beach tonight – not even a tug or a

ship or a single light out at sea. The noise of the waves in the dark is frightening and I hurry to the bus stop with the wind whipping around my ears and face. When I get to his house I can see him through the window, putting logs on his fire, and everything in his room seems warm in red and orange and gold. He sees me coming across his yard and a light flashes on over his door. He smiles when he sees me and he says, 'Welcome' and he opens his arms.

For dinner there is lamb with rosemary, peach chutney, roast potatoes and baby peas. It is all simple and fresh and laid out on a red and white gingham cloth. He has lit a big fire and he says, 'We should both sit on the same side of the table to keep our backs warm.' And outside the wind picks up and somewhere far away is the sound of the night sea. I imagine what it would be like if we were married and like this, feeling the cold together and getting old. He talks easily about himself. Producing awful facts and incidents without any embarrassment or thought. 'Mortality' is mentioned again and he says that for some reason he is the last person other people see before they die. When I ask him about his family and his friends he says that most of them are dead.

'Vietnam,' he explains simply and he takes a forkful of food. He makes two mugs of hot chocolate for dessert and hands one to me with the handle turned around.

'Now,' he says, 'get out the Scrabble board.' The fire dies down but the room is warm. There are no draughts in his house and there is a cowskin rug on the floor. We move to the couch and lay out the little white tablets and pews and in between making words and pretending to find it difficult he offers up more information around his life.

'The women I meet,' he says, 'tell me I can't commit.'

'I'm a widow and I'm dyslexic,' I reply and for the first time I manage to really smile for him and he puts back his head and laughs.

His first word is 'ebony' and then 'bison' and then 'squaw'.

'I am an American after all,' he laughs. And I come up with 'feet' and from that 'toe' and I am in Scrabble hell. He offers me five-letter words and American culture and I reply with four-letter scores and body parts.

We talk about women and men and how it is impossible to know anyone.

'I mean to truly know them,' he says. 'For example, your parents, how well do we know our parents? What sort of people are they when they're not with us? Is it possible to know another person fully – or would you want to?' and he asks this question of the room and of himself.

My letters are 'Q' 'X' 'T' 'Y' 'I' 'I' and he begins to suggest words to me and in the end we agree to accept abbreviations and my next effort, added to 'toe' is 'i.e.'.

'I thought I knew my last girlfriend,' he says, as if I am no longer in the room. 'When I met her. I thought she was beautiful – she was – and then I thought, "Puppy from the pound".'

'What do you mean?'

'The first time I went to touch her, she pulled back. It was involuntary. When I lifted my hand . . . she didn't know what was coming next.'

The door behind us creaks suddenly and I look up quickly and he smiles.

'Then she told me she had been abused by someone, but she was telling me something I already knew. I did care for her. I took her in. One night she told me I was her umbilical cord. I never thought she was dangerous but you know . . .' and his voice trails off.

'She was wounded,' he goes on. 'It wasn't her fault. She learned to trust me. I was the first man who treated her with kindness – so when I wanted to end it – it was like she got all broken up again. She was so lonely . . .' and here he gets up and fills the kettle and there is a part of me that is tempted to look at his letters before he turns back around.

'Lonely people,' he says, 'can invent extraordinary lives for themselves – she was like Robert De Niro in *Taxi Driver* – and I began to realize she would do anything to get to me.'

'And what did she want?'

'Revenge. Against men. The ones who had hurt her. And because I broke her heart – that definitely included me.'

'But she wasn't dangerous . . . ?'

'Who knows . . . ?' and his voice answers in the softest whisper now.

And the shutter behind him suddenly flaps open and I jump up and give a little cry and he runs and closes it and then walks over and puts one protective arm around my shoulder. Somewhere in between being careful with me – he is amused by my distress.

'Honey, there are no devils or ghosts in Wellfleet – you're in America . . . there are usually enough scary things happening in the house next door.'

And we sit back down, our legs touching now, and we look in silence at the Scrabble board.

The fire crackles and it makes shadows and I am suddenly looking at him and how he holds his chin, watching the letters on the board. I cannot stop looking and suddenly he takes his glasses off and looks right into my eyes. I am waiting for him to say something. To tell me something. To explain why I suddenly need to be around him all the time – and instead he says in a quiet voice, 'You know you're a beauty . . . right?' and he smiles. He smiles so that his eyes sparkle and there is light and energy coming from him and filling the room. I can't speak. I don't have any answer here.

'The minute I saw you . . .' he says and his voice trails off. We both see me then as I am walking into the hardware store with red cheeks and tangled hair and his words are lifting me up and up again from my own dark place.

He lifts his hand and places it gently against my cheek. His hand is rough and callused, so much so that I almost move back involuntarily. 'Puppy from the pound', that was how he described her. The girl who would not leave him alone. To me his skin feels like work and pain and fingers pressed against rough walls by someone lost in the dark.

'There have been others,' he says, 'but you have walked into my life and I have followed and looking at you now . . . as you are . . . I can't turn around, even if I wanted to.'

There is a bright flashing current running between us. It moves and curls and twists in each electric flash. It is so obvious we could almost say it out loud to each other, even though we have only just met. It is like an undertow and the rain hits the windowpane in one sudden dash and the wind makes the green shutters creak.

He leans into my face and we kiss and I can feel his breath on my top lip and every sense is magnified. He kisses my neck – my forehead – my face – my lips. And he sits back and watches me as if I am made from some kind of gold. I am wondering what he is going to say to me. If he will tell me that I amaze him, if what is happening here between us is amazing for him as well.

When he speaks his voice is suddenly young and innocent.

He is smiling, almost laughing, as if he can't disguise his own surprise.

'I'm so glad I met you,' he says simply.

He kisses my breasts and then my stomach, once – twice – three times and then he begins to move his lips further down. The cowskin rug feels warm underneath us and there are two reindeer antlers to protect us overhead. In my mind I am seeing Indian ponies and braves who ride bareback through the prairie wind. And deep down inside I still miss him so much that I am in some kind of constant pain but . . . life goes on . . . that is what everyone says . . . and I am trying so hard to make a start . . . and so yes . . . life goes on . . . but it will never be the same again. But Arthur Glassman kisses and sucks and draws the pain out of me until I believe in one sudden bright flashing moment that a world of pain is gone.

In the morning the sky is clear and lilac and there are gulls circling and crying when I kiss him on the steps. He is wearing a red sweater and his stubble and his fingers are rough when they touch my face.

'Come back and have breakfast,' he says and I smile and as I walk away I have a strange feeling that makes me want to turn and see him – and so I turn and expect to see him, hands deep in his pockets, his glasses on his nose, but his door is closed and he is suddenly invisible. He has already disappeared and gone inside again.

Email to Hope Swann 5.38 p.m.
From Matilda Vaughan
Hey, I'm just glad you're OK and safe. I love Cape Cod –

we spent summers there too you know. That guy sounds interesting . . . and yes . . . I think it *IS* a date . . . (by the way what's his name?).
Matilda xx.

Email to Matilda Vaughan 12.00 a.m.
From Hope Swann
Hi Matilda,
We kissed. I don't really know what I'm doing. He's way too old for me – fifty-one – can you believe that? – He's an artist, making something from glass . . . romantic I guess.
Hope.

Email to Hope Swann 12.01 a.m.
From Matilda Vaughan
Hi Hope,
Sounds like you had a great time. Not much happening here . . . by the way what's that guy's name?
Matilda.

Arthur is sitting in his studio. He is wearing an old grey sweater with a red bandanna tied around one wrist. He apologizes because he needs to work today and because the air is full of 'glass dust'. There is a fire lighting in the black iron grate behind him and next it, an old green wicker chair. The grey velvet curtains on the window are moth-eaten and beginning to fall down on one side. I sit on the wicker chair and watch him work and now and then he tilts his chin up a little and frowns down into the glass. He holds each piece in his fingers as if it is precious and confusing or like an unusual shell he has just picked up on the beach. To one side are two fishing rods and there are two big wooden crates. His name, *Arthur*

Glassman, and his address, *1029 Prince Street, Manhattan*, is written in clear black print on one side.

'I'm not sure what it is,' he says suddenly and he slowly puts his head into his hands. He looks sad and broken by it and as if his life is quite suddenly a waste of time. He holds it up then and turns it towards the light as if searching – and then he gets up and dips it into a bucket of water and holds it up again. And I can see it and wonder that he cannot. It is unfinished and already damaged by someone else. It has suffered trauma and been broken and there has been pain inside every vessel and disease. The pale blue and white of the old sea glass is sacred and ugly and beautiful all at the same time.

'It's a heart,' I tell him and he looks at me.

'The right side here,' and I touch it with my hand, 'and here is the . . . aorta . . . and on this side – you can make the rest,' and when I look at him, he nods down into the glass spread out at his feet.

'Not an original idea,' he says and his voice is sad. 'I would not be the first artist to make a heart from glass.'

'It will be a first for you,' I reply and he hunkers down over the glass again and smiles. His hands are callused from it. His hair is full of white dust. Today he looks tired and pale and ill.

'I don't know how you do this,' I tell him then and he gives a wry smile.

'I don't feel like doing it every day.'

On the beach we wrap ourselves in coats and scarves and walk together towards the pale November sun. We collect shells and smooth round pebbles and now and then I find a piece of old glass in the sand. He takes me to the harbour and we watch a red trawler unload its catch. The fishermen are Puerto Rican and the fish are jumping and slapping in nets as they come in. When we watch he stands behind me, his chin resting on my shoulder and his arms around my waist. Then we have coffee at the stove in Attwoods and we read the same copy of the *New Yorker* again. When we walk I put both red mittens around his hand and we rake out the shells from under rocks and stones. We are quiet then in the warmth of his kitchen and he shows me how to make real yeast bread and seafood chowder – 'New England style'.

And tonight in the middle of getting ready for dinner I remember to reply to Matilda's email.

Glassman

That is all I write and then I run from the beach house, over the sand dunes and into the village, on to the bus, towards the red warm barn, the glass heart and him.

18   *Reason to Believe*

'My father was an Indian,' Glassman said to his mirror image and the words came out, truthful and brave.

'He made me,' and when he spoke again the words fell down and broke into pieces on the ground. The other women were damaged and beyond repair but not Hope Swann. They walked to him like a tribe of broken dolls asking to be mended. They came, looking for something – hurt and in some way broken – abandoned and abused. Their eyes were always blue – why was that? And they could blink and roll but they usually just stared straight ahead. Matilda was the most like a doll. An old-fashioned porcelain figure arriving in tissue paper and in a long cellophane box. How beautiful she was and when she was hurting – how angry and dangerous and cold.

On that last night in his apartment he stood in the doorway of his own kitchen and stared as she picked up a Stanley knife. He watched as she began to cut herself, not a nick or a mark – and had he not stopped her, she was going to saw off her hand.

He ran his fingers back through his hair at the thought of it. And now here was this new girl because that is what she was. And he wanted to hold her and protect her and never let her go. He had seen her cross the street from the library and he had begun to dream about her and the hope of being able to feel love and lust again. She was very young but he needed this last chance at happiness and he needed her.

Glassman could not see her – not as she was that day in the hardware store – and then look away and just carry on. He had seen her on the street in Wellfleet before that and then again at the library and then he saw her sitting quietly at the red stove.

He had wanted to talk to her and tell her – confide in her – about everything – and Jake in that silly hat and Huck with his dour face, and even the log that spat in the fire, grew into mountains and got in his way.

She was different to the New Englanders. She had soft smooth skin, high pretty cheekbones – where did they come from? – and such beautiful – Matilda would call it – 'angel hair'. But her real beauty and what made her precious and somehow more breakable was that he could see she was feeling sad and broken deep inside – and she was consumed by it – and completely unaware that for someone else she had become a ray of light. And his illness suddenly shifted and became smaller around her and it gave way to boyish ideas of how to impress and convince her that he was great.

When the sun came out – even Huck was surprised by it – it lasted only an instant and just long enough to make a perfect round circle of light on her head. It was as if she was blessed or had an aura or was an angel and sent by someone else.

Anyone except Glassman would have been taken aback by it, but he felt something click and release inside his chest and he began to feel – what? He did not know – but it was like a vessel in his heart opening and a fresh narrow river of blood feeding him something bright and new. 'The feeling of life . . . that is how life feels,' he would tell her later. And anyone else would have been surprised by a girl like that in Wellfleet, but not him, not really – Glassman was romantic and he had hoped and prayed and longed her here.

In the dark afternoon when she was gone, his mind returned to the scar on her stomach and he spanned his fingers in front of his eyes and against the fading light and reminded himself that he had touched her – and right there and then he wanted to get out of bed and walk over hundreds of dunes to find her at the beach house and bring her here.

He loved her and he wanted to keep her – that was all. In his mind his endorphins were like coloured butterflies now. They had escaped from him and went fluttering away and now because of her, he could catch them and try out a different one each day.

There were suddenly so many things in the city that he wanted to show her. He wanted to re-present the city, tired and grey as it was, and smelling of warm rubber and gasoline and garbage all year long. He would take her to Angelika and they would watch documentaries about the First World War and the next night they would go to Times Square and eat popcorn and watch some silly movie with Meg Ryan.

From now on when he woke in the mornings he wanted to turn over and always see the crease between her shoulder blades or the tiny line between her eyebrows because he already knew that she frowned in her sleep – or at least he wanted to wake and hear her rattling in the kitchen or running downstairs to collect the newspapers or cursing his shower curtain that had a tendency to fall.

But he did not want to frighten her off and so he went to the studio and thought about Matilda a little and then to numb out the memory of her he took a hit of pot. He could wait until after six o clock to call over; he would have her for ever after that.

And he still collected words – ones that he had learned from her.

Rashers

Feck

and

Bollux – and he wrote these with pride on his whitewashed studio wall.

'See ya later, Arthur,' Hope had said and he watched her leave his house and walk in minutes over the first sand dune. And at the highest point she turned and he was standing, waiting as she gave a big dramatic wave.

19 Between Lightning and Thunder (December 2001)

*Missing adj. – 1. Not present in an expected place, absent, or lost.
2. Not yet traced and not known for certain to be alive, but not
confirmed as dead.*

Matilda is sitting on the front porch. She is wearing a light
cotton dress and rocking in the white wicker chair. The wind
from the sea blasts into her face – and her hair which is very
white now stands on end. Her arms and legs are turning
blue from the cold and when she sees me she turns her head
slowly, and her eyes are red and streaming, from crying or from
the cold. There is a small yellow suitcase beside her, an old-
fashioned green vanity case and a white straw hat. The sand
has moved up on to the porch again. It is getting dark on the
beach now and the wind is full of rain and seaweed and salt.

'Matilda . . .' and I say her name very quietly and in my
mind the letters are blowing apart and beginning to make new
three-letter words in the sand.

She breaks into an easy smile and when she blinks slowly
her face seems to transform itself. She walks across the wooden
porch and hugs me. She is wearing red shoes with very high
heels and peep-toes. She feels cold and thin in my arms and
her skin is rippling in goose bumps.

'What's wrong?' I ask and she shrugs. I am thinking about
the night she took me in, when the first snow was falling and
Thanksgiving in New York began to feel like the end of the
world.

'Sometimes the city is too much for me,' she says quietly.

'This morning I woke up feeling . . . so alone,' and we wrap our arms around each other again in a hug. She has been crying. I can hear the tears in her voice.

'May I come in?' she says and she is smiling again.

The gulls are circling and crying and they swoop down low over the roof. It is as if they are expecting a picnic of breadcrumbs and sprats but there is no food here.

Inside the stove is still alight. I put some more logs on and begin to make tea. Matilda looks around. She picks up a pink conch and then puts it back in its place.

She walks then to the pirate chest and picks up a book Arthur gave me last night.

'Walt Whitman,' she says quietly.

'Here,' I say to her and I hand her a mug of tea.

' "I Hear America Singing",' she says.

'Pardon?' I reply and she looks away again.

Upstairs I find one of Arthur's sweaters and I bring it down to keep her warm. It is a red burgundy colour and I bring it to her and smile.

'Put this on,' I tell her. 'People used to die of cold down here.'

She turns and faces me, her pretty face creasing a little into a frown. She stares down at the sweater and her arms fold themselves now.

'Here . . .' I tell her again and my voice is gentle and low.

She takes it, both hands held out flat for it, and then she just looks at it lying across her bare skin. Last night we ate fillet steak. We left it to thaw in the kitchen sink and it made a small thin river of blood. It was the same colour as his favourite sweater. I wore it in bed last night. She sits down on the sofa and then presses her face into it and I can hear her inhale. She just sits there really quietly, breathing deeply, with her face pressed into the wool.

'Matilda, are you sure you're OK?'

'You spent the night with him,' she says and here each word comes out with a smile and in a tiny childlike voice.

And I can feel myself blush.

'I guess I did,' and I'm frowning and trying to look away from her and around the room.

'You really like him . . . don't you?'

'I guess so.'

In the background the whistling kettle is beginning to rattle and boil.

'He's coming over for dinner, so you can tell me what you think.'

'Why would it matter what I think?' and here her voice seems to change a little and she lights a cigarette and blows smoke to extinguish the match.

There is silence now and I ask her if she would like some more tea and she shakes her head to say 'No'. And when I try to talk to her about Truro she lights another cigarette and gets up and stands at the window looking out over the beach.

On the Cape we are different and without New York, she seems to have run out of things to say.

'What time is he coming?' she asks and her words come out as she faces the window and they bump a little into the glass.

'Around six.' It is getting dark now, the sun is happy to slip away quickly and dip down into the icy sea.

'I'm going to have a bath,' I tell her. 'Can I get you anything?'

'You better have your bath,' she says and still she will not turn around. Outside the gulls are bouncing in the wind and dark clouds begin to move in from the sea.

'Come back to New York with me,' Arthur said. We were curled up in his bed, under a bright patchwork quilt and a red cashmere rug. His fire flickered and crackled and when he lifted his hands from under the covers he made more long shadows on the stone wall.

'I want to show you the city,' he said and when his voice came out into the darkness it sounded young and proud and strong.

'I'm feeling better,' he said quietly but he still seemed a little frightened by these words.

'The New England air,' I told him, and he replied, 'New England and you.'

This morning we had breakfast on his back porch. The sun was up and we ate bagels and cream cheese wrapped in a rug. In between drinking coffee and talking about New York, he was throwing pieces of food at the gulls.

'We can spend the holidays there,' he says. 'You'll get to see Central Park in the snow and Macy's tied up in a big red bow.'

And then he just looked at me and said, 'I would hate to lose you, Hope.'

And I said laughing, 'I'm not going to get lost,' and then he laughed too and kissed my hand.

The bathroom is at the top of the narrow wooden stairs. There is a tiny landing with a bedroom on either side. The tub is heavy and old, painted green with small pink flowers on the inside. It is like an old boat, one with a flat bottom, and if there was a sudden gust of wind or a secret current, it would give three sudden twirls and sink. There is a bar of lemon-scented soap. A white soap dish. Camomile shampoo. One rough white towel on an old mahogany towel rail.

The taps are heavy and old. I need two hands to turn each one around. There is a slight delay and then a hiss and the hot water begins to gurgle and splash down. I sit on the side of the tub and watch as the water fills in and grows. I dip my fingers into it and the mirror becomes white with steam.

Lately I've been thinking about something Matilda said.

'One big love,' and I am wondering if there could be more than one big love in life. If there is room for several big loves inside every woman and every man.

I take off my sweater and hang it on the doorknob. My jeans are folded over the back of the little wooden chair. My underwear falls in two white cotton crumples on the tiled floor. I turn the radio on and they're playing REM.

And when I look up Matilda is standing on the landing.

She has taken her shoes off and I notice that her toenails are painted red. It is the same colour as the little line over the dado rail and the same colour as her lips. She is carrying a blue mug of tea which she holds out towards me. Some steams lifts from it and I smile and hold out my hand. She stands for a moment and I pull the towel around my waist. She does not move and I sit down a little awkwardly on the side of the tub. She just stands there watching me and I sip my tea and frown and look away.

'There's a mark on your neck,' she says and I put one hand quickly towards it as if trying to cover up a sin.

Last night Arthur left a bruise on my neck and another on my right breast. I found them there this morning and stood and looked at their pretty colours and touched them with my hands. Matilda stands over me and I can hear her breathing and I can smell her perfume – which stays behind her – when she turns and moves back towards the stairs.

⌁

The water is growing cool and so I add some more hot water from the tap. And as it grows warm around me I can feel my body lift a little and float. I imagine the water is a mixture of pale pink and gold circles and that the warmer currents surround me and lift me up. I stretch out and put my head back and then right under the water again.

Every night I do this, even though it still frightens me, just to prove I can.

And I count to twenty and then I come back up.

And then I begin to shampoo my hair and I run more water and I sing a little to the radio and some old Christmas song.

And then down again. I need to go under three times before I feel that I'm brave enough.

And the third time I am under and counting and beginning to feel thankful for one or two things and so I don't hear the bathroom door – opening and closing again.

And in that brief moment I see Matilda, miles of water away, with all her edges moving and flickering, and I have the saddest feeling I have ever had.

Fingers point into the water.

There is an emerald ring and a gold bracelet on one hand. A manicure that looks new. Her fingers are long and strong and the slim bones in her wrists twitch and move as her hands join together around my neck.

Legs, mine – swinging up and over the edge of the tub – and arms, mine again – thrashing – thrashing – thrashing and there are bottles flying around the bath and a sponge falls from somewhere, and then a face flannel, but my head, my mouth, my lips do not come back up again.

A second or two, that's all it takes and – we – I – am over and there are no prayers and no hope left.

⌇

Yesterday Arthur brought me to the Chequessett Neck Cemetery and he told me that the men who were digging out a cottage there once found some old Indian bones. 'An adult male,' he said and when he spoke I noticed that the wind had chapped his lips, 'with an arrowhead in his spine, buried with his knees drawn up to his chin. And with him the skeleton of a female child.'

We sat in the coffee shops of Wellfleet and talked about it and about life and death and how frightening real people can be. 'What had happened to the Indian? . . . and the child? . . . who was his daughter . . . perhaps,' Arthur wanted to know, and I said, 'Everyone has a story, Arthur,' and he smiled even though my voice was sad.

Under the water – my life – my story – and it has been at times noisy and difficult – is beginning to get quieter and fade. I am trying to imagine Arthur putting his outdoor jacket on, and then his gloves and his scarf. And how he will bang the front door behind him and then check his pockets again for his keys. The car lights at my window. And how he is almost here. He is almost here. Please.

Any minute now.

But it is deep.

Deep.

Deeper, dark and down.

Any minute now.

He will come over the sand dune, carrying a bottle of wine, or a cake, his cigarette making a red dot in the dark.

Arthur who makes everything better.

Arthur who makes me feel safe and calm.

Any minute now.

Any minute now.

He's a little later than he said.

But any minute now.

Arthur is never late.

From this warm bed it is so quiet.

Now that the splashing has stopped it is so quiet and there is no hurt or pain. There is peace and through the water I can still see her face and she is smiling and it is a smile of real life and love. Tomorrow people will read about me. I will become a few inches tall in a newspaper space.

'Girl drowns in bath tub'. And who will read about me? The people I know. The ones I hoped could save me.

Arthur, where are you?

And as the room begins to grow dark I call each face I know to me and try to remember their names to say goodbye.

There are small shooting stars. How beautiful, in this room that is growing dark. And now and then they bump together and explode and fall. Outside there must be lightning and thunder, one on top of the other with no gap at all.

Pappy. It's me, Hope.

Mum. Here I am again. Look, I'm all grown-up.

Daniel. Please wait so I can catch up with you.

Juna. How I've missed you.

Larry. Where have you gone?

Larry. Why is everything so dark?

The face leans towards me. It is someone I know but I can't remember how we met. He leans into my face and puts his mouth on mine and when he blows warm breath into me he looks deep into my eyes as if he is praying for me and for my life. His voice calls out to me.

It is my name but I am not able to wake up.

I want to but I would prefer to sleep instead.

And then I see Daniel and he is standing near the water and smiling and – I miss him so much – and he says, like nothing is a problem, 'Come on, Star.' We are both ten years old again, and without any worries or pain. The man leans into my face and blows his own breath into my lungs again. And now he is crying and crying and trying to breathe slowly in case some oxygen escapes. The strange thing is that I am alive because I can see him and at exactly the same time I am somewhere else. We are all in slow motion and trying to decide if this is the beginning or the end of life.

And I am slipping again – I want to see Daniel and just touch the warmth of his face.

And up over us in the bathroom with the steam and the lime-green peeling paint, is a bright orange puff.

'Danny,' I whisper and then I open my eyes and he says, 'Hope,' and he is crying again.

'Hope,' he says and I answer, 'Jack?' and we are back together in the same old life.

Matilda has left the room. She has crawled out on her hands and knees. I see that one of her shoes is here and the mug of tea has fallen and broken into pieces and there is water splashed all over the floor. In this moment we are like a ship that is trying to decide if it will float or sink. Jack reaches for a cushion to put under my head and the one he pulls from the chair is fat and full of goose and duckdown.

'Don't leave me,' I whisper and he says, 'I won't.'

The noise that comes from the landing is terrifying.

One sudden explosion and there is smoke and bright blue

and silver sparks through the glass in the door. In the same moment the mirror over us shatters and it falls into big jagged pieces near my feet. And I am pulling my feet back towards me and Matilda is gone. We can hear the sound of her crying as she runs down the white wooden stairs.

Arthur blames himself. Not so much for Matilda but because he was fifteen minutes late. He works in silence making bandages and gently bathing my feet. And then he lifts me up in his arms and carries me down the stairs. There is a bullet mark on the wall of the bathroom and we do not know where Matilda has gone. She has taken her car and by now she will have made it to the freeway and she is probably on her way to New York or into another state. Jack picks up the phone to call the police and then Arthur stops him. Instead we all sit on the couch drinking mugs of tea and he tells us everything he knows.

Jack listens in silence and at the end of it all he shakes his head and says, 'Arthur, you sure know how to pick them,' and then he looks at me and says, 'So do you.'

Then I look at both of them and say, 'How come the men I meet . . . are always late?'

And who knows the meaning of anything now? We will wait until tomorrow to call the police. Right now if they asked us any questions we would not know where to start.

20 *Please Do Not Disturb*

On 22 December, Matilda walked towards the reception desk at the Waldorf Astoria. A man in a black twill jacket smiled faintly at her and waited as she moved across the white marble floor. Around her, husbands were meeting wives for coffee and drinks in the foyer and then planning out the rest of their day. Boyfriends met girlfriends and there were small blue Tiffany bags. Lovers greeted one another with a smile and a nod, and a last attempt at love before the goodwill holiday feelings sank in.

The Christmas tree stood in the lobby. It was twenty feet high and silent and beautiful in white and gold.

'Welcome to the Waldorf Astoria,' the concierge said and she noticed how the spotlight over his desk made a golden circle on his head. There was a thin gold stripe on the cuff of his jacket and she remembered how he had managed to retrieve a pearl earring from the U-bend in her bathroom sink three years ago. She had forgotten to put the 'Do Not Disturb' sign on her door and he had disturbed her from her pills and her sleep. He had come to the door and saved her life without knowing it. But he did not remember her now – with her blonde hair, she was like any other New York woman today. And he, like everyone else, was beginning to tingle with thoughts of men in red suits and jingle bells and holidays. He smiled as she handed her credit card to him and he nodded and said, 'Thank you, ma'am.'

She had booked a concierge suite in the Waldorf Towers and it would cost $640 for one night. It was a lot of money and the same amount would have bought her a week at The Beacon on the Upper West Side. But tonight, she wanted to stay here, and wish herself a Merry Christmas in a very special way. Did the money matter now? She actually smiled when she thought about the numbers notched up on next month's Visa bill. On the day before Christmas Eve she didn't care about anything and with it came the first real feeling of freedom – and not for the first time she looked at herself in the mirror and asked, 'Why did I not do this a long time ago?'

That morning she went to a hair salon on West Broadway and had her hair styled and coloured while someone else massaged her feet and buffed and painted her nails. When they offered her the tipping envelopes she smiled very sweetly and said 'Merry Christmas' and put a $100 bill into each.

She took a cab to Barneys and went first to La Perla and then to Chloë and finally to Chanel on the fourth floor. The suit she bought was pale cream cashmere, with a short fitted jacket and large buttons in a double row. The skirt was pencil and fitted her perfectly and fell modestly just below her knee. And her shoes, bought at Chloë, were black stilettos, and she felt a warm rush of love for the designer when she saw the red under-sole. On the way out the staff smiled at her and inwardly thanked her for their commissions and she stopped for a moment near the doorway and allowed a young man in a grey suit to spray her once on each wrist with Chanel No. 5.

In the bathroom of Starbucks she took off her jeans and sneakers and left her black raincoat in a roll on the floor. She stepped into the underwear and her suit and in that moment, surrounded by balls of tissue paper, for the first time in her life, Matilda felt beautiful and new.

The suite was as she expected – three tall windows with long silk drapes in colours like a fresh meadow in spring. The furniture was red brocade and the coffee table was inlaid with walnut and cherry wood. She breezed lightly through the doorway and walked from room to room. And the porter stood awkwardly, not knowing if he had earned a tip because there was no overnight bag. Then she walked to the bathroom and back into the bedroom again and she smiled at the king-size bed covered in the same green silk, and the orange ottoman at the end.

'I am bound to sleep well here,' she told him and she tipped him with a $50 bill. Somehow in that moment she did not want him to leave her and every stranger was suddenly important to her now. She opened the buttons on her jacket and sat for a moment on the end of her bed. Then she lay back and looked up at the pale cream ceiling. She moved further up on to the bed and lay back with both arms outstretched, and now she really knew and understood that there was no longer any reason to be afraid. So she lay like that, surrounded by the smell of her own perfume and the feeling of new clothes and silk – and far away the cabs honked on Park Avenue as everyone else went on and on and kept trying to live out life. And she turned over and for the first time ever she slept deeply, without any pills.

In the end The Chief would blame Christmas. And later, when he told Maggie, his wife surprised him by hugging him suddenly and telling him that he was 'getting soft'. But when she turned away and continued with her turkey stuffing he could still see the trace of a smile on her face. She did not grumble when he said they needed to go to his mother on Christmas Day, the same as last year – and later as they sat watching the first of the holiday movies together, he saw the same little smile flicker across her lips. And she was quieter too, as if what had happened and what he had managed to do had provoked some unusual and happy thought.

On 23 December the Midtown North Precinct was busy and he spent the morning at his desk and in meetings about the Mayor – and he quietly cursed how every movement was becoming like a military operation for him now. In between talks about security checks and crowd barriers, he saw through the glass the drunks, the down-and-outs and the usual pre-holiday suicides that came in. They would watch him as they sat and answered questions, and now and then, when they glanced up at him from under a dirty hood and with bloodshot eyes, they seemed to ask, 'What am I to do?' And his answer was to drain his fifth cup of coffee and look down again at his work.

For once Gallagher wanted to make a difference and not just chip away as he always did without any real feelings or thoughts. Since Glassman had come to visit him, he had felt different and as if, at long last, after twenty years in the force, he felt he could do something and change. Until that day on his back porch when he watched his friend blow on his hot chocolate, there was nothing he had not seen and nothing that could create even the slightest ruffle inside. Maybe that was why Maggie was so amused by it – and maybe now, close to retirement, he was in fact 'getting soft'.

On his first December in the job he had walked down to the subway and had helped to pick up body parts from under the train. Then there was 9/11 and by now he had accepted that this was just a job too and soon he would be old enough to retire and use his holiday home on Long Beach.

It was close to 6 p.m. when Lieutenant Joe Wexler walked across the noisy precinct floor towards his office. Around him there were policemen talking and going off duty with gun belts slung over chairs and bulletproof vests hanging over desks. He nodded to The Chief through his glass door and without knocking opened the door and stepped in. They shook hands even though they were old friends and drank a cup of coffee and talked about their holiday plans. It was only as he was leaving that Wexler mentioned 'some freaky woman' who had been found in a room at the Waldorf and who looked a lot like Marilyn Monroe. He said he was on his way down there now and as he turned and walked away The Chief created a picture of Arthur Glassman in his head and this was followed by a second picture of Marilyn Monroe. He called Wexler back and without explaining anything, he took his own gun from the drawer and told him he wanted to come along. He surprised them by telling them to 'step on it' and even though they moved easily through the traffic it still took nearly twenty minutes to get there.

As they passed the fairy lights in every shop window, he felt as if he was on a different planet to the rest of the world – and he had no idea what Christmas had to do with any of it any more. He did not want to go, and yet for the man who had saved his life, he felt he needed to be there and then at least he could bring some good news to his friend.

Matilda called Room Service and then turned on the TV and curled up on the bed. She ordered one bottle of vodka and some ice in a tall glass.

The knock on her door came and then the voice – young and boyish – called 'Room Service' and she called back, 'Come in.'

She curled a little more on the bed, knowing that he would see the shape of her buttocks in the cream cashmere suit and how her breasts leaned and fell one over the other. He came in and opened the table and set down the small circular tray. He spoke to her politely and to Matilda he just seemed sweet and handsome and young.

'Is there anything else, ma'am?' and she smiled without speaking for a moment and asked him if he could please close the curtains and turn down her bed.

Then she asked him if he could mix her a drink and if he would like to have one for himself. And to this he smiled, an easy, mischievous smile, and told her that he would like to but he couldn't as he was still at work.

She stood for a moment and watched as he turned back the bed. She opened her cigarette case – and as he worked, the bed became a perfect square of white cotton and linen with a small mountain of white down pillows for her head. He reached for the matches on the bedside table and when she leaned towards him, she wondered if he would notice that her eyes were full of tears and that she was suddenly feeling afraid.

She did not want to be alone and so she said, 'Could you just sit with me, for a little while?' and the boy, lifting dark eyebrows and smiling, poured vodka for himself and sat down. And they drank half of the bottle and neither of them said a word.

The light began to fade, and outside the whole of New York pretended to be happy, and Matilda wondered how many people were like herself and the waiter at the Waldorf, and really had nowhere else to go. He had done his duty and she reached for her bag and handed him a roll of dollar bills and he looked at them for a moment and said, 'Thank you, ma'am – Merry Christmas.'

She knew what he thought of her. That she was some sad

woman heading towards forty, drunk and with lots of money and never any kind of man – and then, in case he became suspicious, and also because she did not want to frighten him, she asked if he could bring her the *New York Times* the following day.

She had only taken her purse with her, a black leather pouch bought at Barneys, and inside she had one lipstick, two packs of cigarettes and four bottles of sleeping pills.

When she lay on the white sheets she was still wearing her make-up and a white towelling robe. She thought about that day in New York with Hope and wished she had also taken her for lunch in Barneys – because Hope would have liked that. And then she took the first eight pills and swallowed them down with a drink and this time she remembered to get up and put out the 'Shh – Do Not Disturb' sign on her door.

She had written the note that morning. She had used her favourite black ink pen and wrote it on her kitchen table with Godot at the bay window, still staring out at the snow. Whatever happened she did not worry about her cat. Somehow he always knew he couldn't fully rely on her.

She left the note on her pillow and, swallowing ten more pills, she lay back and waited – and waited – until she was no longer conscious of the wait.

At 4 p.m. as it grew dark in New York City, Matilda slipped quietly and without causing any further trouble to anyone, out of this world. In the morning she had great hopes that she would wake up somewhere else and in that somewhere else place she would no longer be so alone. The next day the note was read by one of the younger officers and then passed with a frown to The Chief.

'I never cared about fame . . . I just wanted to be wonderful.' Marilyn

Later that day an old lady who lived in the subway visited the bathroom in Starbucks and found a nice black raincoat and a pair of Chuck trainers and smiled to herself as she wore them home. The city was almost ready for Christmas and in the middle of the noise and the carol singers and the lights, no one knew or cared that one more star was gone.

After they found her body they took a small room off the foyer and The Chief sat leaning against a table as the officers interviewed the hotel staff. They asked the receptionist how she checked in and took her credit card details. They questioned the concierge about any special requests. They interviewed the Room Service waiter and he owned up to drinking the vodka with her in her room. There were two porters standing side by side and one of them had just come in.

'Did you see anything at all?' he was asked.

'No, sir,' he replied. 'My shift started after she checked in.'

'How long have you worked here?'

'One week,' he replied and here he gave a smile.

'So you're working over the holidays?'

'What holidays?' the boy asked and The Chief grinned.

There was nothing else anyone could do, except tell again what had happened and what was said at the front desk or in her bedroom before she died.

Gallagher suddenly felt tired sitting there and he told the Lieutenant he was going home.

He called Glassman from his car on his way to Brooklyn.

He waited for him to answer and when Hope picked up the phone he spoke to her briefly and then said, 'Put him on.' Glassman listened and then said, 'Thank you, John,' and The Chief could not remember the last time he had heard Glassman use his name.

He knew that he had helped him at last and yet deep down something worried him and he began to wonder if he could also bear – if he had to – to take all that happiness back and away.

He had already seen them together.

He was old and she was so young.

There was nothing that surprised him in Manhattan and yet Glassman seemed to glow too much whenever she walked into a room. The Chief could not understand women but he could feel some sort of worry held back, as if his friend felt she was somehow too special for him or just on loan.

He drove his jeep through the Brooklyn Battery Tunnel and all the way out he thought about Matilda and listened to Christmas songs. As he drove his jeep up the small hill to his house he stopped at his garage and waited with the engine on. There was something about one of the porters that bothered him but he did not know what it was. He had only started at the Waldorf that week and still for some reason The Chief felt he already knew his face. It was Christmas Eve and his family was waiting. He could see his wife inside the kitchen window and as the garage door began to lift slowly and without turning his engine off, he turned the jeep around and headed into Manhattan again. On the way back he called the Precinct and told them to bring the boy in.

On the night before Christmas Eve Glassman wanted to stay at home. After three days they had begun to settle a little now and it became a gentle game between himself and Hope. He would cook dinner in the evenings and she would sit at the table in the kitchen, eating Saltines and reading things out to him from *Time Out* magazine. 'The Rant Show' at Mo Pikins or TJ Monkeys at the Red Room, or what about 'Suddenly Stand-up' on Christopher Street?

Whenever they did venture outside, she said they would both need something to make them laugh. But they thought about these options and then she would come and stand at his elbow and check that his pasta was not overdone. Then she would agree over mixing the tomatoes and anchovies that maybe they would just stay home. They thought about that while they had dinner. The snow building up on the window-sills and the fire crackling in his living-room grate. So far neither one could offer a good enough reason to be away from the open fire and outside in the cold. Later he worked in his studio and she made a jug of hot chocolate and then called him down to bed.

And it was that moment that he lived for – and when they were both safe under the duvet he knew for certain that he had never known such happiness as when Hope was near and curling herself towards him to keep warm.

He was surprised to hear from The Chief again and he had no idea what he was going to say. But he would not come upstairs to the apartment and so Glassman had no choice but to wrap his muffler around his neck three times and turn the pasta down. He noticed as he kissed her cheek when he passed her that the broccoli was making the kitchen window steam up. She had even convinced him that it was good for him and he ate a little now as part of his daily homage to her.

'Honey, open the air vent,' he said and he told her that he wouldn't be long.

They met at the deli at the end of Prince Street, where there were long open counters of salads and sausage and ham. When he saw The Chief eating a doughnut with his coffee at a small white table, his heart lifted a little and he wondered if maybe he was wrong.

The Chief talked about Matilda again and then he stopped for a moment and looked out on to the street. As the silence grew, one of them sighed and at this point The Chief felt he could begin.

He talked about illegals. Hotel staff and bus boys. People who were not documented anywhere – so after 9/11 it was difficult to know for sure where they were gone.

'The truth is, if someone is not registered then it is as if they're not here. So when a bunch of people go missing – it's hard to know for sure – if that person is actually dead – or just hiding – or gone.'

The Chief said nothing for a little while and when Glassman lifted his coffee cup, he could not stop the shake in his left hand. The Chief's words had begun to frighten him. They felt like stones and bricks that could break him right down. But The Chief looked into his eyes and he was suddenly steady and strong about it.

'Arthur,' he said, 'they're so young.'

Glassman swirled his coffee in his cup and turned his face to the dark window and only his ears paid attention to his friend's voice now. She had already decided, and he believed that and this was not about choosing now. He knew that sometimes when she looked at him, it was with the slightest hint of pity, and that she did not want to leave him because it would cause more pain. He remembered how she sat in the hair salon the day before and read a magazine while he saw his own hair, all grey now, fall like dry feathers on to the floor. She had watched as it landed on his shoulders and he had seen her eyes in the mirror – and how she looked away again.

'He was mugged in early September,' The Chief went on. 'Some junkie took his watch, his wallet and his wedding ring.'

But Arthur would not listen or see him. Instead he looked out at people buying late stocking fillers from a stall on the street. The Chief ordered two more coffees and as he turned back from the man behind the counter, Arthur asked, 'How can you be sure?'

'He knows everything about her . . . and when I told him that she had been looking for him . . . you would want to have seen his face . . . Arthur . . .' and here The Chief was almost begging.

'They're just a couple of kids,' The Chief said.

'And his family?'

'Apparently there's no love lost there.'

'And he didn't try to *call* her?'

The Chief put his bear-paw hands on his forehead for a second and he stroked the lines on his face gently as if this would somehow make them go away.

'Of course he tried to call her,' he said quietly and he watched his friend's eyes now for some sign of recognition. And Glassman lifted his hands and finished the point.

'And she was over here.'

The Chief took a sip from his coffee and looked away and then looked back into Arthur's eyes again.

'They're just kids, Arthur,' and his voice was almost pleading for him to understand.

'Arthur . . .'

But Glassman held up his hand. He did not want to hear any more.

21 *Love Itself (24th December 2001)*

*Angel n. – 1. A divine being who acts as a messenger of God.
2. Somebody who is beautiful and kind. 3. A picture of an angel as
a human figure with wings. 4. A spirit that protects and offers
guidance. 5. A member of the lowest order of angels in the medieval
Christian celestial hierarchy, ranked below archangels.*

She taps the white cane and sings on the subway. Her voice is
beautiful and she says, 'Bless you' when a coin falls into her
cup. The song rises up between Bleecker and Spring Street
and at first it only comes through in patches, in between the
bang and rattle of the underground train. Her voice is lifted
up and when she comes closer to us her face is black and lined
with worry and age. But when she sings it is like something
from a gospel choir or a schoolgirl on a June holiday afternoon.
She sounds like Billie Holiday, or as Jack would have said, the
one that didn't make it in New York. Outside the brothers
stand in a circle around a sparking fire in a barrel and warm
themselves in the snow – and inside she sings in the crowded
subway because it is still the one thing she does better than
anyone she knows.

The last words rise and seem to come from her small
bursting heart and in the train people look away from her
because she makes something inside all of us want to well up
and cry – but she sings like a bird and there are no tears from
her as she sings out the last line –

'*Merry Christmas . . . Everyone.*'

Arthur is quiet today. He got up early and then pulled back the curtains and crept back into bed. He took me in his arms and outside it was still snowing and it had been snowing all night. I still have that feeling around a new snowfall and with it, the city is all clean and quiet and bright. He wants to be outside today. So we put on our parkas and our mittens and hats. He wants to show me his favourite New York – and all the things that make this city his home.

We call into Pips for breakfast and he orders pancakes and maple syrup and side orders of eggs and fries. I have never seen him eat food like that before. He is usually looking at labels and making sure everything is organic and free from pesticide. But today he has a real breakfast and then he buys a pretzel and we share it as we walk together on the street.

He takes me to see the Statue of Liberty from Brooklyn Bridge and she is green and tall and standing there surrounded by boats and ice.

'What do you think when you see her?' he asks and I say, 'Pride,' and he smiles and says, 'I think Hope.' Then we go to the Metropolitan Museum and see the pencil sketches by van Gogh. We eat hotdogs for lunch on a bench in Central Park. And around us the dog-walkers make their way through a foot of snow and the ice skaters make slow smooth circles on the rink.

'We need to buy the tree,' he says and his nose and ears are red with cold. It is the kind of frosted air that makes your eyes stream and your head ache. 'Then we might have dinner in Jules.' He knows this is my favourite restaurant and that I love the beaded partitions and how the candles flicker when the door opens and another customer comes in. Then he says, 'If we have time,' and I don't know what that means, so I go, 'Of course we have time. We have all the time in the world.'

The Christmas tree is more than six feet tall and we choose it together after a long debate. On the way back we push it and pull it and everyone laughs when we meet them on the street. We stand with it in the elevator and when the door opens no else can fit inside.

There are pale blue baubles and some are see-through and others are white and gold. We attach each one carefully and neither of us says a word. Now and then he glances at the window and then he says, 'It's getting dark.' He does not have a star and I tease him about this and instead he takes out a tired-looking angel with one wing and dried-out yellow hair. He smiles that smile he has, the one I will always remember seeing in the hardware store, and then he says, 'May I?' and he climbs the ladder and puts the angel up high.

When the telephone rings he does not move to answer it and then when I reach for it, he frowns and says, 'I'll get it.'

'Hi,' he says and then there is a long silence as he lets the other person talk. Then he says, 'OK. Four o'clock,' and he puts the telephone down and now for some reason he won't meet my eyes.

'I have a surprise for you,' he says slowly. 'I want to take you to Gapstow Bridge.'

And when he speaks he is already walking towards the closet for his coat. It is still bright outside but there are more snow clouds gathering over the skyscrapers and the Park.

'We need to hurry,' he says and he is still avoiding my eyes. All day he has been different and I go along with it and only ask, 'We need to be at Jules for six, will we make it back?'

'We'll make it,' he says.

⬡

Central Park is almost empty. The last remaining people walk hurriedly towards the nearest gate. The trees stand like dark people with wild black hair and the lights are blinking on and there are still people laughing on the ice-rink. He walks quickly beside me, and then one hand reaches out for me and we hold mittened hands. We reach the bridge and it is silent and empty – a snow-covered stone bridge that curves romantically upward and then gently slopes back down again.

The branches from the trees are white and ahead of us is the Chrysler building and a grey damp mist. The air feels thick with another snowfall and I'm feeling worried because it's getting dark. Arthur stands for a moment on the bridge and looks into a deep copse of trees. He breathes slowly in and out and his blue eyes squint a little in the cold. Lately I have begun to see things about him and sometimes now he just seems . . . so . . . old.

'I want you to wait here,' he says.

'Here? Why?'

'Because – I want you to – don't be afraid.'

'But . . . I want you to stay with me.' But he says nothing and just looks out over those dark trees.

'Please,' I tell him and he turns and looks right into my eyes and says simply, 'I'm going to wait over here by the gate.'

'But why can't you wait here . . . Arthur . . . Arthur?' and then he answers and with only one glance backwards.

'I can't.'

Glassman did not wait at the gate as he promised. He saw the younger man approach before she did and with that he began to walk away. He would not think about her now and how beautiful her eyes were or how fresh her skin was in the cold.

He would not think of how she had curled herself into him that morning and how he had clutched her and wondered how he would ever be crazy enough to let her go.

'Let her decide,' The Chief said. 'She deserves to know.'

A part of him had always known she was on loan to him and that one day she would return home to be with someone else. He had wanted her to love the city and somehow believed she would grow to love them both. As he walked out on to Fifth Avenue he was elbowed at the subway entrance as people rushed to make an early train. The wind lifted and like the other New Yorkers he bent a little and went on bravely, because they had no other choice but to face the cold.

He told himself that he did not really care for her. That their connection had not gone below her lovely face. He would not think about her eyes now either and that unbearable fragility and then that surprising bright smile in between all sorts of pain. He would tell himself other things about her now and as the wind lifted mufflers and sucked at umbrellas, he would not turn around and see her, looking puzzled and covered in new snowflakes, because he knew he would fall in love with her all over again.

When The Chief called he answered, 'Yes' and 'Yes, it's done,' and The Chief made him promise to have Christmas with him. He said, 'The holidays will be rough for everyone this year,' and he cleared his throat, and in the background Glassman could hear Maggie answer the front door and the sounds of laughing people coming in. And The Chief said gruffly over the noise of their visitors, 'Arthur, you're not on your own.'

But when he sat on the floor of his sitting room and turned the Christmas tree lights on, Glassman felt his heart breaking and he wanted to call The Chief back and say, 'Yes, I am, John.

I am alone.' He did not know how long he sat there for, but he seemed to wake sitting upright with his back to the wall. He wondered if any minute there would be a knock on his door or if the phone would ring – and he even wondered if he might find her waiting for him in Jules. So he waited and as the city grew quieter and quieter, the only sound was the switch on the wall which he kept pressing with his fingers and making the white Christmas tree lights flash off and on.

He sighed then and looking up at the roof he reached the same decision he had reached when he met his good friend at the deli the night before.

Glassman did not turn the bathroom light on. He walked towards the medical cabinet and felt for a new syringe and the bottle of morphine.

'He has good veins.' He remembered how a doctor had once praised him for that. And in his sickly state he had managed to feel some sense of pride.

He avoided the hallway mirror and the one in the kitchen – and he threw a sweater over the one at the end of his bed. He took a deep breath and then calmly drawing the morphine into the syringe, he placed the cold needle against his skin.

He noticed for the first time that the small green flowers on the wallpaper were in groups of three and then two and then one. 'Three and then two and then one' and he thought it was some kind of irony that was his life. Then he smiled at the idea of that. And how when a man dies he should have something more profound on his mind.

'Here lies poor Glassman, he hated broccoli and eggs.' She had even persuaded him to eat greenery. Now even his dull epitaph would not be safe.

He liked to imagine that when his spirit lifted it would be transparent and invisible to the naked eye. That it would turn into glass and then some fine sparkling crystal and then shatter and send him into a million pieces across the Manhattan sky.

'There goes Glassman,' people would say, and outside, it would hardly be noticed that the snow for a moment had turned to hail. He wanted to feel that he was ready and that he could go – as he wanted to – without seeing himself in the mirror and knowing that the last face he saw was the face of Hope Swann.

'A real beauty,' he said to himself and his fingers tightened around the syringe and his thumb tensed a little, ready to push the needle in. He thought about the people he had loved in his life – his mother – Elsa Graham – Hope – The Chief – Trudy – and then he thought about Matilda whose face seemed to move towards him in the darkened room.

'It would be just my luck to meet her in the next life as well,' and even now his own words made him want to laugh. He managed to smile and at the same time he thought about Hope's face again and wondered what she would have to say about all of this.

'What on earth are you doing, Arthur?' He could almost hear her voice.

He swallowed slowly.

His right hand relaxed its grip.

He put the syringe back on the locker and sat up again.

Whatever happened he knew now that she would come back to tell him. She was the kind of girl who would want a proper goodbye. She would be cold and hungry and she would like some spaghetti. And he knew how to make a good Pasta Putana now – amongst other things, she had also taught him that.

⇆

It is cold on this bridge and I am thinking about Matilda and all the things she taught me about New York – the shutters shooting up on Broadway on a bright fall morning, ten different kinds of coffee from a paper cup, those ferocious red leaves and the yellow taxis, and yet she never once mentioned how beautiful and quiet it all gets in the snow. Yet that one line is the thing I remember most from her

– *One big love*
– *One big love*
– *One big love.*

And I just keep saying it as I wait here for Glassman to return to the bridge. In my mind I can see Jonathan and his fresh white shirt. I can see Arthur and then a man who lives on a boat. All these people, and why did I meet them? Did any of them come close to being 'One Big Love'?

Around me there are fewer and fewer people and the lights on the ice-rink are going off now one by one.

And then I see a man on his own. He is coming towards me, just walking with his head down and his shoulders rounded into the wind.

He is just like any other man in this city, wearing a coat and a muffler and gloves. His hands go deep into his pockets now and his ears are red with cold.

The man walks past the last remaining people and he is walking towards the bridge and getting closer all the time.

The sky over us is heavy with snow and it's getting darker every minute now.

> – *One big love*
> – *One big love*
> – *One big love.*

And then my heart seems to move a little, and then just open up inside – if he had fallen and broken into a million pieces I would have known how to put all those parts together again – one by one – and we have changed, both of us now – and we stand and stare at each other as he puts one foot on the bridge. There is a world of trouble in his eyes as he watches me and there is another world of trouble in mine and I wait as he takes one step closer and then a single snowflake falls between us and it is followed by another and another and then I look deeper into his dark eyes.

There are so many things to talk about. There are too many things I have to say. I don't know where to begin with it and in my mind I am already mixing up all the words. I look right into his eyes again and when he looks back, I see the beginning of his smile.

And so I just say it – straight out – the same way I always say it.

'Larry – when are you coming home?'

Acknowledgements

Patricia Deevy, my editor at Penguin Ireland, has been hugely helpful in the fine-tuning of this book. Sincere thanks also to Michael McLoughlin, Cliona Lewis and Brian Walker for helping to bring it all to life – and, as always, my agent, Faith O'Grady. Suzanne Costello, Deirdre Harrington and Juliet Prendergast read the earliest drafts and gave me much encouragement and advice. I would like to thank my family, Mum, Dad, and my brothers and sisters for their constant interest and support. My friends Melanie and Ardal O'Hanlon and also Nick Kelly did their best to help me with the title. While in New York I stayed with David Bourke and Geraldine Collins, who, apart from showing me the 'ins and outs' of this amazing city, were extraordinarily generous in giving me a place to stay and write. Finally, thank you, Steve Schwartz, for your help with the Cape Cod references – and for making me laugh.